To Sue,
Enjoy.
Lenore Rowntree

CLUCK

LENORE ROWNTREE

thistledown press

Thistledown Press Ltd.
410 2nd Avenue North
Saskatoon, Saskatchewan, S7K 2C3
www.thistledownpress.com

Library and Archives Canada Cataloguing in Publication

Rowntree, Lenore Ruth, author
Cluck / Lenore Rowntree.

Issued in print and electronic formats.
ISBN 978-1-77187-108-2 (paperback). – ISBN 978-1-77187-109-9
(html). – ISBN 978-1-77187-110-5 (pdf)
I. Title.

PS8635.O887C56 2016   C813'.6   C2016-905248-6
                                C2016-905249-4

Cover and book design by Jackie Forrie
Printed and bound in Canada

Canada Council   Conseil des Arts
for the Arts   du Canada

SASKATCHEWAN
ARTS BOARD

Canadä

Thistledown Press gratefully acknowledges the financial assistance of the Canada Council for the Arts, the Saskatchewan Arts Board, and the Government of Canada for its publishing program.

For Cortes Community Radio
CKTZ 89.5 FM,
the spirit of independent radio

ONE

1970 Uncool

ONLY HENRY AND HIS FRIEND Tom from next door sit in the front room of the house by the white plastic fencing that snakes around ten miniature cows. Henry admires the finely coordinated movement of Tom's hand when he tips a thimble-sized bucket just to the edge of a small brown cow's mouth. He hopes with all his heart things will remain calm until it's time for Tom to go home for supper. He wants to beg Tom to stay with him, to be his friend no matter what happens. But he's frozen in position, his hand clamped on the seat of the rubber tractor from his *Farm Folk* set.

What are you staring at? Tom asks.

Nothing. Henry smiles.

He bends so Tom won't see the smile and rushes the tractor through the golden carpet, making furrows in the wheat field that stretches across the room and down the hall to the front door that leads to forever.

Brmmm. Brmmm. Brmmm.

The night Henry's mother turned this room into a bedroom for him, she said, The light's good in here, nice and cheery for my Little Ducky. Henry, tucked between a feather pillow and down quilt on his mother's bed, couldn't understand why he had to change rooms right then. But he knows now that's just the way it is with her. And most of all, he knows it's best to do as she says and always to fake being happy. Even when happiness is cracked.

He swoops the tractor around by the foot of his bed, and speeds it up as he heads back toward the barnyard where he crashes through the fencing and into the cows grazing on the carpet.

Watch it, Tom shouts. You almost killed Daisy.

Tom and Henry laugh. This is their routine. Tom rights all the cows while Henry zooms around once more before screeching to a stop beside the barn. He picks up a small black and white collie and drags her through the carpet. Lead the cows home, girl, he shouts. His thumb rests on a speck of yellow paint at the collie's neck, left from the time he tried to change her colour so she'd look more like the real Lassie. He uses his other hand to pull bunches of protesting cows through the carpet.

Moo. Moo. Moo.

Sooie, sooie, Tom yodels to round up the hogs.

It's noisy and soon enough Henry's mother bursts into the room. She's out of breath, and has a curious mix of annoyance and emergency on her face. As if she's run in to put out a fire.

You boys are getting too old for this kind of play, she says.

Only ten, Tom answers back.

Still — too old to be making such a racket, she says.

Not that noisy, Henry says. Busy scattering popcorn kernels among the chickens, he barely looks up.

His mother puts her foot in the middle of the fenced circle, right on top of one of the cows that hasn't been herded into the barn.

Time to clean up this mess, she says. Now!

He doesn't like that she's upset by the noise, but he's glad Tom's ruckus has distracted her from the popcorn. Last time he *wasted* corn, she made him wash the inside of the cupboards in the kitchen, and the next day he had to skip school to help her perm her hair. He stood at the kitchen sink all afternoon running warm water over her head, the smell of perm solution sticking in his throat. Then when she was finally satisfied with her own hair, she tried to use the leftover mixture on him. He had to run into the backyard and hide behind the laurel bush. He couldn't have his hair corkscrewing out like the curly-tailed mice in the grade-five science book. The teacher had told the class those mice were mutants.

Henry's mother reaches her hand down toward him. He shrinks back, unsure where the invitation is leading, but she grabs him anyway and pulls him onto his feet.

Let's dance, she says. Her face suddenly alight.

No, Mom.

Come on baby, it'll be fun. Tom, turn the record player on.

Tom switches the knob and carefully sets the needle down onto the record sitting on the turntable. Henry can't remember what record he left there and holds his body rigid praying it won't be "Wooly Bully". He found the album in an alley on the other side of Fourth Avenue where the wealthy people live in Kitsilano. The people who have views of the ocean and enough money to throw away a practically new record, one that's not even scratched. He keeps it hidden under his mattress and pulls it out at night to read. The back cover says it was recorded in 1965, and the front is a thrilling scary picture of Sam the Sham and the Pharaohs. He knows his mother won't like them, especially if she finds out he dances to their music in his underpants when she's at work over at the drugstore . . . He's relieved when the record begins and it's the children's choir singing.

When the red red robin comes bob-bob-bobbin' along — along.

Henry's mother begins to bounce and tries to make him bob on his feet. She tugs at his hands, moving his arms up and down, then pretends they are jiving and scrunches down to swing around under his arm.

Isn't this fun? she says.

No, Mom, it isn't.

He shrinks back, wishes he could hide in his *Farm Folk* set. She ignores him and reaches under his armpits, trying to lift him up into some sort of overhead loop. Perhaps because he's heavier than she expects, she falters for a moment and he escapes. But instead of stopping she begins to jump up and down by herself, frantically, like a small child.

She points at Tom. You're afraid of me, aren't you?

Henry looks over. Tom doesn't look scared, he's rolling and laughing on the floor. While Henry's head is turned, his mother grabs him again and pulls him back in under her bouncing tah-tahs. Her breath is heavy on his neck, and he hates being in so close. He can hear her dress scratching against the lace of her nylon slip. He tries not to breathe in the smell of her, all hot and pungent, a smell he can't quite put a finger on except to name it eggy.

He leans into the dance routine for a second, hoping it will hold off one of her rants about how she used to dance at the Cave nightclub, men lining up to partner with her before her figure got ruined from childbirth. How one man in particular, a talent promoter from Toronto, still might come back and help her get into show business. It's excruciatingly embarrassing to have this happening in front of Tom.

He can't help himself. He takes in a big gulp of air and wails, Mom this isn't fun.

He thinks his voice is lost in the muffle of tah-tahs and music, but Tom hears him.

It is pretty funny, Tom says, still rolling on the carpet.

Henry feels his face burning as his mother wiggles him around the room in that jerky way she has sometimes. The song screams in his ears.

No more sobbin' when he starts throbbin'.

Tom kicks his feet up in the air laughing.

The harder Henry pushes, the more his mother pulls him in. Soon his face is wet with sweat and snot. For a moment he thinks his world may come apart. Bits of himself may fly off his body as his mother jiggles him across the room. When he begins to believe he really might suffocate, he gives her a mighty shove and she falls back against the window, her hand striking the glass.

Get up, get out of bed. Cheer up, cheer up, the sun is red.

Although the window doesn't break, his mother does have to hang onto the windowsill to steady herself before she's able to reach down and fix her brassiere, which is threatening to unleash a breast.

Oh, Mrs. Parkins, you look so funny doing that, Tom says.

Doing what? she demands.

I dunno. That . . . Putting your hand down your dress.

You're a bad boy, Tom Lawson.

Sorry Mrs. Parkins. I . . . I . . .

Quiet, you ungrateful little brat. And don't call me Mrs. Parkins. I'm Alice.

Tom's eyes grow as wide as the cucumber slices she puts on her face at the end of a bad day. Henry knows this is getting serious, her eyes are turning black, and strangled sounds are starting to come out her mouth.

Gggrrrooom. Gggrrrooom. Fffriginggrrroom . . .

He is powerless to stop any of it, things will only escalate if he tries. Instead he begins to laugh in his nervous way, laughing at things that aren't funny but that need a little happy. It's a habit he picked up to mask these weird interactions, of which there have been so many lately the laugh has grown into a startled grunt that comes out his nose in short puffs.

Hmphf hmphf hmphf.

His mother crosses the room and picks up the tractor from the farm set. She gets down on her hands and knees and runs the tractor through the carpet, revving it with her grumbling mouth. She rushes the tractor toward the bottom of Tom's pant leg.

Fffuddinggrrooomschidt!

Henry puts his hand in the tractor's path. This doesn't stop her. She keeps the tractor moving right over his hand. By the time she gets to Tom's sneaker, he's caught on and tries to move away. But he traps himself against the window and she runs the tractor over his foot. Hard.

Ow!

Tom kicks but she holds his foot down with her free hand while she tears the tractor up his leg, narrowly missing his winky.

Henry does not want to watch, but keeps staring because he owes this much to his friend. When his mother finally takes her hand off the tractor, she lets it fall to the carpet.

Aaahhh! Tom doubles over on the floor beside the bed. He lies still, his mouth open.

Henry thinks for a second that Tom might throw up; his lips pucker and the back of his hand goes to his mouth.

His mother picks up the tractor and walks toward the bed holding it in the air like she's going to do it all again. But as she gets to where Tom is lying, she turns and throws the tractor into the metal wastebasket. Thud.

All finished playing for the day, she says.

The record spins silently between songs until the cheerful band of children begins a new tune.

Ee-i-ee-i-o. Old MacDonald had a farm, ee-i-ee-i-o. And on his farm he had a cow, ee-i-ee-i-o.

Henry's mother sings along, Ee-i-ee-i-o. And on his farm he had a duck.

Neither Tom nor Henry sing.

After a time of solo warbling, she rakes the needle from the record.

SSSZIP.

Then go home! Both of you, she wails, and stomps out of the bedroom.

What did she mean? Tom asks.

I don't know. Sometimes she says that, tells me to leave.

And do you?

Course not. Where would I go?

To my house?

They look at each other. They both know Henry wouldn't go to Tom's house. Tom's mother doesn't like it when Henry comes over. And she'd be insistent Henry not come if she thought it was something his own mother wanted. She'd be angry even if she knew where Tom was that very moment. Tom has started lying to her, saying he's going to play with other friends down the street.

Okay, I gotta go, Tom says. See you around sometime.

Sure, Henry says, watching the back of Tom's head. He tries to smile, but Tom does not look at him. He just leaves the room.

Henry sits on his bed waiting to hear the front door close. He worries Tom won't come again. Only when the outside knocker rattles does he make his way to the wastebasket and his desk. On one of his mother's happy days the two of them walked to the hardware store on Fourth Avenue to buy paint for the desk. By the cash register there'd been a set of stencils of the planets and stars. He told her about the constellations they'd studied at school — Pegasus the flying horse, Canis Major the big dog, and Bootes the herdsman — and she was proud of him for remembering so many and because of that she bought the stencils to make his desk fancy. They decorated it in the backyard, setting out newspapers to catch the drips.

Henry pulls the chair, which has been painted to look like a rocket, out from under the desk. He squats in the cubbyhole where the chair had been. It's the place he goes to get away from things. He knows his mother is crazy. And sometimes he wonders if he's a bit off too. If only he could be more like Tom, smooth and assured. He decides he needs to watch Tom more carefully to see how it is to be him, but it'll be tricky to do that if he doesn't come over anymore.

He reaches to pull the wastebasket in and fishes among the soiled tissues until his hand hits on something hard. He digs out the tractor and spins its wheels to make sure they still work. He sets the tractor on the rug and drives it in circles under the desk.

Thurrrrr. Thurrrrr. Thurrrrr.

The vibrating tongue on the roof of his mouth is calming. He huddles and drives. The tractor holds steady. Yes. Consistent. Confident. Yes. All is quiet, except for his whirring tongue. Maybe everything will be okay this time.

A pot crashes. A small one. It could be a mistake. Then another. A bigger one. Not a mistake. Now the muttering. That's the word Tom used when he first heard it. Your mother mutters, he said. Afterward Henry had to look the word up in the dictionary. The meaning seemed to fit. *To murmur, grumble, say in secret.*

The muttering gets louder, loud enough for him to hear what she is saying.

Daffy-Duck, Daffy-Duck, Daffy, Daffy, Daffy. Shut the duck up!

By the time his mother is slamming cupboard doors and shouting about Cuban spies, Henry's thurring tongue has lost all its power to soothe. He crawls out from under the desk and across the rug to close the French door to his room. He wedges the rocket chair under the doorknob. He doesn't like that his mother can see through the windows on the door, but at least now she can't get in. He tests the setup, and once he's certain it will hold, he begins to pack away the farm set. It's a good collection and he needs to take care of it.

There's an order to packing. First, he takes the lid off the box and lines the edges with the plastic fencing. Next he dismantles the barn, unsnapping the joiners to nest the pieces one against the other. In the centre, he settles the cows on their sides with legs interlocking. The pigs lie beside the cows, and Lassie has her own corner with a cardboard partition crayoned to look like a doghouse. The white chickens and their eight baby chicks fit in beside

Lassie's house, and the rooster is housed on the other side so he can't bother the chickens while they sleep.

Henry saves the chocolate-brown chicken for last. There is only one brown hen, and he takes a fresh tissue and wraps it carefully around her. The comb is nearly torn off from too much *roughhousing*. He's very sorry he let Tom play with her today. He doesn't think he could bear it if there is ever any more damage done. He gives her a gentle pet before he makes a final fold on the tissue and tucks her in beside the other chickens. He scoops up the popcorn from the floor and puts it in beside the brown hen so she has something to eat if she gets hungry in the box.

He's reaching up to put the box back on the shelf when he realizes the house has gone quiet again. He can even smell supper cooking. Maybe it isn't going to be one of those nights after all. He knows his mother is trying to be normal, and he has helped by staying out of the way. He takes the rocket chair out from under the doorknob and opens the door slowly. The room fills with the smell of spaghetti sauce, his favourite.

He feels proud at supper when she tells him, You're a pillar of strength.

Henry is getting ready for bed when his mother calls from her bedroom. He walks to her door, and finds her sitting at her mirrored vanity table with its array of lipsticks and fancy coloured perfume bottles. The makeup lights are on. It's like a movie star's set-up, with as many light bulbs as outside the cinema. The glow from the bottles is mesmerizing — turquoise, lime, blueberry, cranberry, peach. His mother holds out a small round hand-mirror.

Would you like this for your farm set? she asks. It could be a pond for the animals.

Sure, he says. Thanks.

You can invite Tom over again. I promise I won't bring my hyper self next time.

He takes the mirror and puts it in his pocket. He watches her select a lip colour and feels sad about Tom. To distract himself, he thinks instead about looking up the word "hyper" in his dictionary. His mother rolls the lipstick tubes up one by one. Scarlet, crimson, ruby. He wonders if the word might mean over-excited. Plum, misty-rose, purple. Maybe it will mean unhappy. Eventually she settles on a bubblegum pink. She lets her lower lip go slack, then tightens it, and runs the tube back and forth, back and forth, so many times lipstick threatens to spill over the edges of her lips. Just when the lips can take no more, she purses them and touches a tissue to the edge of her mouth, fixing everything.

How do I look? she asks.

Like a raven-haired beauty, Henry says.

This makes her smile. It's something Tom's father, Mr. Lawson, used to say whenever he saw her sitting on the porch. How's the raven-haired beauty next door? he'd ask.

But he stopped saying it after Mrs. Lawson overheard him one day and smacked him on the back of the head. The houses on the street are nice wood homes painted pleasing colours, but the lots are narrow and the front porches practically touch. The incident left Henry thinking about his own father, who he might be, what he might be like. If everything hadn't felt so uncomfortable he might even have asked his mother then, or if not about his father about his only other relative, his mother's sister in England. He's thinking again about asking, but now is not the time either.

His mother surveys herself in the mirror and, satisfied with the result, squirts her favourite Shalimar perfume at her throat. Then she looks one last time before slapping cold cream across her lips and all over her face. Once the lipstick has mixed in and turned the cream a pale pink, she invites Henry to play. He sticks his finger in the goop and draws faces with it. First he makes her a happy sort, then a sad sort. *And on down the yellow brick road*, they sing together. It's a routine they know by heart.

When they're finished taking the cream off her face, she leans into him for a goodnight kiss. She smells warm and sweet, like a flower in the sun. Then she reaches under her vanity and pulls out a turquoise transistor radio.

I got this for you at the drugstore, she says. I know you like music.

She turns the wheel on the side of the radio and the jingle for a radio station plays.

CKLG radio 73, and we love you.

She rolls the wheel again to silence the radio and hands it to him. Should we finish our other song? she asks.

Okay, he says. Together they sing.

And on that farm there was a chicken. Ee-i-ee-i-o. With a cluck cluck here. And a cluck cluck there. Here a cluck there a cluck. Everywhere a cluck cluck.

Later, when Henry is alone in his bed, he sings softly to himself.

Ee-i-ee-i-o.

He wonders what it means, but knows it won't be in his dictionary. So he picks up the tiny radio and turns the wheel. It vibrates gently in his hand with the voice of a disc jockey on the other end.

It's the Midnight Spinner here, playing all-night requests. Bringing you some psychedelic funk from San Francisco's Sly and the Family Stone "Hot Fun in the Summertime" — hit bound 1970 after their blowout in Woodstock last year!

He shoves the radio under his pillow and falls asleep feeling connected to the world.

TWO

High School Radio Junkie

GOOD MORNING. GOOD MORNING. HOW *the devil are you? H-E-double-N-E-double-S-Y. Hennessy we love you. That's not bad gang, but next time can you sing it on key. Roy Hennessy here, CKLG Vancouver and 7:03 in the morning. I'm coming to you live or as close as I can get and reminding you a week Friday we'll be giving you a chance to rip us off for the new Stones album* Black and Blue *just released for their European Tour '76. The hit line is open! CKLG — the station with the happy difference — Boss Radio. 7:04 on a beautiful sunny morning with Hennessy. And here comes the chart topper from 1975, KC and the Sunshine Band, "That's the Way (I Like It)" — a-huh a-huh, I like it!*

Henry lies in bed listening to KC fading in and out under his pillow while he pulls at a couple of scraggly hairs on his chin. He's going to have to buy new batteries soon and maybe a razor. He doesn't like the thought of starting to shave, he's only in grade eleven, but it's that or have fuzz hanging from his face at school. And new batteries are a must. For him, falling asleep and waking up to the radio is the greatest pleasure. Ever since he figured out he can buy four packs for cheap at Woolworth's and extend a battery's life by putting it in the oven when it starts to fade, he can get lost in the radio all day long.

Fridays, he has a routine. After school, he takes the bus to Woolworth's on Hastings Street to pick up the Top-30 list for the week and batteries if he needs them. This year, now that he's almost a senior, he doesn't have last period on Friday so he has time to stop and look at the budgies on the way to the record counter, then to sit at the lunch counter and pore over the brightly coloured hit list while he eats an ice cream. On a week when he has enough left from his earnings cutting lawns, he'll pick out a new 45 and every few months he'll splurge and buy a whole album. He keeps the Top-30 lists in a shoebox in his cupboard, and the records arranged along the wall of his bedroom in alphabetical order.

As KC finishes up, he gets out of bed and puts in the white ear speaker button from his transistor. He doesn't want to disturb his mother while he listens for details on how to get the new Stones album. More and more his mother sleeps in. She says it helps with her blues, but he isn't so sure it's working. She looks puffy and tired all the time. He stands at the mirror in the bathroom and thinks he looks puffy and tired too, but he feels better after he uses the nail scissors to snip his chin hairs and remembers today is A-V day. The audio-visual club is about the only thing he really looks forward to in a school week. Every Wednesday at the end of class, he and two other guys meet in Mr. Bromley's homeroom mostly to trade record lists and look at each other's blurry photos — Mr. Bromley lets them use the lab to develop their black and white film — and occasionally to discuss more serious things like Betamax versus VHS, or who will get the hall pass to cart the projector to the next school assembly.

Henry eats a banana and a bowl of Special K while his battery burbles in the oven. When he walks out the front door toward Kits High School, he has the radio in his pants pocket and the speaker in his ear. Once he's at school, one of the surly grade nine boys comes up to him in the hall and begins mouthing words. It's a joke they started after somebody mistook him for deaf because of his speaker wire. He just keeps walking. The halls are a nightmare for him and the radio is all that really matters. He carries a touch of California and a touch of Britain when he's plugged in, and he feels naked as a rat when he's not.

Class time is a serious drag because he's not a good student and he has to take the ear speaker out or risk having the radio confiscated. Mostly he just waits the day through.

At 3:15, Mr. Bromley greets the A-V club members at the door.

Hey guys. Got news for you.

Henry is not really listening, he has his speaker in, and Donny, the skinny Chinese kid, is hitting two rulers on a table like he's drumming to "In-A-Gadda-Da-Vida".

Okay guys, listen up. Henry, speaker out. And Gene Krupa, drumsticks down.

Not Gene Krupa, Donny replies, Ginger Baker.

Not Ginger Baker either, Henry corrects, Ron Bushy — Iron Butterfly.

Okay, whatever, Mr. Bromley says. Now that I have your attention, good news. A week Friday, the A-V club is sponsoring the dance here at the school.

What's that mean? Donny asks.

It means you all get to be disc jockeys. Spin your records.

Cool, Nathaniel says as he wipes cracker crumbs from his face. I can help set up, but I don't think my mom will let me come.

Donny jerks his thumb at Henry. He's got the best collection anyway.

Henry says nothing. He watches Nathaniel open another pack of crackers and worries about not being able to catch the bus to CKLG's Richards Street station that Friday to get in on the Stones album giveaway. Besides he's not sure his mother will let him go to a dance either.

Come on, Donny persists. I'll help you.

Okay, Henry finally says. I'll bring some records if you guys get the equipment together.

All right! Donny leaps out of his seat and starts drumming with his fingers on the tops of Nathaniel and Henry's heads. We'll have two turntables just like the pros, he shouts.

On the way home from school, Henry decides the best way to deal with it is not to tell his mother about the dance. She works most Friday nights until 9:00 anyway, so he can take the records to school and get everything set up to spin a few and be back home before she is. Donny can spin from 9:00 until 10:00, when the dance ends, and no one will be the wiser.

But word gets out at the school that Henry is going to be the main DJ for the dance, and for the first time his classmates begin to come up to him in the hall and talk to him like he's a regular guy. He doesn't know how to be with them exactly, but he listens seriously to their requests and he starts a list on a pad of paper that he keeps in his breast pocket. On Tuesday afternoon on his way to French class, a pretty blonde named Debi bounces up to him.

Do you have "Sister Golden Hair" by America? she asks.

No.

Oh it's so good. Can you get it?

I'll try.

Thanks! She giggles and walks past.

He is breathless. Debi makes him feel anxious but also deeply warm. He doesn't have the vocabulary to describe how the sight of her thick ponytail and her adorable rear-end turns him on, but there it is. He's turned on.

Next day at A-V Club he asks Donny, Do you have "Sister Golden Hair" by America?

Yeah, it's on *Hearts*.

Can you bring it Friday night?

Sure.

During Thursday's French class, he works on the final set lists. He's decided to go with a mix of Canadian content and other. He can tell some of the Boss Jocks at CKLG don't really like having to play CanCon, but he loves a lot of the Canadian bands, and even though most of the kids don't ask for them either, he figures it's the right thing to do. While the teacher does dictation — *bleu, gris, rouge* — he writes out the first set:

1. "Spinning Wheel"   Blood Sweat & Tears
2. "Misty Mountain Hop"   Led Zeppelin
3. "One Way Ticket"   McKenna Mendelson Mainline
4. "Shining Star"   Earth Wind & Fire
5. "American Woman"   Guess Who
6. "Maggie Mae"   Rod Stewart
7. "For What It's Worth"   Buffalo Springfield
8. "Takin' It to the Streets" Doobie Brothers
9. "Sunny Days"   Lighthouse
10. "Crocodile Rock"   Elton John
11. "Up on Cripple Creek"   The Band

He purposely puts one extra quasi-Canadian song in, as he's going to have to slip in "Sister Golden Hair" whenever Debi shows up at the dance. He knows Buffalo Springfield is no more than a quarter Canadian, what with Neil Young being only part of the band, and more and more an American, but he can't help himself, "For What It's Worth" is just such a good song. Still it's important to keep the list balanced.

The night of the dance he is in a pretty good mood considering he's at school. He's wearing his best ultra-suede shirt and a new pair of corduroy jeans. For the first set, he is going to spin the Canadian tunes, and Donny, the American and British ones. Donny designed a sign that Nathaniel helped paint — *CanCon Dance: be there or be square*. The sign hung all week in the cafeteria advertising the dance, and now it hangs over the door to the gym. Henry protested at first — No one will come if they know it's CanCon — but standing at the record table in front of a packed gym, he realizes most of the students don't know what it means and the sign looks good. Mr. Bromley helped them put up the lights that spiral and pinwheel as the students begin to dance, and soon shafts of purple and red zigzag across a mass of gyrating teenagers.

Henry keeps his eye on the door to the gym so he can spot Debi and cue up "Sister Golden Hair". But by three-quarters of the way through the first set he's starting to worry she will not show before he has to leave. Then, as Lighthouse is finishing "Sunny Days", instead of Debi, he sees a horrifying sight — the mad frizz of his mother's permed hair is unmistakably backlit at the door. Someone at the drugstore must have told her about the dance. She stands for a time under the blue and pink squares of Donny's sign before she starts to move through the gym toward him. Without saying anything, he slips under the table to hide while Donny spins "Crocodile Rock". But like some relentless swamp reptile, his mother keeps coming, so he begins to pretend there's a one-way glass wall between them, and against all odds his mother seems to respect the wall when she leans down to look at him and makes no further move forward.

He stares right at her and she at him. Then out of the corner of his eye he sees Mr. Bromley move in from behind. Mr. Bromley taps his mother on the shoulder, and when she jumps up to take his hand and makes a Lindy Hop step all in one quick motion, Henry thinks, Oh no, she's mistaken this as Mr. Bromley asking her to dance. *Hmphf hmphf hmphf.* He feels his stupid laugh snort out from under the table while his mother grabs Mr. Bromley's arm and begins to jive rock with him. Mr. Bromley looks confused, but being a good sport follows along. Henry, frozen by the sight, is afraid to move until the unmistakably cute bum of Debi goes bouncing by and he hears Elton singing — *Laaaaa, lalalala laaaaa, lalalala laaaaa, lalalala la-a, lalalala la* — signalling the end of "Crocodile Rock".

He needs to get up and organize for "Sister Golden Hair". Fearful as he is, he emerges on the final *la* and pulls America from its sleeve. Holding the album carefully by the edges, he puts it on the turntable, but he's so nervous he miscues and sets the needle to the end of the previous song. As the last bit of "The Story of a Teenager" plays, he can see everyone in the crowd looking confused, except for Debi. She knows what's coming next. Then when the opening chords sound, she swoons into the arms of the boy she's dancing with and Henry realizes this must be *their song*. He's so relieved he can no longer see his mother's permed hair when he scans the gym, his disappointment that Debi has a boyfriend barely registers.

At the end of the set, Mr. Bromley comes up.

Was that kooky lady your mother?

Yes.

She can dance, he says.

At least Mr. Bromley is smiling.

When Henry gets home, his mother is asleep. He's expecting a temper the next morning, but instead she's in a good space and asks, Is that man one of your teachers?

Yes.

Did he say anything afterward?

Not really. He said you can dance.

I know that, but did he say anything else?

He does not have the heart to tell her Mr. Bromley called her a kook. He decides to embellish because he knows it will make her feel better, but he wants to pour cold water on it at the same time so she won't get carried away like she can when she gets too excited about things.

I think he's married, Mom. But he said he had fun dancing with you.

She smiles and the conversation ends.

For a long time nobody except for Henry, and maybe Tom and his parents next door, really know anything is seriously wrong with his mother. But soon after he starts grade twelve, the whole neighbourhood learns how odd she can be. Nothing is good about grade twelve. Mr. Bromley is gone so there's no more A-V Club, Debi transferred to the mini-school for the arts, Donny hardly talks to him, and even Tom mostly ignores him. So the last thing he needs is for his mother to have a very public meltdown.

It happens the night the house up the street burns down. In front of everyone, she runs out onto the road and holds up a branch, several dried leaves still attached, to catch it on fire from the flames of the house. Then with the crown alight, she leaps along the street chanting, *I am the Fire Mistress.* Henry is the only one who understands she thinks she's doing an interpretive dance. Everybody else judges her crazy and wonders if she has had something to do with the fire. The neighbours talk so much about it afterward, the fire chief himself comes by to investigate.

His mother holds the door open a crack until she understands the imposing man on her front porch is with the fire department. Then in her unbridled off-kilter way, she throws the door wide and urges him in.

Don't mind the mess, she trills. Please call me Alice.

The fire chief steps into the hallway. It's crowded with boots and running shoes, some so tiny they go back to when Henry was a child — a smelly stew of footwear mixed with old newspapers, a broken umbrella and empty milk cartons. From where he's standing in the hall, Henry can see his mother is embarrassed. For some reason, she quickly ushers the chief into Henry's bedroom where she busies herself straightening the quilt and pulling the rocket chair out from under the desk for the chief to sit on. She sits on the bed, crossing and uncrossing her legs while they speak. Each time she moves her leg, her bathrobe falls more precariously open. Henry is transfixed by what he can see going on through the French door. It has been a few years since a man has been in their house and his mother is behaving badly. Finally the chief calls Henry to join them.

Have you got anything you can add, young man?

Henry remembers flames shooting from the house, and sparks flying from the rooftop, he remembers a whoosh as the fire moved up toward the roof, and the popping sound of windows as they blew out. Then there was the roar of people, though honestly he didn't know whether they were roaring at the fire or at his mother — she cut quite a sight with embers from the branch dropping into her hair, and her white nightgown so close to the flames the hem got singed. And he remembers praying their house would not catch fire because he couldn't imagine how he and his mother would carry on if it did, but at the same time he recalls thinking it might not be so bad if she caught herself on fire because she looked so miserable that night. But the thing he remembers most is that nobody, himself included, tried to stop her.

He doesn't tell any of this to the chief. Instead he says, My mother can't make lightning bolts fly from her head.

Why on earth would you say something like that, Henry Parkins? his mother asks.

Because it's what the kids are saying.

He's right, ma'am, the chief says.

Whether it's the chief siding with Henry or just the general excitement of having someone over at the house, he can't be sure, but something causes his mother to turn all serious and convincing. She stands up, pulls her robe tight and says, I know what caused the fire.

Tell me then, the chief says.

She puts her head back to answer.

The man who rents on the first floor cooks French fries every night after work. Some of the fries in his basket are so old, they're like charcoal. Besides, he drinks.

When she's finished pronouncing, she sits down and refuses to say anything more. The chief makes some notes in his pad and then says, You know I don't usually do this, but somebody from Social Services might help out here. Do you mind if I contact them, send someone around?

Henry watches his mother's body stiffen. Why? she asks.

Some of the neighbours have concerns, that's all.

Like who?

I'm not at liberty to say, ma'am. But one of the ladies on the street said you've been acting a bit manic.

Well I never. Do as you must, she says. Then with her head so far back she's looking at the ceiling, she says, Henry, please show this gentleman to the front door.

As soon as the chief is out, she goes into one of her rages. The slamming pots and banging doors quickly escalate into shouting and screaming while she stalks in and out of Henry's bedroom, smacking him on the shoulder, pounding him on the back, shrieking that she needs a real man not a snivelling child. When he doesn't respond, she gives up and runs down the street in her bathrobe. From the front window, he watches her stop Mr. Gheakins from three doors down and lean into his car crying.

An hour later, her robe torn and brambles in her hair, she returns and he tries to help her into the bath. But she begins battering the side of the tub with her fists, and he has to yank her out half-wet and shove her through the bathroom door so he can lock himself in. He sits in the tub until the water is icy cold and his body is shaking.

A week after the chief's visit, a Giselle Martin from Social Services phones. She makes an appointment to visit the following Monday after school. For the first time ever, he and his mother spend a weekend cleaning. Things at the house begin to look almost tidy, though most of the junk is simply being shoved into cupboards, or under beds. But when it comes time for his room there's a commotion over his record collection. His mother, failing to appreciate there is any sort of system, starts to hurl records randomly into cardboard boxes. He lets out a loud wail when several fall from their plastic sleeves into a heap of black on black. He can't stand to watch the one corner of his world that is organized fall into a stack of scratches and imperfection. The only way he can get her to stop is to threaten her with dismantling the TV antenna, although he isn't sure how he will accomplish that if it comes to it.

When they're finally finished, he sits at his desk and inserts his ear phone.

Thank you for standing by. Have you had a chance to get on down to Vancouver's best menswear, Brandy and Wine at 557 West Broadway? They've got loads of Johnny Carson suits in, and they're on special just for you. It's 4:33 sock-it-to-me-time and here comes an oldie but goodie from Three Dog Night, "Jeremiah was a Bull Frog".

Henry can't stand the song or how soft the station has become. Good thing he's learned about Burns and Webster on CJOR talk radio. He pushes the dial around until he hears the distinctive voice of Pat Burns talking over some cranky woman who's on the Hot Line trying to make a point about pornography on television. The two of them get louder and louder until Burns is simply saying the same word over and over . . . *Doll* . . . *Doll* . . . finally he cuts her off with a snap of the phone line. Henry's hands shake. Radio is still his best friend but it is deserting him.

On the Monday the cheerful little social services woman arrives in a yellow polyester pantsuit.

Howdy, Alice. It's Miss Martin. Mind if I come in?

His mother waves her into the TV room and points at the wingback chair, then takes a seat on the couch. Henry, not wanting to sit too close to either of them, brings a chair in from the kitchen.

How are things, Alice? Miss Martin begins.

Fine.

And Henry, how about you?

I'm good.

So, Alice, you told me on the phone you work at the drugstore. How long have you been there?

Since 1968.

Nearly ten years.

Almost.

That's good. And how many hours a week do you work?

Maybe 15. Some weeks only Friday nights and Saturday afternoons.

Really. So how do you afford this house?

I inherited it. We come from a family of some substance, you know.

Henry hates it when his mother bluffs about their background, and Miss Martin must have sensed it because she keeps on.

Well, the house is better than a lot of my families can afford . . .

His mother interrupts, *We* are not one of your families. What makes you think that we are?

Well, I don't know . . .

If you don't know then stop asking. Clearly we can afford to live here.

Henry is not entirely sure how his mother has so quickly reduced the perkiness quotient in the room by half, but all of a sudden Miss Martin seems to disappear into the wings of her chair. He tries to help by making a little conversation himself.

Mom, do you think you should tell Miss Martin that you lived in this house when you were a kid?

Henry, I thank you to not refer to me as Mom. I am Alice.

Instead of him helping things, Miss Martin's questions become more rushed and mangled, and by the time she departs, her calling card left in the centre of the coffee table, it's fairly certain they will not be seeing her again. All in all, Miss Martin's biggest concern seems to have been that he and his mother can afford to live in a better house than she does.

Not long after the visit, Alice loses her job at the drugstore. Although she will never admit it, Henry figures it's because her mood swings are worsening. Too often they culminate now with her marching outside his school in her dirty trench coat and yellow rubber boots, hours before the final bell, calling for him to come home. And although she never actually does anything terribly dangerous, he feels the constant pressure of it coming. Then one day, a day she did not show up at the school, he comes home to find she's put her fist through the kitchen window and ripped an angry six inches on the underside of her arm. Blood seeps from the wound for a couple of days but she refuses to put a dressing on it. Her sheets are bloodied, and he has to wipe up drips of red from all around the house.

A month after that, he finds her sitting in front of the television with an ice pack on her hand. She is crying and doesn't seem able to talk, merely opens her mouth wide and lets tears roll down her cheeks. When he asks to see her hand, she holds up her palm. The shape of a stove element is plainly visible.

Why'd you do that, Mom?

I don't know, she mouths. When she calms down, she tells him she's seen the talent agent from Toronto, the one she met at the Cave, walking along Fourth Avenue.

I thought he'd come to find me, she says, to give me a part in a show. But the man said he'd never seen me before, that he worked in a bank. I don't know why he would lie like that.

Henry knows she is disappearing into herself with sadness. He thinks in some way it is his fault, but he doesn't know how to make it stop.

A week later, Tom stands in front of him in the hall at school. He knows by the way Tom's eyes avert it isn't going to be good news, but in no way is he prepared for what Tom has to say. Tom sticks his hip out nonchalantly, which makes his bellbottoms flare.

We're moving to Guayaquil, Ecuador, he says.

Henry says nothing.

Tom leans in to add, My dad's being transferred by the mining company and my mom wants to live near the beach — they compromised on Guayaquil. Then as if he's saying nothing more than where the family is headed for summer vacation, he puts his hand up to wave goodbye and says, We'll be gone for a while, maybe we'll catch up later.

Henry mistakes Tom's gesture as a handshake and grabs his hand, hanging on for too long, and when he finally does let go, the two of them do an awkward teenage shuffle before Tom ducks into math class. *Guayaquil? Ecuador?* Henry straggles to chemistry and slumps at his lab desk where he has plenty of room to sprawl because he's the only one who has no lab partner. He is in a daze, barely paying attention to the teacher who is conducting another one of her bizarre experiments, her wild Afro hair presiding over a stinking, flaming concoction. He failed chemistry once already, so he is taking it again and he knows Afro is going to make bubbles that float. Once she has a bubble airborne she will light it with a candle, and the bubble will sink.

All is relatively calm, until unexpectedly one of the bubbles triples in size as soon as it is lit. The burning orb moves across Afro's lab desk and heads for the girl named Sharon, or Shannon, or something like that, who sits across the aisle from him in a too-tight Charlie's Angels T-shirt. Henry comes out of his slump and wanders toward the fiery ball. A part of him thinks he might impress Shannon-or-whatever-her-name-is if he can stop it, but a bigger part of him doesn't really care. Once he is directly under the bubble, it lands on his head and the smell of burning hair fills the classroom. He lists a little toward Shannon-or-whatever, who recoils and says, Ew, as he comes close. He knows it is not the fire she's upset about — it went out as quickly as it started — it is the proximity of his head to her too-tight T-shirt.

Afro shuts down her Bunsen burner and yells, Henry, what are you doing? Why would you walk into the bubble?

I don't know, he answers.

I'm calling down to Mr. Sogland's. You go there directly. Understood?

Yes.

Mr. Sogland, fresh out of teacher's college, is the new counselor. He has a pointy nose and the joke around school is it's built to stick into other people's business. Henry has not met him before, but he's listened from his solitary seat at the end of the grade twelve's cafeteria table to the others laugh about *the nose*.

He is having trouble concentrating on what Mr. Sogland is saying, and wonders if it's because he's too focused on the nose.

It says here in your records that last year you were recommended to go into the trades. Do you think things might be easier in that stream? Mr. Sogland asks.

No, I like my classes. Especially chemistry. I'm doing better with my own lab desk. *Why are you making me feel bad? In trades I'd have to work with others, and I'd just be in the way. Probably cut my thumbs off.*

Do you have troubles at home?

No more than most. *No point in telling you about my mother, her crazy marches in front of the school? Surely you know anyway. It's your job, right?*

Any recent changes causing you difficulty?

Nothing recent. *Except my only friend, who is the slimmest shadow of a friend, but just the same my only friend, is about to leave for Ecuador and I have no one who gives a shit — no father, no brother, no sister, no functioning mother, no one at all. Even you, pencil-nose, must have someone.*

Well then what would make you deliberately want to harm yourself?

It was just meant to be fun.

When he says the word *fun* Mr. Sogland's nose goes high into the air, as if he is sniffing for more. Henry feels the glimmer of a smile. It feels good in a terribly inappropriate way to be smiling.

Do you find this funny?

No, sir.

Okay, no more cutting up in class or you will be in for detention. Clear?

Yes, sir.

Henry puts his ear speaker in and moves on down the hall and out the front door of the school.

The day before Tom's family is set to leave for Ecuador, there's a knock on the front door. When Henry opens it, Dieter Lawson seems to be hiding in the shadows of the entrance. Even though it is a gloomy spring day, he is wearing a straw hat that partially obscures his face. Henry thinks he must have come to see his mother so he twists to call her, but Mr Lawson puts his hand on his shoulder to stop him. The two of them stare at each other for a moment.

Don't worry, son. God tests those he loves the most, Mr. Lawson says.

Henry waits for more. He likes the way he's been called son and he wants to know about the test, but instead Tom's father walks down the porch steps. At the bottom, he looks up, squinting as if the sun is in his eyes, even though there is none. He tips his head so the brim of the hat obscures his eyes. He opens his mouth as if to speak, but says nothing. He turns and walks across the lawn. It isn't until he is back on his own porch that he speaks again.

Tell your mother goodbye from me, he calls.

I will, Henry answers. But knows he won't. If he does, she will either berate him for letting Mr Lawson leave without telling her, or berate him for letting him come to their house at all. He isn't sure which, just certain that mention of Tom's father and the move will set something off.

Tom himself never does come over to say goodbye.

But on the weekend when the young couple who've rented Tom's house show up with a van full of furniture, Alice marches right over and through the front door before most of their stuff is even off the front lawn. Henry, nervous about what might happen, follows her.

Hi, I'm Alice, she is saying. Haven't been inside this place in years.

Somehow she's already figured out they are newly married and have moved to Vancouver from Guelph so the husband can take a job with Federal Fisheries. She walks into the living room.

I see they never fixed the crack in the chimney, she says. Smoke'll be pouring out of there soon as you light a fire.

The pretty young wife, whose name is Patsy, looks concerned. She holds her hand up to her mouth and calls to her husband who is struggling onto the porch with a precarious load of dishes.

Dave, come and look at this.

I don't think it's a problem, Henry says. I've never seen smoke come out of there.

How would you know? his mother retorts. You were never over here.

He could say the same about her, but he lets it drop.

Dave comes into the room and sets the dishes down. He is a good-looking man, trim and youthful, but with an over-serious quizzical expression, like someone who's spent a lot of time staring at fishes. Alice sidles up to him holding out a long and unkempt fingernail toward the chimney.

See. Look way up, she says. See the crack?

I do, but I agree with your son — Henry is it? Not a problem, Dave says.

Henry wonders how Dave knows his name and not knowing what else to do he starts to make his embarrassed strangulated laugh.

Hmphf hmphf hmphf.

Shut up, Henry, his mother says.

He stops, his attention focused now on his mother's expression. Her face has clouded over and she is giving the *I dare you* stare. The stare is meant for Dave, but he knows the *I dare you* part is meant for him. He wants them to leave before there's a scene. She is silent for a moment and then holds her finger up to her lips as if imploring silence. Instead she speaks.

I'll never tell how much I know about this house. And *Henry* doesn't know everything, that's for sure. She laughs and points at him.

Well, nice meeting you, Dave says. We've got lots to do here today.

Dave turns and walks down the front steps to pick up a bureau that is too big for him to carry alone. Henry jumps to help, but Dave says, I got it.

Still, Alice does not take the hint. She stays swaying slightly in the centre of the living room. Patsy looks a little panicked after Dave disappears down the hall into the back of the house. Eventually Henry takes his mother by the arm and steers her toward the front door. To his surprise she comes easily. Once they are home, he expects her to admonish him, but she quietly disappears into her room and shuts the door.

That evening after Henry has cooked fish sticks for dinner — a scoopful of instant mash and frozen peas on each plate — she doesn't say anything about the new people, about Tom's family, or their move. Once she's finished supper, she sits in front of the television and knits. She says nothing at all, not even good night, when she slips into her bedroom.

It turns out she was saving it all up for the darkness. Well past midnight, he hears the chanting in her room begin. He switches off his transistor radio to monitor what is going on.

Dear Dee, Dear Dee, Dear Dee in the fire. Dear Dee, Dear Dee, Dear Dee make the fire, Dear Dee, Dear Dee . . .

It sounds strange and it goes on for a long time, but he is grateful it never turns into a full-on rant. The first thing that comes to mind is the sound of Mrs. Lawson calling her husband from their porch. *Dieter light the barbeque, Dieter bring in the garbage cans.* Henry lies in bed and wonders if his mother is chanting about putting Tom's father into the fire.

He knows what is happening when the noise wakes him up. It is an odd but recognizable sound, a solid crack followed by a plopping swish as the yolk streaks. He is too tired to do anything about it except turn on the bedroom light to scare the kids away. When he gets up in the morning he's dismayed to see they have egged Dave and Patsy's house too. He knows from experience it is almost impossible to remove if left long enough to cook in the sun, so he hoses the egg from their place first, hoping they are still asleep and will never find out.

By the time he is finished, it is just after 7:00 AM, and he walks to the laundromat at Fourth and Macdonald. He isn't sure why he goes there except that he knows it will be open, it will be warm, it will smell clean, and it won't be his house.

He sits on one of the hard chairs between the extruder and the cigarette vending machine. No one else is in the laundromat except for the woman with no front teeth who takes in bundles of laundry from the people too lazy to wash for themselves, and a jockish guy who's trying to wrestle a heap of training shorts and singlets, all of them the same greyish colour, into an orderly pile. While Henry sits watching the pile of grey grow, he fingers the coins in his pocket and realizes he has seven quarters — enough to buy a pack of cigarettes.

He slips the coins one by one into the vending machine. It feels reassuring when each one hit its mark and registers in the brain of the machine. He pulls the knob under the duMauriers and a red crush-proof pack vaults out of the guts. He runs his fingernail over the customs stamp and pushes the tray of cigarettes up. He removes the silver foil from one side and twelve virgins, all erect and stiff, stare up at him. He runs his fingers over the tips. It makes a seductive fluttering sound enticing him to bend down and smell the tobacco. The virgin in him realizes he is beginning to get a boner from molesting cigarettes. He rubs his hand slightly over the fly of his jeans.

He doesn't get very many erections. Or more correctly, he doesn't get very many he can do anything with. He knows in this he is different from most of his male classmates who spend half their time whacking off, and the other half talking about it.

And the laundromat is an odd place to have this happen, not all that comfortable to be feeling a stiff urge in front of a toothless hag and a jock with too many grey singlets. But still, since this erection has already lasted longer than usual without hedging back into itself, he decides to go with it and see where it takes him. He tries to think about the blonde girl in the front row of English class, the one with the black eyeliner, above and below her eyes, and the tight sweaters — pink ribbed, red ribbed, white ribbed — all of them taut over giant boobs. He rubs his hand a bit harder over the zipper of his jeans. His right leg jumps out in a two-step motion and he recognizes it as the same movement his mother makes sometimes when she is dancing. Next thing he knows black-eyeliner girl is fading, and all he can see is his mother's ruby lipstick, her yellowed overlong fingernails, and her gut. Then he is smelling her, her breath, her underarms, and feeling so sad his erection dies. It's very disappointing, along with the money wasted on cigarettes when he doesn't even smoke.

He is sitting in a demoralized heap with barely enough energy to get out of the chair when the woman who runs the place shouts over to him.

Get out of here. No loitering.

Sorry. Henry leaps out of his seat.

And don't come back, she yells. I saw you.

He knows what he's been doing is inappropriate, but he hadn't meant to cause the woman any trouble. He sort of thought he was in his one-way glass case again, and he's so used to people not paying him any attention he's almost surprised she noticed him at all. Outside, his hand trembles as he tries to insert the transistor's speaker into his ear. He's having trouble getting it straight, and his hand shakes so much he drops the radio on the sidewalk. The turquoise case shatters. The radio's contents splay in front of him in a terrible array. He picks up the useless pieces, pockets the battery, and chucks the rest in the garbage can at the corner.

The next day Henry quits school. He just can't keep going day after day to that brick and mortar warehouse for teenagers who look like him, who dress like him, but who won't talk to him — a place where he has no friends, no one even to get an erection over. He is always alone. It feels worse than being bullied. He and his mother are a disgrace, they have no rights, no right even to ask for help.

When he tells the school secretary he is dropping out, she doesn't say anything, simply buzzes Mr. Sogland, who sticks his head out of the counselor's office and motions him in.

So, are you finding your studies too difficult? Mr. Sogland asks.

Henry thinks it's better to say yes than to admit his real problems.

Which studies are too tough?

Socials, math. All of them I guess.

Well it's not too late to go into trades.

No, no trades.

Have you thought about a tutor?

No.

Why not? Is it the cost?

No.

What then?

I just don't think a tutor would do any good. I was wondering . . .

Mr. Sogland cuts him off to ask, Should I contact your mother, perhaps send a social worker to the house?

Gosh, no . . . that . . . I think that . . . that would not be good.

He stops talking. He can see Mr. Sogland is busy looking through the window in his office door at black-eyeliner girl who is sitting in a ribbed sweater in the waiting area. Mr. Sogland's eyes are completely on the girl.

No, he continues, no need for a social worker. We have one.

Mr. Sogland swings his focus back. You do? Who?

Giselle Martin from Social Services.

Mr. Sogland makes a note, then looks up and asks, How are things going with her?

Good. She recommended I take a year out from my studies.

She did?

Yes. She thinks I need a break.

Henry isn't sure why he is lying, he just knows he needs to get out of Mr. Sogland's office, get away from the school, and away from people like black-eyeliner girl whom he believes is probably feeling squeamish at the thought of sitting in the same chair as him after he leaves.

Well, Mr. Sogland says, you're old enough to make up your own mind about this, so if you really want to withdraw you're always welcome back next year.

Okay, Henry says.

Mr. Sogland's face lights up with a goofy grin as he motions black-eyeliner girl in.

Henry feels her veer away from him as their paths cross at the threshold.

THREE

Snake Eyes

A YEAR LATER, HENRY CAN STILL feel that veer. He's certain he's a failure. He's a high-school dropout. He has acne — the blond moustache on his upper lip barely covers any of it — and he has no job. No friends. When the front bell rings and no one is there, he just stands at the door. The lawn badly needs cutting. He doesn't want to go out because the kids have probably written swear words in black marker on the hood of the car again, or put dog shit under leaves where he or his mother walk. It isn't until he sees Dave and Patsy's white cat pounce and come up with a limp snake, its head dangling as if it has been severed, that he moves off the porch. He doesn't want the cat to hurt itself again from a razor blade stuck in snake meat.

Scat, he calls. Scat.

Stamping his foot finally makes the cat drop the snake. When he gets close he can see there is only a dead snake and no blade. What else have the kids done? He avoids the mouth as he picks the snake up — he's heard snakes have a biting reflex even after death — and he walks it to the curb. A rush of liquid hits the side of his head. His free hand goes to his temple and green algae drips from his fingers. The tip of a super water gun is sticking out over the hood of the car parked across the street.

I see you, he calls.

Two early-teen boys and a younger girl laugh as they run down the street.

The boy carrying the gun yells, Your mother is psycho.

I know, he says.

After the kids are out of sight, Henry holds the snake over the sewer grate. He sees the tiny black coal bubble of an eye and the flash of white belly as the body twists and falls.

Lying on his bed that afternoon, he thinks, Maybe dead things shouldn't go into the sewer. Maybe it's better to give them a proper burial. He gets up to turn on his record player and distract himself. He drops the needle randomly without looking at the turntable, and he's flat out again, too lazy to get back up, when he discovers it's Roger Miller's "King of the Road". He hates the song, mostly because he's worried he's that man of *means by no means.*

After listening for a time, he gets off the bed and pulls the needle. But once he's back down, visions of his mother's failures start to swim in his head. The nasty words the kids wrote in black magic marker on her car, the ripped and dirty underwear they left on her antenna, her inability to protect herself, her confusion. When one of them threw a stone knocking her sunglasses to the ground, she just stooped to pick them up.

These thoughts twist in Henry's mind together with thoughts of his own failures and rejections until they're a writhing mess, worse than a nest of snakes. A panic starts to rise in his body and swirl around, landing for a time in the pit of his stomach, then settling in his penis. The tip is tingling. He yanks it out of his pants, tries to make it do something, stand on its own, transport him. He thinks about Debi's bouncy cheeks, about black-eyeliner girl's tits, even virgin filter tips and grey singlets. But none of it works. The more he yanks and pulls, the more the shaft collapses. Soon he's limper than the snake he let fall through the hole in the sewer lid. He zips his pants back up, gets off the bed, walks out the front door and across the lawn to Dave's house. He knocks, and because it's a Saturday afternoon, Dave is home.

Are there any jobs at Fisheries? Henry asks. I like animals, and fish too.

I'll ask around, Dave answers.

I worry about animals mostly, Henry says. I'd like to work with animals although fish would be okay, and so would reptiles. He doesn't know why he is babbling, maybe it's the dead snake, the white cat, a limp penis, all of them muddled into one giant concern. He takes in a big breath, stifling a nervous snort. He hears Patsy at the back of the house, in the kitchen. She's washing dishes, making a lot of noise. A pot crashes against the side of the stainless steel sink when she calls out.

Ask him about the hooligans. Ask why they keep coming here. Why they egg the house?

It has nothing to do with you guys, Henry says. I'm on it. I'll take care of it.

Maybe there's something in Agriculture, Dave says. But even if there is, it could take a while.

That's okay. Thanks for looking.

Henry walks with resolve down the steps and around the side of his own house toward the garden shed. He moves the garbage cans away from the door. Inside he puts his collection of rosette pine cones out of harm's way, then takes the push mower off the wall. He presses the mower forward down the sidewalk and out onto the front lawn. In no time the grass is trimmed and looking much better. Once he's hung the mower back up, he walks into the house and positions himself in front of the bathroom mirror. He picks up the razor and takes the blond moustache off his upper lip. It's lighter than his hair, but it looks darker in the sink. He stands back. Other than the small trickle of blood from where he nicked his lip, he's pretty sure he looks better too. His face is regular and balanced, if a bit pale, but there's less acne under the moustache than he expected.

You can only do what you can do, he says to his reflection.

He takes a piece of toilet paper and wipes the whiskers from the rim of the sink. He drops the paper into the pile of junk that has reaccumulated in the hall. Then he opens the front door and shoves all of it onto the porch and down the steps. He uses a rake and shovel to push everything toward the street where he makes a starter pile on top of the sewer lid, another bigger pile beside it. He sets a match to the small pile. The smoke is thick and black, especially when the wax on the milk cartons begins to melt. The trio of kids from down the way are attracted to the smoke and eager to join in, help him tend the fire. They bring the super water gun loaded.

There, Henry says pointing to the edge of the pile where the flames are threatening to get out of hand.

The middle boy expertly directs a stream of water to the trouble spot.

Henry picks up a running shoe that had been his when he was a child and hands it to the girl. He motions with his hand to her to throw it in.

Cool, she says as they watch the sole of the shoe begin to bubble, then spew like a rubber volcano.

Cool indeed, Henry says. In a weird way he's more comfortable with these kids than he is with people his own age. No more egging the houses. Okay?

Sure, the eldest boy says. The other two nod in solemn agreement.

After the embers of the fire die down and the kids have left to go home for supper, he hangs the rake and shovel in the shed, and he lines up the rosette cones in descending order of size on the windowsill. He walks into the house and down the hall to his bedroom, where he turns on the Sony desktop radio his mother gave him for Christmas. He likes the new FM station CFOX and he's standing by the radio thinking how nobody needs to know his only picture of Tom was in that pile of burning junk when he hears the DJ say, *Save your Cadbury wrappers for the Cadbury $100 record rush contest . . . Drum roll please, and* *now the moment you've all been waiting for, announcing the first regional winner of the Cadbury wrapper record rush contest, and the winner is . . . are you hanging from the ceiling yet, boys and girls . . . ? and the winner is, wait for it gang . . . more drum roll please . . . and the winner is Henry Parkins in Kitsilano. Henry if you're listening and can get to the phone in the next five minutes, call us at 685-CFOX and all those records are yours including this new one from the Stones, "Far Away Eyes".*

While he dials, he hears Mick singing about a girl with *far away eyes.* The pedal steel and country twang in the song is truly cool.

FOUR

Longer Nails

SIX MONTHS INTO THE JOB at the Burnaby office of Agriculture Canada, Henry sits anxious at his desk sorting mail. It's a Monday morning and already he's behind because he's been too focused on peeping through the slot of a window on the other side of the room. Despite the building being a grey bunker with little natural light, and erratic heating that bangs on when the sun comes out and hisses off when temperatures drop below freezing, he is happy enough working here. He likes that he's mostly alone in the mailroom and, although people don't necessarily come around to befriend him, they don't go out of their way to avoid him either, don't draw back like they did at the high school. So he really doesn't want Alice showing up in her dirty yellow boots to ruin everything for him.

He's done what he can to be vague about where the office is exactly, and he's managed to make it sound like he's out most of the time (which is true at least in aspiration — one day he does hope to become a poultry technician, a job that will take him into the field), but he can't help getting up every few minutes to check to make sure she's not outside. She was so agitated over the weekend, at first too loving in her barely hidden sexual way, and then when he told her to *back off,* raking his face with her fingernails. Her nails have grown so long they are beginning to curl and twist like dirty roots on a radish. The full-on physical attack frightened him and he wanted to tell her so, but at the same time he did not want to hurt her feelings.

This morning when he was applying some of her pancake makeup to cover the scratches, she sat slumped and depressed at the kitchen table with the phone book open to the Federal government listings. She said she was looking for Agriculture Canada so she could come to work with him. To make her stay at the table and not follow him to the bus stop he promised he'd come home early and they would do something fun. In reality, he'd made her an appointment with Dr. Davis.

When he gets home, she is not happy to learn they're going to see her physician. Why? I'm not leaving the house.

Mom, you are making me scared.

Really? she says, her eyes wide with hurt or perhaps fear.

Yes, really. You attacked me. You know I want the best for you. I want to find out if the doctor can help.

She sags in resignation.

At the clinic they wait with two pregnant women and a clutch of sniffing children. Across from them, a poster features a chorus of colourful characters washing their hands under the banner: *Flummox the Flu*. A cartoon bubble above one of the creatures exclaims, *Keep nails short!* Henry thinks briefly about pointing this out to his mother, but worries she'll react and frighten the children.

When the nurse comes to usher Alice into Dr. Davis' office, she turns to Henry.

Will you come and listen to what he says this time?

The doctor doesn't get up from his desk, and his shoulders seem to drop when he looks at them over his glasses.

What brings you here today, Alice? he asks.

Her only response is to slump again, so Henry jumps in.

She's been acting kind of erratically, seems a bit out of touch. Show the doctor your fingernails, Mom.

She holds up her hands, and the doctor's shoulders drop even further. She's tried to make things look better with some purple metallic nail polish, but it's only made it look as if she carries some kind of gangrenous disease.

What's this about, Alice? the doctor asks.

It's a sin to cut any part of the sacred body, she says.

How've you been feeling? A little more down than usual?

Yes, she answers.

Henry feels his neck disappear into his shirt collar as if he were a turtle. When he looks round, they are all slumping in their different ways.

Then the doctor sighs and swings around in his chair toward Henry. Your mother suffers from depression, he says. Not the ordinary sort of blues, a more serious pathological sort called manic depression.

He shoves his glasses back up his nose and extends a pamphlet toward Henry. You read about it, he says. It can be hereditary. It's tragic when these things happen. And there's not much we can do about it.

The doctor turns his focus back to the patient, What do you think, Alice — should we up your medication?

Yes, she says.

Henry is shocked. He didn't know she was taking medication or that anyone, let alone a doctor, had known there was something so wrong with her she needed it. There's silence in the room.

Any questions? the doctor asks.

What do you mean hereditary? Henry says.

Dr. Davis shifts in his chair, pushes back on the swivel seat and asks, How old are you, Henry?

Twenty-one, he answers.

He doesn't know what the doctor's nod means. Panic starts to rise from his stomach. He's tasting it at the back of his throat, waiting for it to clear, when he notices the doctor looking impatiently behind him. He turns to see the same big-faced clock on the wall that they'd had in the classrooms at school. He knows then he's no more important than the frog whose heart they had pithed in biology. Suddenly he is that frog who can't talk, who barely has energy to breathe. The sound of Dr. Davis' voice brings his focus back to the room they're sitting in.

Look I'm sorry, the doctor says, I have many other pressing appointments this afternoon. I'm happy to talk to either of you on another day. Call if things get worse.

Henry and Alice leave the office, Henry with a pamphlet in hand and she with a prescription for a daily dose of something called chlorpromazine.

When they get home, he opens up the pamphlet in the solitude of his bedroom. He smooths his hands over the folds as if straightening out the paper is going to make the reading easier. Even ordinary words like exercise, good nutrition, regular sleep, are frightening when they're printed on a pea-green sheet folded in three with the title *You and Mental Illness* stamped on the front of it. He scans the leaflet looking for a few words of solace. *Engage the family in the solution*; that's a good one — how do you do that when the only family member is the problem? The more he scans, the more he finds truly scary words, words that freak him out: *bipolar, manic, psychotic*. Then he reads about the anti-psychotics, how they don't work for everyone and can take some time to kick in. He paces the bedroom before walking into the living room where Alice is planted in front of the television, knitting what looks to be yet another pair of pompom slippers.

Mom, I need to know a few things.

Like?

Like who is my dad?

She stares straight ahead at the television.

Your father died in the war. You know that.

Please, Mom. I was born in 1960. What war are you talking about?

He lets a few minutes pass while they watch a rerun of a Carol Burnett show. At the end of the show Carol tugs on her ear. Henry knows this is Carol's code for saying hello to her grandmother.

Well what about my grandmother? he asks. Your mother, what was she like?

She died before you were born.

I know that, but what about her?

She left us this house. She was a good woman.

Mom, did she have depression or some sort of mental problem?

Snip. Snip. Snip. Three new pompoms fall off a cardboard slat into his mother's lap. She scoops them up and throws them into the air. She catches two and tosses them at him.

Catch, lover. Let's have some fun.

He lets the pompoms fall to the floor. He hates it when she turns coy. A Pepsodent commercial comes on the television when she stands to retrieve the pompom she missed. She throws that pompom at Henry too and sings him the line, *You'll wonder where the yellow went*, then blows him a good-night kiss and walks out of the room.

Three weeks later, Henry comes home to a surprisingly clean kitchen. Alice sits with a pot of pink nail polish and a pile of freshly cut fingernails beside her. The drugs have kicked in, he thinks.

I don't know what I was thinking with that horrid purple polish, she says.

Looks good, Mom. He moves over to the fridge and pulls out a few wilted carrots and a beef pot pie.

I bought a bunch of spinach and some onions today, she says.

Really? Good.

After supper, while they sit in the television room debating whether to watch the Fonz or Meathead, she pulls out her knitting bag and hands him a pair of number 9 needles.

I'm going to teach you to knit, she says.

You did that already.

I only taught you how to knit and purl. Tonight I'm going to teach you basketweave.

He really isn't interested, but knitting is something she's good at, and it's a focus they can retreat to when needed, so he lets her. While he casts on stitches she starts to talk.

Dr. Davis called, she says. He told me I might be able to get a job at the *Vancouver Courier*.

Wow.

It's part of a program.

Good. What will you be doing?

Bundling newspapers.

Sounds okay. Does it pay?

Of course it pays.

Just wondering. You said it was part of a program.

It is, but still they have to pay. I used to work at the drugstore you know.

Yeah. Yeah. I know. Shhhh, the Fonz is on.

He's relieved she'll be working. If she's working, her curiosity about his job will wane, and she won't have the time to follow him to the office. Which is good, especially now. He really couldn't take her showing up at work, what with his new responsibilities and all.

On September 12, 1981, the Federal Government had installed a fax machine. To most people the machine is a miracle, and Henry — the only one trained to change the heat-sensitive rolls that allow the text to travel — is treated like a miracle worker. Everybody is in love with the technology. Lunch orders are faxed to restaurants around the corner, confidential medical information is sent all over the Lower Mainland, and smoochy love messages are sent everywhere. Henry knows who likes pastrami on rye, whose gum disease is becoming an issue, and who's having a romance across town. It's been terrifying and exhausting. He isn't used to having so many people around, sometimes he can't breathe properly, and if there are too many in the queue at once his heart races. To get through it, he focuses on the piece of paper and not the person handing it to him, especially when the paper has eye-popping words like *rectal and vaginal prolapse*. Even though he's figured out the woman who gave him that message was actually reporting on a herd of cattle, he still can't look her in the eye.

At first HR tried to control the crush around the fax machine by issuing an office-wide memo saying Henry was to be responsible for recording the number of pages and the nature of the information contained in all the faxes. He was relieved; this meant he could spend part of his time alone figuring out which of the HR categories — commercial, medical, family, or other — the various messages fit into. But what to do with the order to a florist for a dozen red roses going to a Dr. Ulla Martine, veterinarian, with a note that says *Until your chickens grow new feathers*? When he asked, even HR couldn't decide which category that one belonged in, and after debating whether they should create a multiple category, the powers that be decided to outright ban all personal faxes. But by then everybody had gotten to know Henry and the title *Fax God* had pretty much stuck to him. And he doesn't mind the machine so much anymore because it's through the fax that he's met the chief poultry inspector, a man everybody calls *Chief*.

Chief likes that Henry has a nickname too, and calls him Fax God every chance he gets. Henry likes the way Chief says Fax God, and he's begun to think about how he might work up the nerve to tell Chief that what he really wants to be is a poultry technician and go out on inspections. Rows of blinking hens and collections of eggs just seem so right to him. Something indescribably soft and ordered overcomes him when he thinks about the chickens. He knows not all of them will be like the chocolate-brown hen in his *Farm Folk* set, but thinking about this job does remind him of a time when his mother used to be easier and he had a friend next door. A time when he fantasized about turning out cool like Tom. Perhaps it still isn't too late to learn to move with precision and athleticism instead of being clunky, stunned Henry.

One evening, after Alice has been working at the *Courier* for a few weeks, she and Henry are in front of the TV trying to decide whether to watch *Three's Company* or *Different Strokes*. Lately he hasn't cared what they watch because his mother has been calm and just lets him sit and veg after supper. He's been allowed to let his mind drift to whatever he feels like, which mostly has been a lot toward Kitty, the girl he met at the Arbutus Mall, the one he still can't believe actually talks to him. So it's really upsetting that on this evening his mother is agitated again. She's already asked him three times why he can't get her some more glamorous work at Agriculture Canada, and she is going in for a fourth.

Well why, Henry?

Why what?

Why can't you at least ask if there is a job for me?

Because we don't bundle newspapers.

That's not all I can do.

I know.

I could run a fax machine. I could have glamorous work too.

It's not that glamorous.

I'm the mother, I'm the one who should have the better job.

Your job is good, Mom. It's right in the neighbourhood.

It's so dirty, and that awful noise.

Henry has heard it all before, but doesn't dare say it's the noise that makes it work for her — the printing machines are so loud everyone wears earplugs and no one can hear what anybody else is saying. He can see she's going to keep at it unless he does something to stop her. So he lies.

I might be fired next week, he says.

Because of a girl?

No. Why would you think that? Just because.

Oh, she says. That's not good. But maybe a job will open for me.

Mom! We need the money from my salary.

This works. She leaves the subject — perhaps she's even a little worried for him. For a time they sit in front of the television knitting. Things stay peaceful enough through the beginning of *M*A*S*H* that he can even allow his mind to wander back to Kitty again. While Radar and Hawkeye bicker about who should go first in the canteen line, he starts detailing in his mind what has gone before with her. He hopes by going over it he might come up with some new strategy he can use to push things forward.

They met in the lineup at the Woodward's Food Floor. He was in front of her, his cart full with a week's worth of groceries. She stood behind him with nothing.

Want to go ahead of me? he asked.

That'd be great, she said. I only need to buy a pack of cigs.

It was a tight squeeze for her to get to her Winstons, and when she pressed by him he smelled tobacco on her coat, and something else indescribably arousing. He was scared to go back the next week — What if she was there? But what if she wasn't? — so he took a line with him he'd heard one of the guys in research use at the office. It was simple, just a few words, but the potential for him to mess it up was high. He would just have to stay relaxed, not let that nervous snort happen or anything else stupid like his hands flying up in the air, which had started to happen lately whenever he got nervous.

So when he arrived, and she scooted in behind him again with no food cart, he could hardly believe it. He turned sideways and showed her the way.

She nodded and said, You.

How goes it? he said.

He got it out. He used the line from the guy in research, and it worked. He was actually looking at her and he could see she was going to answer him.

Good. Good. And you?

Oh you know. What goes comes back.

What? she laughed.

This is where he knew to disengage as he couldn't necessarily handle correcting himself, but he didn't want to blow it either, so he looked down like he was working the fax machine and everything just sort of flowed. He could hear her talking.

I'm gonna get a coffee after I buy some smokes, she said. Want to join me?

He didn't like coffee but he was happy to order them both a cup from the thatched-roof Koffee Kiosk in the middle of the mall. On the counter there was a basket of cookies and Nanaimo bars, but when he turned to ask if she wanted one she was inhaling so deeply on a cigarette he decided not to interrupt her. She didn't look like much of an eater anyway.

They sat on the benches by the simulated indoor park with its Astroturf, potted plants, and giant playjungle. He had bought vanilla-flavoured which turned out to be a mistake as she took her coffee black and strong, but he sort of liked it and she drank hers anyway while she finished her Winston. Normally smoke bothered him, but her cigarettes were American and smelled exotic, and he was glad when she decided to have another. While she finished her third, she said she'd like to stay and chat, but she had to get back on shift at the dry cleaners.

See you next week maybe, she said.

Hope so.

Back home, his mother threw a small fit when she smelled cigarette smoke on him. But she calmed down after he explained he hadn't been smoking, he'd been sitting beside a woman at the mall who smoked.

The second time he came home smelling of cigarettes, Alice asked, Were you sitting beside that girl again? When he said yes, she smiled and asked, Did you get her name? He mistook the smile as encouragement.

Her name is Kitty, he said. She works in the dry cleaners at Arbutus Centre.

It worries him now how much he has told her, but it was fun at the time to share the news with someone and a sheer pleasure just to say Kitty's name out loud.

By the time the *M*A*S*H* theme song "Suicide is Painless" is playing, Henry is in a state of deep regret that he told his mother anything. He's not sure what she might do with the information. His anxiety spikes when he notices that instead of knitting pompom slippers, she's knitting what looks like a female voodoo doll. He wonders if there is going to be a burning Kitty effigy in the middle of the night. She is busy stuffing the small knit figure with cotton batting when he asks, What is that?

It's dead, she says.

Who's dead?

Alice Parkins. Me, she says.

She gets up from her chair and retrieves a magazine from the stack in the corner of the room. She sets a *Woman's World* in his lap. The cover shows an array of cheerful knit figures with the caption, *Make your own Mexican Day of the Dead Fiesta*.

Why are you making these? he asks.

Why not?

We're not Mexican.

Immediately he knows he should not have said this. She holds her hand to the side of his face. Her fingernails press into his cheek. The message she is giving him is that nails as weapons can return at any moment. This makes him want to ask again about the mental health of his father and his grandparents, but the timing is definitely not right.

Later, when he tries to sleep, the knitted dead figure and the fingernails keep him awake. He imagines nails pressing through the flesh on his cheek. Every time a nail penetrates, psychedelic colours flash in front of his eyes. His heart races as he tries to figure out whether these flashes are hallucinations marking the beginning of his own mental illness. He turns so many times in the bed the sheets are a twisted mess and eventually he can't lie there any longer, so he snaps on the light and searches in his desk drawer for the green pamphlet. The words *You and Mental Illness* burn through his fingers as he reads that an hallucination *is a sense of perception for which there is no external reality.* His mother's threats with the fingernails are real and the colours have disappeared with the light on. This calms him enough that he can continue reading, believing for the time being anyway that he does not have a mental illness, though he concludes he does have a problem. He reads with renewed interest the line about involving family in the solution.

After about an hour, when he hears his mother's deep drug-induced snoring, he creeps into her room. One by one, slowly and carefully, he opens her dresser drawers until he finds the little book in which she keeps handwritten addresses and phone numbers. Under the hall light, he flips through the pages. He's surprised to come across an old calling card from a talent agent named Bob Toronto, but he keeps thumbing until he finds his aunt in England. He met her once but remembers little about her except that she's his mother's older sister and his only relative.

Next day at work, he searches through the pen and elastic collection in his desk looking for enough quarters to make the long distance call from the payphone outside the lunchroom.

Hello, it's Henry from Canada. Is Esther there?

Who?

Esther.

This is Esther. Who's calling?

Henry. Alice's son.

The line is silent for so long, he thinks it's broken.

Hello, are you there? he asks.

What do you want?

My mother, she's not well. Is there . . . Well, is there any history of illness in the family?

We're all dead or dying. Who isn't?

I mean any history of . . . I don't know —

Henry feels ridiculous. This is his aunt he is speaking to, and he can't even say the words he needs to say. Can't spit out *mental illness, craziness, nuttiness,* or any variation. Surely she knows what he's getting at. But if she knows then it must be true, and he doesn't want to hear that either; he so much doesn't want to hear it, he holds his breath for fear of it. He nearly drops the handset into the wastebasket when she starts speaking again.

What do you think? his aunt says. She's nuts just like my mother. Your grandmother was nuts, you know. But your mother's the one who got the house and all the money, and I got nothing. So she can't be that nuts. She even took my husband. I got absolutely nothing. Be grateful.

Click.

The line is dead. He knows she's hung up, but he tries to reconnect by jiggling the coin mechanism. He didn't even get to ask about his father and now he has to wonder if his aunt's husband might be his father. Who is or was his aunt married to? He uses the remaining quarters to call again. He listens to the strange double burr of an English line, but no one picks up. After three tries, the phone does not return the quarters and he has to give up.

He walks back through the lab to his cubicle to find a stack of reports for faxing. In a strange way he's relieved by the amount of work piled on his desk. He likes work.

He's good at it, it's his oasis. He picks up the first report and reads 47 *hens kept caged on slatted floor, all hens have extremely long nails that are used as weapons.*

Jeez, he mutters.

Henry's in a good mood on the Saturday morning as he readies to go to the Arbutus Mall. Things seem back to normal with his mother after the incident earlier in the week, and he's since learned they weren't even as out of whack as he'd thought. It turns out she'd been told that day her work program was going to end, so it wasn't entirely crazy to be asking him to help her find work.

He puts on the new black T-shirt and blue jeans he bought from the Mark's Work Wearhouse on Fourth Avenue. Kitty wears a lot of black and he thinks she'll approve. He plans to ask if she has time to go for a spin and catch a coffee away from the mall. He's cleaned out his mother's car, throwing out stacks of old mail and remnants of takeout food. He shaves extra carefully and puts a bit of water on his thick blond hair to hold down the cowlick at the back. He notices his hair is darkening a little, wonders about the genetics of having a dark-haired mother. His father must have been fair. When he's ready he tries to slip quietly out the front door, but Alice hears him.

Why are you wearing that awful black shirt? she calls.

I like it.

Makes you look like a workie.

I am a workie.

Where are you going?

To do the shopping.

I'll come.

It's okay. I can handle it.

No, I want to come.

It's too far for you to walk.

I thought you said you were taking the car. You don't even have the shopping cart with you.

No, I'm walking. I'm just getting the cart now.

He disappears into the front hall cupboard and makes a lot of noise looking for the cart. After he finds it, he stands in the dark closet for a time until he's pretty sure his mother has distracted herself and is no longer waiting to go with him.

But as he emerges, she's standing right there. I need the exercise, she says. Give me the cart, I'll walk with you.

Maybe I will take the car after all, he says. The load might be too big for walking.

Okay, I'll drive with you then.

Henry shrugs. All right.

I just wish you'd take that awful shirt off, put on something with a little colour.

Quiet, Mom.

They load the cart into the back of the car and Henry drives as fast as he can to the Arbutus Mall so that they can get in and out of the Food Floors before Kitty goes on break. He lets his mother load the cart with cookies, pastas, two tubs of ice cream, sausages, all the things he knows are not good for them, because in the end it's quicker to do this than to argue. He's walking stooped, he's so tense in the neck. It isn't until they've paid and are leaving the Food Floors that he lets his shoulders drop from around his ears. They're almost out the mall door when his mother spins on her heel and says, I want to check out the dry cleaners.

No. You can't, Henry says. The ice cream will melt.

But she's already off and he has to drag the too-full shopping cart behind him. He's keeping up with her until a bottle of apple juice hooks on one of the benches by the playjungle and smashes on the tile floor. He stops to pick up the big pieces so nobody will get hurt, and by the time he catches up, she is already talking to Kitty. From the doorway he hears her say, Why would you turn a perfectly good name like Catherine into something so slutty as Kitty?

Mom, Henry wails, I can't believe you said that.

Kitty says, This is your mom?

He feels his ears begin to burn hot and a snort of anguished embarrassment move up his throat. He tries to suppress it, but a sound like the stifled choke of a dying hyena comes out his mouth.

Chaaanggh-Chaaanggh-Chaaanggh-de-topukh, please.

Only the last word comes out at any sort of normal level and volume, and he has to wipe his eyes when he's finished speaking. He'd been trying to say, Change the topic, please.

Kitty and his mother look at him with alarm, but he sees behind the expression on Kitty's face — *he's just another weirdo guy at the mall, with a crazy mother.* Any chance he had with her is over.

Pull yourself together, Mom, and come with me. Now! he barks.

Alice looks at him with a mixture of confusion and hurt, but says nothing. He can't tell whether she's being disingenuous or is simply so socially inept she really doesn't know what she's done. Either way, he needs to get out of the mall. He doesn't want the dying hyena routine to be just the warm-up.

After they get home, he takes the container of Häagen-Dazs Vanilla Swiss Almond to his bedroom and eats the entire thing. He wolfs it fast. When Alice calls to ask where the ice cream went, he doesn't answer. The skin from one of the almonds sticks between his incisor and front tooth where it starts to annoy the shit out of him. When he hears her opening the cellophane on the lemon cookie pack, he stalks into the kitchen, snatches it from her, and throws it on the floor.

Well, I never. What has gotten into you, Henry?

I think you know.

I don't know.

He feels like weeping. His gut tells him he should move away from this house, but he can't bring himself to abandon his mother or the cocoon of his bedroom lined with his albums, the one place where she mostly leaves him in peace. He goes back to his room, pulls a pad out from his desk and tears out all the sheets and tapes them onto the windows of his door. Then he rips off the black T-shirt and blue jeans — they're too sophisticated for him anyway — draws the front drapes and thumbs through the records until he finds Sam the Sham and the Pharaohs. He jams the rocket chair under his doorknob and turns the volume way up. He drops the needle on "Wooly Bully" and dances alone in his underpants.

FIVE

New Occupants

I'M GOING TO START WITH Beginners' Basics and work my way up to the Jane Fonda Burn Class, Alice says as she lays the Kitsilano Community Centre fitness schedule on the table.

Henry is not sure this will ever happen, and in time he's proven right, but his mother does start a routine of walking to the Centre a few times every week where she relaxes in the hot tub and even gets on the stationary bicycle for a couple of spins. This is good because the drugs have increased her appetite and she's put on more weight. The Centre also has group music lessons, and she tells him about sitting in a circle singing with a bunch of other people and playing the ukulele. Her favourite tune is "Think of Me".

Remember that one? she says. Skeeter Davis sang it. It's got only three chord changes, but it sounds so good.

She sings, *Think of me when you're lonely.*

Henry remembers Skeeter, but he doesn't remember her ever singing the song. Or maybe it's just the way Alice sings it, but it doesn't matter. She's been getting out of the house and she's met some people who will listen to her for more than three seconds. And that is what's important.

She often mentions two brothers, Jim and Chas, whom she first encountered in the hot tub. She tells Henry about them over supper, tidbits about their lives, along with new recipes for rhubarb cobbler, ideas for spring colours. One night, after six months of talk, she waggles her fingers in front of Henry's face. Her nails are meticulously painted in a showy silver polish — a colour Chas has apparently recommended.

Don't they look beautiful and, oh, I've got an income stream again, she says.

This too is a new thing for her, running two completely different thoughts together in one sentence and both of them rooted in the real world. He has to admit it's a relief to hear she might have work again. Although she's refused over the years to give any details about her savings — Don't want Little Ducky troubling himself — he knows, even with his job at Agriculture, money is becoming a concern. All the previous winter they were having to turn the heat off during the day. Then in the spring she broke down and applied for a mortgage on the house, something she'd apparently promised her own mother she would never do.

You have a new job? he asks.

Yes, I'm a landlady.

Where?

Here, she points downstairs. I've had Hydro turn the power back on down there.

Years before, a couple lived in the basement suite, but no one had been down there since he was five or six. As a teenager, he tried to convince her to let him sleep there or at least use it as a study, but she claimed the key was lost and it wasn't safe to inhabit. He knew better than to argue back then.

After supper, they push the suite's door open. It creaks like an old person startled by a visitor. The place smells musty, but appears livable enough. Alice goes directly into the kitchen where she turns on the stove. While the elements heat up, she removes the dishcloths jammed into the freezer and fridge doors to keep them ajar. She sticks her nose inside the fridge and sniffs.

Whew. We'll need baking soda to get the smell out.

He watches while she flits, keeping his eye on the now fiery-red elements. It's an age-old concern he'll probably never lose. Whenever she's near a big pane of glass, a burning candle, a hot stove, some part of him will always watch for the quick flash of the hand. He wants to be there to stop it.

You could help, you know, she says.

He reaches over and flicks off the stove elements.

Two days later, Jim and Chas show up ready to move in. Mrs. Krumpskey, the nosy neighbour from across the street, watches from her porch and even ventures once to the edge of her lawn where she looks poised to say something, but doesn't. Possibly she's intimidated by Jim's impressive size. In no way do these two men look like brothers. Chas is delicate, maybe a year older than Henry, mid- to late-twenties, with a well-shaven face and impeccable clothing — creased khakis, a fresh white dress shirt, and stylish loafers. He seems excited to meet Henry and moves gracefully in and out of the door carrying his matching leather bags.

Jim is a tall, sprawling man with a bushy beard and a thick thatch of greying chest hair popping from the neck of his flannel shirt. If they are brothers, Jim is the elder by at least ten years. He stands imposing as a horse in the frame of the door and has to stoop to walk through. He grunts something when Henry sticks his hand out, but he doesn't take the hand, simply walks past and throws his duffle bag into the bedroom. It seems to be all he has brought with him. He lies down in the middle of the bed, his feet extending over the end of it.

Not much room for me in that bed, Chas giggles.

For sure these men are not brothers, but Henry's not certain his mother has caught the gist of it.

Could you help me with something at the car? Chas asks Henry.

Henry walks with him toward a beautiful Mustang convertible.

Nice car, he says. Is it new?

Only to me. It's a couple of years old already, an '82. The last year Ford made the blue glow.

Chas reaches in the back and pulls out a strange piece of rosewood furniture with a pair of pants hanging on it. He sets it on the sidewalk.

What's that? Henry asks.

A trouser press, Chas says and hands him a wine-coloured silk robe still in its dry-cleaner's bag. He watches Chas put the roof up and lock the doors. The plastic on the bag flaps in the breeze like a kite waiting to take off. He walks down the sidewalk behind Chas, who reaches over to take the robe from him at the door and kisses the air.

Thank you so much. You're a dear.

Before Henry and his mother leave them to unpack Chas asks, Can we set up a barbeque in the little patio area at the back?

Henry is expecting this to be a problem, but Alice answers with a breezy, Sure.

Super, Chas says. We'll have you down for a cookout the first weekend there's good weather.

Three weeks later, on a sunny Saturday evening, Chas and Jim invite Henry and his mother for dinner. Chas has cleaned the moss off the old paving stones that for years have been stacked at the back, and he's laid them out with a border of pots filled with purple and pink petunias. Four new webbed folding chairs lean against the kitchen table that someone has dragged out from inside the suite. Chas snaps open a chair and gives it a pat. Have a seat, Alice. Make yourself comfortable. What can I get you two to drink?

Do you have any soda? Alice asks.

Cherry Coke and orange, Chas answers.

I'll have a cherry Coke.

Me too, Henry adds.

Chas ducks inside and returns wearing an apron and carrying a tray with drinks and an assortment of canapés:

asparagus rolled in salmon, smoked oysters nestled on cheese puffs, and skewers of shrimp interspersed with tiny-tom tomatoes. Alice piles her plate high and proceeds to remove all the *fishy* bits. When she becomes aware everyone is watching her, she looks up and says, What?

Save room for dinner, Chas says. Jim has some delicious steak he's barbequing for us.

I will, don't worry, she says. I could eat a cow. It's the drugs.

Jim looks at her with interest for the first time since they've arrived. Henry feels as if he and his mother are the kids sipping on their cherry drinks while smiling Chas and glaring Jim, who is maybe a little drunk, are the parents. He's grateful no one is making a fuss over Alice wasting the expensive seafood that's now piled in an inglorious heap by her plate.

Once they're all sitting around the wobbling table sawing at their steaks — the meat overcooked — Alice breaks the silence with a question Henry is surprised she doesn't know the answer to, given all the crowing she's done about what friends they've become.

What do you fellows do for a living?

Jim answers by lifting his fork toward Chas, He's a hairdresser.

Stylist, Jim. I'm a hair stylist, Chas corrects.

Whatever, Jim says.

Oh, maybe I can come in for a trim sometime, Alice says. Which salon?

Derrick's of Liverpool, Chas says.

I've heard of Darryl's of London but not Derrick's of Liverpool.

Jim snorts, Not surprised. What a stupid name for a hair shop.

Jim, just because you don't like where you work doesn't mean you can make fun of where I do.

Where do you work, Jim? Alice asks.

Jim doesn't answer. Finally Chas does.

He's a longshoreman at the grain elevators in North Van. It's not really his scene.

The conversation suddenly has become awkward, and it's clear the subject of jobs is a touchy one. Henry is glad nobody asks where he works as he has just that week — after years of fretting about whether or not to lobby Chief — been given a chance to train as an apprentice poultry technician. He's waiting for the right moment to tell his mother, and this moment is clearly not it. In the silence, Chas begins to clear plates and offers coffee. Jim gets up and pours himself a shot of something topaz-coloured from a bottle he has stashed beside the barbeque. Chas asks him teasingly, What about our guests?

Jim ignores him and Henry says, Neither mom nor I drink anyway. But thanks.

On the way back to his chair after serving everyone sponge cake, Chas stops behind Jim and gives him a head massage.

New shiatsu technique I learned, he says.

Jim swats his hand away, and Chas looks a little hurt, but undaunted he moves on to Henry.

Fine head of hair you have here, he says. He begins to massage Henry's scalp, but Henry is concerned that Jim, who is now glowering, does not like it. Neither does he, particularly; he's not used to having people so close to him and he's kind of surprised how easily Chas is able to do this. Chas is making a short tapping motion along Henry's shoulders, cooing about how strong he feels under his shirt, when Jim snaps.

Cut it out, he hollers. He gets up and leaves the table with his cake untouched.

Well, says Alice. I guess we better get going.

Thanks for coming, Chas says. Sorry about the scene. Jim'll get over it. He's had a hard day. He really is a good provider. I don't know what I'd do without him.

Same as my Henry, Alice says.

That night, lying in bed above Jim and Chas' bedroom, Henry tries very hard not to think about what might be going on down below him. He's sad for Chas who seems to be trying hard to be a good guy, and maybe he's a little sad for Jim, too, because he seems stuck. He thinks he understands a little about that part of being Jim at least.

Around one in the morning he hears the suite door slam shut. When he looks through the crack in his curtains, he can see Jim walking alone across the lawn toward the street. He goes back to bed and lies quietly for another hour wondering what must have happened as the night progressed and where Jim might be going. Eventually he leaves thoughts of Jim and Chas and finds his hands on his tackle, his thoughts focused on, of all people, the new receptionist at work.

Janine, he thinks her name is. She's not really his type, that is if he can even say he has a type, but there is something about the way her front teeth overlap that makes her look like a bunny rabbit. He sort of likes that about her. And also, strange to think, her bad breath that fills the lunchroom when she talks — he doesn't mind that either. It's at once human and horse-like, the same odour he smelled when his grade six class visited the stables in Southlands. The horses' breath came out in snorts of steam that smelled of fermented hay.

He debates whether he will do anything with his semi-erection. Things were so discouraging after Kitty he vowed to forget about women, and then after that when he did try to arouse himself, thinking first about black-eyeliner girl from school and then, despite his vow, Kitty again, nothing happened, which made him feel inadequate all over again. But right at this moment, drumming on the head of his big fella, it feels okay. And if it works it might actually help him to go to sleep.

He jigs and he jags with his right hand and eventually when he does come, he is thinking about Janine's breath and horse balls at the same time. Lying there afterwards, he isn't even sure whether it was balls or horseshit he'd been thinking about, but whatever it was he's pretty sure he won't ever be able to look properly at Janine again.

In a jabbering dream, he sees himself, Chas, and a woman that could be Janine, with a horse that he is sure is Jim, walking down a forested path in a place like

Southlands. When they stop at a crystal pool, stones slip from their glittering eyes and one falls from the horse's nose. Two green, two orange, two yellow, and one large white stone — quite a nice collection. That's it, or all of it he can remember when he wakes in the morning. He doesn't usually pay attention to dreams, but he wonders what this one means.

Later in the day he is out cutting the back lawn with the push mower when Jim and Chas come to sit on their makeshift patio. The two of them look relaxed, as if nothing untoward happened the night before. Jim even holds up what looks like a glass of orange juice and says, Mimosa, Henry?

Henry and his mom don't drink, Chas says.

Oh right, I forgot. A cherry Coke then?

Sure, Henry says.

Jim disappears inside to get the Coke, and Chas slips Henry a couple of discount cards from Derrick's. You and your mom are welcome to come and get a cut anytime, he says. I'd love to get my hands on your hair. We could have such fun.

Henry's hand instinctively goes to his head and he pats down his cowlick, Oh I don't usually get fancy with my hairdos. Maybe Mom can use these, though. Thanks.

He slips the cards in his pocket before Jim returns.

SIX

Turkeys and Chickens

APOLICE OFFICER WALKS ACROSS THE lawn toward him. Henry thinks, It's come to this — she's been arrested.

Henry Parkins? the officer asks as he mounts the stairs to the front porch.

Yes.

I'm sorry I have some bad news, sir. Can we step inside?

Even though he's a little scared of what he's going to hear, his mind goes to the paraphernalia his mother had scattered in the front hall before she left for the day — an old dance costume, a clutch of Day of the Dead figures, her badly tuned ukulele, a glitter hat, and a bag of kitchen garbage that hadn't made it to the curb.

I'd prefer to talk out here, he says.

Okay sir, your choice. I'm sorry to tell you your mother died earlier today in a single vehicle accident.

Henry knows he needs to react, needs to show some emotion. He shouldn't just stand there dumbly staring at the officer. In his mind he runs through the reactions he's seen on television — the scream, the faint, the sob, the rapid succession no-no-no — but none of them suit. He feels more like a man who's been submerged in water and is struggling to breathe. Yet, strangely, words seem to be forming in his mouth. He has no idea what they're going to be until they spill out alphabet-soup style. He halts between each word to give the soup man time to make the next one up.

They — should — have — taken — her — license, he says.

Sorry sir, who should have taken her license?

You — The cops — You should have. He points to the officer.

Sir? I should have?

No — I didn't mean it that way. He looks at the ground.

She hit a cement abutment, the officer says. The car's been towed to the wreckers. We pieced together who she is from the mail in her back seat. But she wasn't carrying a license, so we'll need a next of kin to positively identify her.

There is nothing positive about this, Henry says.

He's aware he is close to speaking nonsense, but his insides started to crawl when he heard the words *next of kin*. The officer could have no idea what the words set off. Flashes of Dr. Davis holding out a sickening green pamphlet with *You and Mental Illness* on the front, a phone call to an aunt who sounded as crazy as his mother, a deep fear that now that he is the only kin on this side of the Atlantic; all the craziness of the clan will float into him, take up residence and wreak havoc with his mind.

And the fingernails, the fingernails of his mother, his kin. They are at that very moment curving, flapping like wings, in the front of his mind. He wants to reach out and grab them but knows that would be real craziness, so he clenches his hands into a ball and struggles to speak. He needs to get the officer off the porch.

You'll know her by her nails, he says.

Sorry, sir? Her nails?

Her fingernails. They're long and well-manicured.

Right, sir.

The officer looks confused and uncomfortable. But Henry has at least succeeded in one thing: he's getting ready to leave. The officer takes a card out of his book and presses it into Henry's hand.

Take this to St. Paul's Hospital with you.

Henry looks at the card with the case number on it. She's nothing but a case number now. Still he can't react beyond wanting to grab for the wings she's sent to him — a French manicure with soft pink polish and tiny seashells pressed into the nails.

Sorry again, sir, the officer says as he leaves the bottom step.

As soon as the officer's gone, Henry reaches out to touch the wings but they vanish. He heads toward his mother's bedroom thinking she was in a good mood that morning, if perhaps a bit overexcited to be driving out to New Westminster to find a wig for a costume party that he was not clear she'd actually been invited to. Recently she'd been delusional again but not in an unhappy way.

She'd taken herself off the meds — *I'm too fat,* she'd said, *I'll never get a job dancing looking like this.*

As he enters her room, he starts to feel guilty, afraid she'll catch him here. He shrugs his shoulders as he thinks how old habits, even feelings, die hard. He pulls open the drawer on her vanity table in search of her phone book then slams it shut when he spies the cold cream jar sitting beside her makeup mirror. The lid is precariously set, not screwed down. Clearly she thought she'd be coming back to attend to this, she hated it when her creams scummed over. He backs out of the room, then runs outside to the suite downstairs. He bangs on the door.

While he waits, he fears it will be Jim not Chas who answers. Things have become so strained with Jim since he had to take a leave from work and check himself into drug detox. One day after he returned, Alice, impatient with the rent always being late, pushed Henry down the sidewalk toward the suite, insisting that he *Just go in and take something. They owe us!* Jim had heard them coming and opened the door to fling out their television set, which shattered on impact. *Take this, you bitch,* he said. Now standing at the same spot and with those words still ringing in his ears, Henry looks up with relief to see Chas open the door.

Mom is gone, he says.

How can I help? Chas asks.

Henry and Chas sit in the basement of St. Paul's Hospital in a small waiting room beside a table piled with old *Chatelaine* magazines. They could be waiting for any kind of medical appointment. The odd nurse or doctor cruises through, all of them with the same no-eye-contact gaze, and when the attendant they await finally comes, a short fat man with beads of perspiration on his brow, he motions them to follow. As they make their way down the corridor, Henry wonders if this is the way his mother's body came in — led down this hall by a fat man dotted with beads of sweat.

They come to a door with a sign that says *No Unauthorized Admittance*. The fat man pulls the door open. A whiff of something like the smell of the lab at Agriculture escapes. Once inside, there's another smell that goes way back. Henry is focused on that smell when the attendant asks him to sign in. It's biology class and the smell of formaldehyde on the fetal pigs. His hand shakes as he signs. He's thinking about the frail fallopian tube in the belly of his pig, how he severed it by accident when he tied the identification string too tight.

Even though the room is chilly, the attendant is sweating. They walk toward a stainless steel cabinet with three doors. His mother is behind one of these. Impossibly, her mind and body are stilled. She will be still. *I will be still*, he tells himself. The attendant pulls open a door and a stainless slab rushes out of the cabinet with uncanny energy. Henry is shocked. She's spread out nude. He takes in the fullness of her hips, the greying pubic hair, sagging breasts with nipples the colour of purple pansies, until he realizes the pansies are bruises. His brain triggers — Avert.

Something's wrong here, the attendant says.

What? Henry asks.

Somebody forgot to finish up.

The attendant waddles over to a pile of sheets in the corner and retrieves one to cover her body, so only the head is exposed.

Henry had hoped he could just look at her hand, under the edge of a sheet, know it was her by the sea-shell jewels encrusted on the half-moons. *Like the sand at the beach,* she'd said that morning to him. He focuses on the spot in the middle of her forehead where he'd trained himself to look so it wouldn't be obvious when he was avoiding her. Even in death he can't look at her eyes. *Look me in the eye when you talk to me, young man.* He sees the temples where she needs a dye job. *Do you think it's time for a touchup, Henry?* He scans the side of her face working from the temples down to her mouth and chin. *Does my makeup look all right — is my lipstick on straight?*

It's my mother, he says.

Looks like she wasn't wearing a seatbelt, the attendant says as he shoves the body back into the cooler cabinet.

Probably not, Henry says. He'd long ago given up trying to convince her to wear a belt. There'd been no point, especially after she'd been stopped and convinced the officer not to ticket her because the belt would wrinkle her dress. The officer agreed that even his own wife did the same thing sometimes.

On the way home, Chas and Henry ride silent. Henry is soothed by the white leather seats, the clean interior of the Mustang, the hum of the wheels crossing the Burrard Bridge onto Cornwall Avenue. The sun slants over English

Bay and across Kitsilano Beach at an angle he could almost walk on. For a moment it glints so ferociously off the hood, he thinks a piece of blue glow might catch in his eye. As they make a left onto Bayswater Street, Chas turns to him.

Her eyes were closed you know, he says. She looked peaceful.

Thanks, he says.

The next day, Chas and Henry check out three funeral homes. They settle on Roselawn where the mortician was most helpful, even giving them templates to use for composing an obituary to go in the newspaper. When they spread the various words meant to sanitize death on the kitchen table, none of them seem to fit. *Died peacefully* certainly doesn't work, neither does *passed away with dignity and courage*. Although Chas thinks it might be good to say *lived with courage*, Henry vetoes it as too dramatic. So they decide to begin with *suddenly and sadly*.

The bit about family is easy since there's only Henry; his aunt might as well be dead. The date of birth is not so easy. Alice would never tell him when she was born — for years she's been throwing out all identification that might reveal it — and although he thinks it was in the early 1930s, he can't be certain. They decide not to put it in. This leaves the hardest part, the line where you're supposed to say something about the person. How do you describe a woman who spent a lot of her time dressing up to go nowhere? Who on bad days still ran out the door in a torn and dirty bathrobe, with hair matted to one side of her head, flailing at cars to stop them so she could talk about inappropriate things? In the end, they settle on:

> Suddenly, Alice Parkins died on July 22, 1988. Family, except for son Henry, predeceases her. She was born and lived in Vancouver where she worked as a drugstore clerk and landlady. She enjoyed cosmetics and manicures, and an array of television shows and magazines. The memorial service is at 10:00 AM on Saturday July 30 at Roselawn Funeral Home.

When the announcement runs on Tuesday, Henry reads it sitting at the window in the kitchen drinking an early-morning hot chocolate. It is the shortest on the page. He almost misses it because it's the only one at the top of a column that is otherwise pretty much devoted to funeral home advertisements and used-car sales. The notice looks lame, even the ads for puppies are longer and some of them have pictures. His cheeks burn red as he rereads. His mother would have criticized him for the number of times he'd used *she* instead of her name. *Who is she, Henry? She is me, your mother. Not some disembodied she-wolf.* He and Chas had even taken out the words *and sadly* because the paper charged for every ten words and those two words put the count over an even sixty, which would mean he'd be charged for seventy. He couldn't come up with eight more words? What was wrong with him? Thinking about it now, he could kick himself for not adding that she was a good dancer and enjoyed knitting. He could have said she danced in the clubs and was an expert knitter, something to make it seem she had talent, wasn't just a dimwit sitting in front of the television doing her nails. And she had been doing other things when she sat there; she was producing for the poor. She donated slippers to the Diabetes clothing box at the corner of Macdonald and Fourth. Her dejected voice floats off the steam of his hot chocolate. *What were you thinking, Henry? Everyone else's family says nice things.* He could have said she was a good and charitable woman.

He debates with himself whether he should go to work today. He went on reflex yesterday, but told no one about his weekend. Few people ever asked anyway, which was a relief because most of the time if he were truthful he would have to say, *I watched some shows on television with my mother and I worried.* But now that this is in the paper, you never know who might have read it. How should he respond to people's sympathy when some measure of what he's feeling is relief? At least that's what he thinks he's feeling. Not wanting to dwell on it further, he gets dressed and heads for work.

He is sitting at his desk sorting through a mound of lab reports on rheumy eyes in chickens, when a young woman he's never seen before appears at the door to his cubicle. She is holding a stack of paper toward him.

I need to send a facsimile transmission, she says.

Henry looks at her with surprise. Nobody calls it a *facsimile transmission* anymore, but she's sort of cute and is young enough to be one of the summer students. Maybe she's trying extra hard. He can understand that kind of earnestness as he too has been trying hard for his promotion from apprentice to accredited poultry technician. He's been stuck nearly three years at apprentice. Failing chemistry in high school has not helped, but still he's more than made it up for it with all the extra courses he's taken since.

Are you a summer student? he asks.

Certainly not, I'm the new poultry inspector, she says. I'm assigned to oversee the technicians and field-testing.

Oh, I didn't know, he says.

Immediately she starts speaking again, rapid-fire in her directions. In a weird way he's glad she's doing this as he is out of energy to say anything. He doesn't know how he will feel working under this new person, especially once he's promoted and out into the field. He's not computing what she's saying, except he does hear her say, And they told me to ask for the Fax God — strange ideas some people have around here.

She leaves the stack of paper on the edge of his desk, taps it and walks away. He takes it that he's supposed to do the faxing for her, which he will do, even though it's no longer part of his job description.

When he returns the fax together with the receipted cover sheet, she doesn't look up from her desk. But he's seen her name on the fax and works up the nerve to say, You're welcome, Elaine. She still doesn't look up. Then while he's on a nervy streak he walks down to the chief's office.

How's it hanging, Henry?

Not so good, Chief.

Why's that?

Well, my mom died on the weekend and what about this new person Elaine?

He realizes this is an odd combination of responses, but he's not going to retract either of them and waits for the chief to digest it all. Chief is a jocular fellow who mostly tries to do right by people, although he would have made a better high school phys-ed teacher than chief poultry inspector. His face registers a mix of emotions. He looks at Henry.

I'm sorry, he says.

It's okay, we weren't close in the traditional way. He's trying to slough it off, but all of a sudden he feels like crying. Maybe it's the impersonal setting of the office that is bringing this out. As he struggles to pull it together, he realizes it's not so much sadness for his mother's death but for her life that's upsetting him. He never really was able to make a happiness difference for her.

Still, it isn't easy, Chief says.

Never easy when these things happen, Henry says. He can feel that stupid nervous laugh of his working its way up his throat so he just stands there waiting for Chief to pick up the conversation.

Well. Sorry. Sit down.

Thanks. Henry's cough suppresses the embarrassed laugh that will fire out his mouth soon if Chief doesn't stop talking about his mother.

Chief looks down for a moment, then back up at Henry. His eyes show an understanding he's supposed to switch topics and he says, I guess you met Elaine and you're wondering what that's about?

Right.

What can I say? She has a degree in agriculture. Ottawa said we had to take her. Chief puts his hand up to the side of his head and looks down before adding, I'll let you in on a secret, I'm still working on getting you promoted to accredited and out into the field to do more testing. Who better for the job than the Fax God?

He and Chief both laugh, a real laugh. He doesn't know whether Chief made it up on the spot, but he's glad for it and chooses to believe it'll happen sooner or later.

On the Saturday, ten people attend the service at the Roselawn. Eight more than Henry expected. Chas convinced Jim to come, and he isn't happy, but that may be because he's stuffed into a three-piece wool suit that hasn't been worn in years and it's about 100 degrees outside. Two people are there from the drugstore where his mother used to work, and Henry is surprised but pleased to see Chief. Of course, now that he thinks about it, Patsy and Dave from next door are not such a surprise. Neither is nosey old Mrs. Krumpskey from across the street. But then there is the man in the last row that he does not recognize. Later, when he stands at the back of the chapel thanking people for coming, he can see the man hanging around the pews waiting for everyone to clear.

Most pass through quickly, mumble a few platitudes. Chief just waves and gives a thumb's-up, which is appropriately Chief. But Mrs. Krumpskey takes her time.

I hear she hit a cement truck, she says.

No, a cement abutment, Henry answers.

Still, hitting something cement must have meant there was quite a scene. Was there a lot of blood?

No.

Well I guess you had to have a closed casket. Too bad.

How so?

It would have been nice to see her again. I hope she went quickly.

Yes.

Well, did she?

I don't know.

He is grateful when Chas comes up behind Mrs. Krumpskey and takes her by the arm to lead her away. As they pass out the door, he hears Chas say, You know, Alice looked as beautiful as I've ever seen, so peaceful and natural.

They're alone in the chapel when the man approaches.

Orville Johnson, he says.

Henry Parkins, but I guess you know that.

That's right, I do. You don't remember me, do you?

Henry nods his head no. His chest is pounding. Is this man some kind of relation? Is a piece of history going to reveal itself? What God takes away he gives back tenfold, isn't that what the chaplain just said at the service?

I used to live up the street from you and your mom. In the house that burnt down. Remember?

Oh yes, Mr. Johnson. Nice to see you again.

I was sort of a friend of your mother's until . . . look, I'm very sorry . . .

Mr. Johnson stops talking, looks at the hat in his hands. His fingernails are dirty, the skin around his knuckles rough. Henry has no idea how this man wants to finish his sentence. *Very sorry about your mother's death* seems too obvious to be causing such difficulty. Maybe he's choked with emotion, but why? Could it be there was more than just a friendship? Henry remembers way back he sometimes would wake in the night and call to his mother. She wouldn't answer, yet he could hear her making soft mewing noises like a kitten, and then there would be harsher deeper sounds, sounds that could have come from a man, could have come from Orville Johnson. *Very sorry . . . I don't know how to tell you, but I'm your father* seems far-flung. But there it is in his head. He is thinking it, and just as he thinks it, he starts actually to want to hear it, is waiting to hear it, preparing himself to put his arms around this man and hug him, welcome him into the fold of the family nest, invite him back to the house, maybe let him stay in his mother's room, a room where he belongs. He watches Orville prepare to speak again, and his arms almost begin to twitch with the desire to throw that big hug around him.

I'm sorry your mother was such a nut, Orville says.

Henry doesn't know what to say. He thinks about mumbling, Oh that's okay. But it isn't okay. It's so very disappointing. He wants Orville to leave. Not to be standing there anymore. Wants very much to be out of this moment and far away.

What a thing to say, he blurts.

She was a nutter and you know it! Orville claps his hat on his head and remains uncomfortably motionless for a moment before leaving.

Henry stands in stunned silence and waits for Chas and Jim to collect him, but after a time he realizes they've left, and he rides the Number 7 alone west along Broadway.

He barely feels the heat as he walks the sidewalk down Macdonald toward home. He passes the Kitsilano Branch Library where there's a sign out front inviting people to browse the *What's New & Hot* shelf. Someone has chalked arrows pointing to the door, where inside coloured footprints are taped to the floor. He steps onto the footprints that lead him to the shelf and picks up a slim book written by a strange-looking man named Stephen Hawking. The newly plasticized *A Brief History of Time* slips from his hands, falls to the floor. The librarian looks up to make a disapproving cluck with her tongue. He stoops to retrieve the book and sweat drips from his brow onto the floor. He feels like flipping her the bird, but doesn't have the energy.

SEVEN

Kluk Transmission

HENRY SITS AT HIS MOTHER'S vanity. It's been nearly a year since she died and nothing in the room has changed, except for the grime settled on everything. He tried dusting once, but after a half-hour of flicking at the tubes of lipstick, the bottles of nail polish, and the vials of perfume, he started to feel too much of a presence. As if she was going to jump out of the closet to yell at him, but just as likely to smother him in kisses and ask for help in choosing a lipstick. He is almost thirty and still a virgin. The situation is not good.

He knows it's time he stopped being an ill-informed ten-year-old boy huddled in a man's body. But he has no clue how to move beyond. He bends and picks up the empty cardboard box at his feet and puts it in his lap. He stares at the array before him. The nail polishes are colour blocked — the reds in front, the pinks clumped in the middle, and the strange colours, the greens, the blues, the turquoises lined up at the back. Tacked to the wall is a chart pulled from a magazine: *Perfect Nail Colour and What It Reveals About You*. His mother has circled

Grape — *you are outgoing and vivacious, popular and talented, but prone to exaggeration* — she's ticked the words *vivacious* and *popular*, and crossed out *exaggeration* to handwrite *liar* above it. It's as if she believed she could pick and choose personality attributes as easily as she could nail colours. Maybe she was on to something.

He continues to stare at the collection on the vanity and eventually the Shalimar perfume with its elegant blue fluted cap practically struts forward like a preening bird. He squirts some into the air. A fine spray of velvety lemon descends. The scent takes him back to a walk in Stanley Park perhaps three years before she died. It was her birthday and all she'd wanted from him was a walk in the park. Shalimar. She often wore too much, but the amount was right that day, little puffs of it coming in his direction every few steps. A golden retriever zigzagged along the seawall between them, head low to the ground, sniffing its own scents, or perhaps the trail back to the lost owner or a coyote that had preceded them.

She was trying to tell him about her childhood, a topic that should have commanded all of his attention, but at first was nothing but a bunch of meaningless words, occasionally an oblique slice from their current life. She was lamenting the shame of it all, asking why things couldn't have stayed the same, and he was aware of a rising level of emotion in her voice; the more the timbre rose the more he focused on the dog, reaching down to pet it, talking to the golden retriever instead of to her. Near the Second Beach concession, she demanded, Look at me, I'm talking to you.

He and the dog both looked at her. Shalimar radiated and for a second cleansed everything.

And then Henry did see. Her full face, her eyes, the clarity in them at that moment. Eyes in which he'd become so used to seeing confusion and fear, he'd stopped looking.

Sit down, Henry, she said.

They sat at one of the cement picnic tables near the concession, drinking tea and sharing a bag of potato chips. The retriever sat with them, under the table, between their feet. She continued on about her childhood, but this time in a more rooted way. She told him she'd been a happy kid who grew scarlet runner beans up the back of the house, planted at the same spot where Chas and Jim made their garden patio, how she'd had a warm bed that she shared with her sister Esther, and how the two of them had their differences but no more than other kids, until her dad had died. He watched her face crowd in on itself as she disgorged the details of her father dying when she was twelve. His breathing, she said, sounded like a horse slopping in water. And then Mother got so very sick. I watched her run down the street, her dress half undone, yelling at the neighbourhood kids, banging on neighbours' doors, shouting and screaming.

Surely she saw the parallels, Henry thought. She too ran down the street, battered neighbours' cars, inappropriately begged people to come home for supper. And part of her must have known he'd endured the mirth of his entire school every time she appeared below the classroom window in her yellow boots and dirty trench coat. And then he saw that she did understand. He watched the connections start to form in clusters across her face. When enough of them had fused to form an insight, she grasped his hand.

I'm sorry, Henry, she said. It's all very disappointing. I didn't mean for it to be so difficult.

Her voice drifted at the end and she slumped back. He could see the colour of disappointment in her face. The hollows below her cheekbones as blue as a dispirited jay, an inky infinity in her eyes. She was exhausted from trying to drown a thousand crazy beasts in her stormy mind. He thought then he should hug her, should cheer her, somehow encourage her, or at least smile at her, but he felt rooted to the cold concrete they were sitting on, unable to move even the tiniest muscle in his face.

I love you, Henry, she said.

I know, Mom. I know. I . . . I . . .

He wasn't able to say it. He was pretty certain he loved her, in a way, but he was also mad and disappointed in who she was, in who he had become because of her. It was impossible to put any order to his emotions, his mind was simply numb. Still, even then, he knew it was the most important thing he could ever have said to her, to tell her he loved her. But he couldn't. YOU CANNOT DO THIS! his mind screamed. His hand had reached down under the table hoping to gain strength or at least a short reprieve by patting the soft fur of the golden retriever . . . but the dog was gone.

He waves his hand around under the vanity as if searching for that dog now. The scent of Shalimar floats up. His hand, which is now possessed by something outside himself, begins to swipe at the lipsticks in front of him.

Fuck, he wails. You jerk — three words, how hard could it be to say them?

He hears his voice bounce off the wall and then, as if it's coming from inside the wall, he can hear Alice's sensical/ nonsensical response. *Henry, watch your language! Use Daffy Duck if you must.* His arm swats at the lipsticks, some clatter into the carton, some crash onto the floor, others roll under the bed. When there are none left to bat, he turns his attention to the lotions. He knocks a few off before he comes to the pot of cold cream. He unscrews the lid, takes a whiff, sticks in his index finger to daub some on his chin and makes streaks at his temples. He smiles. It's Henry the warrior smiling back. Henry the strong guy. Henry the invincible. He jams his whole hand in to take a gob of cream and wipe it across his face. Henry the invisible. Henry wiping out the loser. He moves his face up close to the mirror, his breath a cloud of moisture. Tiny blobs of cold cream blink at the ends of his lashes. He reaches down into the carton and pulls out a tube of lipstick. The top of the stick slants in the characteristic shape his mother used to make. He draws a red smile covering his face from cheek to cheek, then takes his forefinger and sketches a frown of cold cream over top. The frown bleeds red into pink across his mouth.

He throws himself on his mother's bed and drowns in her scent. He breathes in small gasps as he draws the quilt around himself. He buries himself in the sheets and sniffs up the length of the bed. He is the golden retriever sucking up clues. He breathes hungrily. He's become a specialist — a specialist in disappointment. Disappointment is who he is. Disappointment feeds him.

When he stands and walks to the mirror, the cream is mostly off his face except for one bit under his lower lip where it protrudes like the small beard some of the musicians wear. He remembers reading in the liner notes on the back of one of his albums — Tom Waits or Hank Williams Jr. — that this is what they call a soul patch. He leaves it on his chin while he addresses his reflection.

I LOVE YOU MOM!

He makes the declaration because he thinks he owes it to his mother, needs to make it equal between them somehow, massage the purple bruises from her life. Yet even as the word *love* falls out of his mouth, he's not sure what it means. The idea of it seems so hopelessly complex. If he really loves her, is he supposed to have so many uncertainties? The soul patch helps him decide a specialist in disappointment can feel things both good and bad. With this in mind, he finishes clearing the vanity.

When he's done he closes the carton, folding in the corners one by one, doing it in the wrong order only once, before the lid is tight. He stares at the empty space where the cosmetics were. He turns the lights on around the vanity and surveys his profile. He is Henry the survivor going on down the road.

Two weeks later, on a Saturday, Henry walks toward the curb where his new Subaru station wagon is parked.

He's fingering the soul patch, which he's grown in for real and doesn't look like a smudge on his chin anymore. He's excited to be looking good and able to drive himself wherever he wants in his chariot. His mind seems to be firing in a corner he's never felt before. Halfway down the walk, he remembers he meant to deliver the box of his mother's cosmetics to Chas. Chas likes to dress up on weekends, use a little makeup now and again. He turns and runs back into the house. When he re-emerges he's carrying the carton and he walks it around to the suite. As he waits at the door, a shadow moves inside. He hopes it's Chas, then knows by the size it's Jim.

What do you want? Jim asks.

Just thought I'd drop this off. There are some creams and things in here that Chas might use.

Smells pretty girly to me, but I'll let him know.

It's a good collection, Henry says, seems a shame to waste, that's all. He smiles at the closing door.

Even cold-shoulder-Jim can't take the grin from Henry's face. Every time he looks at his Subaru, he feels proud. He handled himself well at the BowMac dealership. He went there the day after his promotion to poultry technician because he needed a car to drive out to the farms. He chose a sturdy 4-wheel drive wagon because he knew some of the roads he'd be driving on would be rutted in winter. He was shocked at the price *all-in* after the features were added, but kept his cool. His mother's estate had been smaller than he'd hoped, so the last thing he wanted to do was give money away needlessly to a car dealer. Especially one he didn't particularly like. One who was sort of vulgar.

They'd been out for a test drive when Henry, making idle talk, said, I like the new-car smell.

The dealer without missing a beat said, Only one smell better — snatch.

Henry wasn't sure he'd heard correctly. But he kept smiling, and after a bit he even started to feel a little good about what the guy had said. He was after all being treated like a man's man, the sort who would dig that kind of comment, would know the smell exactly because he was getting himself some every night. But it hurt too, reminded him the only snatch he had any clue about, the only one he'd ever had a whiff of, was that eggy smell of his mother's. In an effort to be nonchalant, he stuck his arm out the window and tried to drive with only a couple of fingers, but that hurt too. Triggered a pain in his shoulder, so he had to bring his left hand back in and use both. That's when the dealer told him about the little indents on the steering wheel so he could properly position his hands.

Your fingers will start to go there by memory, the dealer said. The last road trip the wife and I took down through the Midwest was so relaxing because of those things, I can't tell you.

Where in the Midwest did you go? Henry asked.

Idaho, the dealer said.

Really? What took you there?

No reason.

Thoughts of snatch and Idaho mulled in Henry's mind for a bit before he got back to cars — a topic he knew slightly more about after Chas' briefing.

So this is the last of the '90s models, he said. The '91s have been in for a while. Yeah?

Yup, said the dealer. Are you interested in one of those?

No, but I am thinking you should be practically giving away these old guys. Maybe some free rustproofing?

Maybe.

By the time they were driving back along Broadway, Henry had struck a deal for himself — $1000 off the price because he'd agreed to buy a manager's car instead of the one he was test-driving.

And it's got one heavy-duty radio in it, the dealer said.

How so? Henry asked.

Well, the manager who had her detailed is a real audio nut. Likes to listen to all kinds of exotic stations.

This suited Henry just fine, and he was only slightly disappointed when he saw that the car he'd agreed to buy had been painted a vibrant neon yellow as part of a promotion.

Won't miss her in the parking lot, the dealer said.

That's for sure, Henry agreed.

For some reason, he thinks about that conversation now as he eases himself into the front seat and looks ahead over the hood. He's getting used to the colour, realizes he finds it sort of cheery. He places his fingers in the steering wheel's memory holes and heads the Subaru downtown, not going anywhere in particular, just driving around enjoying the day. At a stoplight on Georgia Street, he decides to test out the radio. He switches it on and fiddles with the tuner until he gets CBC FM coming in crystal clear. Jurgen Gothe or James Barber, or some other robust food lover, is going on about the delights of Spanish chocolate. Flamenco music plays between remembrances of Barcelona and stews with hints of *mole*. The word *mole* is new to Henry. He gathers it's some kind of chocolate chili sauce, and the way the guy is pronouncing the words, like he's a Spaniard, is interesting. But after a while the sound of *Barthelona* and *mo-lay* coming out his speakers irritates, so with a push of a button, the car switches to CBC AM.

He's on the Lions Gate Bridge when some freak of the sky begins to beam in a faraway-sounding radio station. He's annoyed that country music is budging in on the bandwidth, but amused by how easily CBC is knocked down by a station called KLUK 680 AM. He doesn't want to fool with the knobs while he's driving the bridge, and by the time he's exiting, KLUK is playing one of his country favourites — "Turn It Loose" by the Judds — so he follows the rogue station off the bridge and into the trailer court on the West Vancouver side. He drives around under the bridge through the doublewides, until he finds a spot where the signal comes in pretty well.

The announcer lives up to his name, Goodtimes Charley. He sounds like he's having a great time, and Henry likes how he says he's there for all the country fans in Silverton. He's never heard of Silverton and wonders where it is. Charley ends the show with a plug for his favourite announcer, Jamie Lee Savitch — *she's the prettiest gal in all of radioland bringing you the best in country radio every Monday to Friday at seven o'clock sharp in the afterwork time!* Charley plays a snippet of Jamie Lee fooling around in the studio. She's a livewire, laughing and talking, and so friendly, with a voice as smooth as milk and honey. The clip ends with, *Tune in to me, Jamie Lee, where we have more fun than a chicken in the bread pan kickin' out the dough.*

Henry laughs out loud. He can't believe there's a radio station called KLUK, with a cute sounding announcer making chicken jokes. Ha, he's a turkey and chicken man himself. *Omens come in threes,* his mother used to say. *Pay attention.* He makes a date with himself to be back under the bridge at seven o'clock sharp on Monday evening.

Monday morning, Chief is the only other person in the coffee room, yawning and rubbing his mostly bald head, as if friction will somehow rev up his hair-growing machine.

Morning Henry, Chief says.

Morning sir. What brings you in so early?

Getting ready for vacation.

Oh yeah. Hawaii again this year. Right?

Yes, the bar at Mona Kona awaits. Look, there's something I want to tell you. After I'm back, I'll be announcing my retirement. Next spring, that is. Just giving you the heads up.

Wow, I had no idea.

No idea. What — that I was that old?

The two of them laugh. Henry knows there's no chance he'll be promoted, even though he's a good employee, never calls in sick, always shows up on time, never drinks, has taken all the extra poultry courses, and knows chicken and turkey like nobody's business. Problem is, he's only a technician. But he really hopes it won't be Elaine.

Any idea who might replace you?

I think the job has more or less been promised to Elaine.

Shoot, he thinks. Elaine has been at Agriculture for less than three years. Even though she has that fancy university degree, she's too young. And what pressure this is bringing down — for two years he's been thinking about asking her out, but how can he if she's going to be the big boss? Alice's voice comes into his head. *Make pie with sour cherries. Use lots of sugar.* Odd that she would interfere at this time, and on this point. She never seemed to want him to date anyone when she was alive. Maybe she's mellowing in the great beyond. Maybe she knows he's destined to be alone if he doesn't get cracking.

Soon as Elaine is in her office, he walks down the hall and hangs at her door. She's done something with her hair over the weekend. It looks like she's tried to dye it blonde but it's turned a funny orange colour. Still, she looks pretty.

Hi, Elaine. I like your new colour, he says.

She looks up and scowls. He fingers his soul patch — maybe they are even in looks now that he's classed himself up and she's been downgraded.

I mean your hair colour, he says.

Really? she answers. She plumps up her hair and adds, It didn't really work out like I planned.

Mmmm. Thought so, Henry says.

He doesn't believe he said that, but she starts to laugh, so he does too.

I like your honesty, she says.

He's on a roll, this could work. Would you like to have lunch today? he asks.

Elaine doesn't say anything for long enough that Henry feels that stupid laugh begin to well in his throat. Maybe he's been hasty thinking they are somehow almost equal. Alice's voice hovers again too. *Henry why do you set yourself up? She's too fancy to be interested in you.* This at least is more what he expects. And she's right. Elaine with her expensive spiked heels and purses with gold chain straps wouldn't be interested in the likes of him. Even Elaine with funny orange hair.

I've got lots on my plate right now, but how about coffee or something after work? she says.

Henry would have whooped for joy except for the slightly over-excited sick feeling that creeps into his stomach, as if there's too much Black Forest cake in there. But she's actually sort of saying yes. His date with Jamie Lee and the radio show can certainly be postponed for this.

He is back at Elaine's door at five o'clock, normal quitting time.

She looks at him and says, I'm still working. Come back in an hour.

He goes back to his own office and tackles a stack of files piled in the corner waiting to be closed. The closing checklist mandates that he stamp each file three times and initial up to eight different boxes to indicate all final checks have been made. He gets into a robotic state, stamping and scribbling in more or less the proper boxes, but it's so mind-numbing he's nearly asleep by 6:20, when he gets up from his desk, takes in a few deep breaths, and does a repetition of leg bends from his 5BX Exercise book. The oxygen feeds his brain and gives him the energy he needs to wander slowly down the hall. By 6:25 he's back at Elaine's door feeling stupid for wasting his time. Clearly, she's still working.

Be a dear, Henry, she says. Can we do this tomorrow?

Sure, why not.

His headache is fierce as he pulls out of the lot at work. Sometimes the yellow glare reflecting from the hood pisses him off. This is one of those times. Plus it's too late now from where he is to make it to under the Lions Gate Bridge for the start of Jamie Lee's show. He likes to hear things from the beginning if possible. So because of all this, he decides against the rush of Highway 1 back into the city, and drives the Subaru around Still Creek and onto the Lougheed hoping for a more tranquil trip home. At the first stoplight, the gleam from the setting sun on the hood makes him wonder whether it's too late to return the car to the smarmy dealer. He's only driven it a few hundred kilometres and it really is an embarrassment. Why didn't he buy a car in a regular colour?

He is impatiently drumming his fingers on the steering wheel waiting for the light to change when a car with four teenaged girls in it pulls up beside him. The brunette in the back seat motions to him with her hands and mouths a few words. The last thing he sees as the car pulls away is her candy-coloured lips puckered into a kiss. This is both startling and satisfying. He floors the Subaru to try to catch their speeding vehicle, but they fly through the next stoplight and he is forced to stop on the orange. As he waits, he wonders what he would have done if he'd caught up to them anyway. By the time he's at the next light he's convinced himself they were mocking him and his stupid yellow car, but still the image of the puckered lips lingers.

At the corner of Cambie and Broadway, he feels a boner begin to grow in his pants. He keeps it alive along Broadway with gentle hand pressure on his fly, and every now and again taps his middle finger and focuses on how Elaine looked when she said *be a dear, Henry*.

By the time he's at home parking the Subaru on 7th Avenue he's in a rush to get into the house. But Chas is on the front lawn bringing garbage out to the sidewalk.

Evening, Henry, how's it going?

Good, Chas. Talk to you tomorrow. I'm late.

Late for a very important date?

Something like that. Chat later.

He rushes to open the front door. Once inside, he draws the drapes in his bedroom, hastily pulls off his pants, flops on the bed spread-eagle, and grabs himself. He focuses on the way Elaine sucked in her lower lip when she said *be a dear, Henry*. He's certain she licked that lip, maybe even her upper one too — *be a dear* with each stroke, *be a dear, be a dear* — everything more and more lubricated. Then his headboard begins to pound the wall, and the lubricated word *dear* swims in the scent of his excited penis. He's about to arch his back into orgasm when of all damn-fucking-stupid things, his mother's voice floats into the room. *How to make Little Ducky fly?* Suddenly, he is five again and his mother is laying him down on the bathroom floor after a bath, pulling his legs apart, inspecting his anus, putting cream on it, saying *listen to me, you have to keep it clean down there.* His hand stops moving, his erection goes limp, and the head shrinks into the foreskin.

He tries drumming with his fingers softly just under the tip. Thinking about Elaine's orange hair helps, he takes it to breasts and erect nipples, these thoughts are working but then turn to soapy bathwater, cream in anus, and he has to fight for a time to keep it more neutral, less demanding, Elaine sucking in her lip — all the wild seraphs of love start dancing; but then some of them begin to tread in muck. He yards on his boner — orange nipples, lips on penis, worth his life to take off, to fly. But the seraphs are too crazy and he can't do it. Thoughts of his mother prevail, kissing him while he's in the bath, kissing him in his bedroom, on his bed, the very bed he is lying on, kissing him before his pyjamas are even on. Everything is always damp and boggy when his rod goes numb.

He gets up from the bed; to lie there any longer is pointless. He opens the front door and sits on the top step of the porch. The night has become foggy, the air balanced between the energy of evening and the numbness of approaching sleep. He feels everything, even the individual droplets of fog, but he doesn't know what he's feeling. He tries to organize his thoughts; the margins between dream and reality are almost nonexistent. It's sort of comforting to be in a trance sucked in by the fog, so it's with annoyance he hears the sound of the door to the basement suite closing. He braces himself for it to be Jim coming around the corner, but it's Chas. He comes to sit on the bottom step.

Foggy, isn't it? Chas says.

Unusual to have this much fog in early October.

Want to go for a walk down to Kits Beach?

Okay. Why not.

Thought you had a date. What happened to that?

Ah, it didn't come together. You know how these things are.

Been there, had that done to me.

They walk quietly down Bayswater toward the ocean. Evening turns to night and the fog thickens so that by the time they are at the beach it's difficult to see more than a few inches ahead. Without saying anything to each other, they walk toward the place where there are some swings. When the top of the swing set looms in the fog, each reaches out and takes a seat. They just hang there, they don't swing, don't move at all until Chas begins to talk.

Sometimes I get confused about how to be with you. Part of me wants to mother you. Part of me just wants to be . . . well, you know, be your friend. We're sort of the same. Same age that is.

Henry can't see Chas' face very well for the fog but he is aware that Chas' voice has changed. It is a bit softer. Or maybe it's just the fog distorting everything. But what does Chas mean? Henry can't think in what way they are the same. He feels a little unstable as he tries to give himself a push on the swing. He misses the ground and instead flails his foot into the fog.

See what I mean? Chas says. You need a mother to push you.

Chas gets off his swing and comes around behind to give him a push. He's good at it and he gets Henry flying so high in the air, he starts to wonder if he's going to go right over the top of the swing set. It is exhilarating and frightening at the same time.

You completely disappear into the fog every time I push you, Chas shouts up.

Good, Henry yells back.

Then Chas is finished pushing, and the swing returns to equilibrium.

Do you want a push? Henry asks.

Me? No, I'm afraid of swings, says Chas.

I don't believe that.

Believe it.

As they walk back home, he wants to tell Chas he appreciates his friendship but something stops him. It feels like new territory, or maybe it's just been too long since he made a real friend. Whatever it is, his footing is unsure as he mounts the steps on the porch. He stumbles on the top one. Chas, who has already gone around the corner to his suite, hears him.

Careful now, Chas calls out.

I always am, he replies.

EIGHT

Radio Noise

LAINE IS ON THE PHONE when Henry goes around
to her office to pick her up. This time he's waited
until 5:30. He didn't want to leave it too late in case she
actually finished more or less on time, but he knows how
aggravated she was when he arrived right at 5:00 last
time. She holds up one hand. He is not sure whether this
means *go away, stay out of my office,* or is just a friendly,
I'll only be a minute. Out of a healthy respect for her
unpredictable and sometimes withering impatience, he
stays in the hall. His right shoulder is high with hope, his
left drooped as if he's already been slugged. As he waits
he wonders about his attraction to someone who can be
so ornery. Why does he never go for the sweet girls? Why
this one with the bad dye job and a mouthful of nasty?

After Elaine puts the phone down, she starts talking
before she's even out of her chair. What a day, he can hear
her say as she stands up. Then she walks out of the office
and is face-to-face with him. Let's get this over with, she
says.

He can't quite believe this is what she meant to say, so he doesn't respond. Silently, they walk down the hall, out of the building, and into the parking lot toward his car.

Is this yellow one yours? she asks.

Yes.

What colour do they call this?

Volt yellow, he says.

Did they forget the re?

What?

Revolt, she says.

Now he really doesn't know what to say. He walks to the passenger side and opens the door for her. He is standing with it open when she says, Let's just walk to Denny's on Kingsway.

She makes it sound like Denny's is only around the corner, when it's a good three miles from where they stand, and to get there they'll have to cross the busy eight-lane Trans-Canada highway. Now he is certain she does not want to be doing this. As if the stupidity of her suggestion will make him say *forget it, let's do it some other time*. But she starts to walk generally in the direction of the eight lanes and he decides to be polite now that he's gotten himself this far into it.

I think we better drive, he says.

Okay, she says, turning on her heel back toward the car.

He has always hated Denny's. The tacky mud-brown-and-orange carpet takes his appetite away the minute he walks in, and it's an odd choice for coffee. But Elaine surprises him and orders a full dinner. Then when he orders cinnamon toast, she laughs.

What's wrong? she asks. Have you got gum issues?

What?

You know, bad gums. Only old people or people with bad gums order cinnamon toast.

I don't know. I feel like eating toast.

They sit quietly waiting for the order, as if their first attempt at conversation has been too much. When the food finally arrives, Elaine begins to bolt it down, stuffing mash and Swiss steak so fast he has barely finished one toast finger before her meal is nearly gone. And this, the same mouth he was trying to masturbate over just the day before. Elaine with her mouth full, mushrooms blanketing her front teeth, starts to complain between bites about her boyfriend Bob.

What a tool . . . doesn't he know how hard I work . . . does he have to clip his toenails in the bathtub . . . why are men so inconsiderate . . . every one of them a sex-crazed maniac, humping everything in sight.

Elaine speaks as if he was not a man, as if somehow he should be agreeing with her. He sits in stunned silence until out of the blue she switches topics. With a kinder voice she says, Chief is reassigning the Swift Farms file to me and I'll be taking it over. Then, as if her pronouncement were the whole point of her agreeing to come out with him, she says the word, There!

Swift Farms is the biggest file Chief has given him yet and Henry can't believe he would take him off it completely without discussing it, but then maybe Chief is not happy with his performance, or maybe Elaine is just that much better at everything she does and Chief has no choice. Anyway, that's the way Chief is sometimes, quick to make decisions. This is a very delicate subject and Henry is not sure how to play it. By the time he's gathered himself together enough to say, Really, I won't be running any of the tests out there with you? the waitress is setting down apple pie and whipped in front of Elaine. The sweet takes her attention away from him and his question, and seems to satiate her appetite for slamming men. By the third mouthful her face turns moony.

Do you think it's okay Bob spends every Friday night with the boys?

He decides the switch of topic back to Bob is good for now, and he'll run with it.

It depends, he says.

On what?

On what he's doing. If he's playing broomball then okay, but if he's out in the bars maybe not.

Broomball! Jesus, is that what you do with your weekends?

No. I mean I've played it before, but it's not a regular thing. It's something I . . .

Then why would you say broomball?

I don't know, it just came into my head.

Broomball, what a stupid thing.

He wants very much to have nothing in his head. This date is not in any way going in the direction he had imagined. *Why can I never figure out what's going on? Why do I feel like I have a layer of Saran Wrap over my brain?*

Oh Jesus . . . Why do I still find that stupid orange hair appealing . . . the mouth full of whipped cream a turn-on? Shit, what is wrong with me?

What are you staring at, Henry?

Nothing. I mean your shirt. It's nice.

Thanks. It's Bob's favourite.

When the tab comes Elaine picks up her purse, the chain strap clanks on the table, but she makes no move to open it, no motion to expel any small part of its contents. Not even a few coins offered toward a lousy tip. Though he is happy to pay just to, as Elaine predicted, *get this over with*, he did not anticipate such a large bill. Sure enough, inside the cloth band of his billfold there's only two five-dollar bills.

Can I borrow a couple of bucks?

God, can't you guys ever get it together to take a girl out for a proper meal? Okay, but you owe me.

Finally it's Wednesday. Just before 7:00 PM, Henry arrives at the trailer court under the bridge in West Vancouver. He parks beside a doublewide with red geraniums in a whitewashed tire. He's mad at himself for messing up the night before and hopes the radio date will be a nice break. He tilts his seat back, sets the scanner searching, and is happy to see it stop by itself at 680 — the signal will be strong. He's read in the car manual how to make 680 a preset and he holds his finger on the button till it takes. He's come early enough to hear the evening news, maybe pick up some clues about where Silverton is. While he waits, he stares up into the early evening sky and begins to bliss out on the friendly halos of melon green and indigo rose encircling the bridge lights above.

The first news story is about the $10,000 raised at the Reunion Hall in the Stars for Children show. Then there's a report of an armed robbery at the Wells Fargo in Wallace. He doesn't know where Wallace is either, though now he knows by the Wells Fargo it's somewhere in the United States. It isn't until the weathercaster comes on talking about a ridge of high pressure bringing in expansive Idaho skies that he understands the station is coming all the way from the Midwest. He likes listening to the weather — it's something immediate, something he knows for sure all the people who live in the area have experienced that day.

He sits with his hands in his lap and watches the numbers on his clock flip from 7:03 to 7:04. Jamie Lee's show will start any second now. He's eager to have some fun. Work has been tough, what with Elaine's behaviour, and Chief coming into his office that morning to tell him all over again he's leaving the next day for Hawaii and retiring in the spring, and that Henry is welcome to apply for his job but he won't get it. It's as if Chief thinks he's too stupid to remember being told the first time. And after that discussion he didn't have the energy to ask about the Swift Farms file, although his ears are still burning over that too. Then suddenly, Jamie Lee is purring inside his car.

Hey there, it's the cowgirl inside the radio coming at you. Sure hope you get to soak up this country evening with someone you love. And if you don't have anyone

*to spend it with, stay right where y'are and we'll spend it
together. It's 7:05 KLUK time, Jamie Lee Savitch inside the
radio bringin' you one of Wilf Carter's night hurtin' songs.
Just in case that's the way yer feelin' tonight. Hurtin' that
is.*

Henry starts. Yes, Jamie Lee, I am hurting. How do
you know?

He feels better already just by asking her out loud.
Somebody out there cares about his day, cares about his
hurting. He's going to enjoy this. After Wilf is finished,
Jamie Lee is back on with her sultry voice.

*That makes it all feel better doesn't it, just knowin'
somebody else out there is havin' a hard time too. If you're
feelin' lonely and blue, here's one of my all time favourites,
named by her grandpa after a mosquito, 'cause she had so
darn much energy, Miss Skeeter Davis singing "Think of
Me".*

He can hardly sit through the song, what with the
importance of the connections it's making. He so doubted
Alice when she said Skeeter recorded the tune, but now
his body twitches while she sings about feeling lonely and
blue, and again at the chord change with the words *for
I'll be thinking of you.* He can hear Alice's voice warbling
over top of Skeeter's, her inexpert ukulele keeping time,
and his body fills with compassion and love for everybody,
Skeeter, his mother, and this magic woman Jamie Lee
who put it all together for him. Part of him wants the
song to go on forever and part of him can hardly wait to
hear what Jamie Lee has to say next.

Out of nowhere a phone interview with a parson in England who's grown a giant squash cuts into the bridge of the song. Henry knows it's interference from CBC, but still he jabs impatiently at the preset, trying to make the radio dial back to KLUK.

Ack, he says. Help me. Ack. Ack. Ack.

Precious minutes of Jamie Lee's show are draining away, but still the parson keeps yakking on about his troubles with bacterial wilt. He waits for the heavens to settle but eventually the preacher's sonorous voice makes him sleepy, and he has to give up.

During the next weeks, he's only able to dial in Jamie Lee's show intermittently. He tries several different locations in the trailer park and even drives all the way up Cypress Mountain for clearer skies. But to little avail. Still it's worth the effort — she has the hurtinest voice in all of country radio — and when he does manage to fill his car with her voice, she sounds so pretty. One evening, Jamie Lee tells her listeners about a radio ranch promo package available just for the asking. She's about to give the details on how to get it and he is poised pen in hand ready to take it down, when CBC breaks in with a story about a woman in Lillooet who's shot her fourteenth cougar in as many years. He can feel hot tears of frustration build as he jabs at the radio. *Why does nothing ever work out?* When he finally gets the station back, it's too late to hear where to send for the package.

Next morning at work, he looks through the federal government directory trying to locate the department that deals with radio signals, only to discover that all of the numbers he dials are routed back to CBC. In desperation he calls Environment Canada and asks to speak to a meteorologist, someone he figures who might know about radio signals. The fellow he gets on the phone sounds too young to know much, but he listens patiently to his problem. He says he's sorry Henry is having trouble, how it's curious that Henry gets the station at all, but that something similar happens to him when he heads up to Whistler, how he loses CFOX every time he rounds the bend at Porteau Cove, and it's always right in the middle of a super funny bit by Larry and Willy, or a rockin' good tune by Aerosmith, how his problem is one of land mass where Henry's might be more one of heavy winter crystals, and now that it's getting late into October the signals are only going to get worse.

And for that I don't have a good solution, the fellow says.

Wow, you actually know a lot. But it's disappointing it's going to get worse, Henry says.

Hey. Why don't you call down to the Chamber of Commerce in Silverton? They'll know how to contact KLUK.

Brilliant. Great talking with you.

After a half hour with the maps in the office library and the help of an operator, Henry locates a Chamber of Commerce in Kellogg, Idaho. He uses his thumb and forefinger to calculate that Kellogg is about ten miles down the road from Silverton. Close enough, he decides. He dials and a female voice answers.

Kellogg Chamber of Commerce, home of the Gold Diggers Auction, how may I help you?

What time do you close? he asks.

Five o'clock Gold Diggers time.

Darn, he says. I was hoping to call you from home. I don't want to charge up a long distance bill here at work. So I'll be quick. Do you know Jamie Lee Savitch at KLUK radio?

Sure, everybody in these parts knows her. Great show.

Here's the thing. I want to send away for the radio ranch promo package, but I don't have the station's address.

Oh, I don't either, but I can find it for you. Let me put you on hold.

No, don't do that. Maybe I'll give you my address and you can ask them to post the package to me.

While the Gold Digger gal talks away, taking down his address, saying she'll pass along a package from the station, it dawns on him he should have just asked the long distance operator to locate the station phone number. Why does he always do exactly what other people tell him to do? Why did he listen to that meteorologist? By the time she has moved on to the upcoming fall highlights that Henry might like to take in, Chief, newly tanned, is walking back and forth in front of his office door, and Henry has to pretend he's setting up an inspection. He ends the call with, Thanks for your time, I'll be at the farm by 10:30 tomorrow. He can hear the Gold Digger gal say, What? as he hangs up on her.

What inspection are you on tomorrow? Chief asks.

Just a recheck at Swift Farms.

Didn't know they needed one. Got a new heater file for you.

Henry barely listens to the tale of soft eggs out in Surrey; half his mind is preoccupied with the bizarre end to the call, whether it will mean the Gold Digger gal will not get the package or bother to pass his address on; the other half is on thoughts of why Chief didn't react to his saying Swift Farms, didn't catch him and say, But Elaine's in charge of that file now. Then before he has a chance to say anything about it Chief is up and out of his office. How could something so simple become so complicated?

A week later a large envelope from the Kellogg Chamber of Commerce waits below the mail slot at his front door. Three red, white and blue Old Glory stamps are stuck to the top right hand corner of the envelope and inside is a handwritten note *Come on down and visit one day,* Denise♥. Friendly, he thinks, but he's more interested in what else is in the package. He can see a KLUK bumper sticker and 8x10 glossies of the disc jockeys. He shuffles through the pictures. He doesn't like the look of the morning man with his satin western shirt and greasy smile, and the out-of-focus photo of Goodtimes Charley is so bad it makes him think about using the camera he bought for poultry inspections to take his own shots, but when he gets to the picture of Jamie Lee, she just looks pure pretty. Her blonde hair is tousled, and a hint of breast pokes out the top of her blouse. And even though she's what his mother would call a *cheap piece*, he doesn't care. Jamie Lee understands things about men like him, understands they don't want to be alone, didn't ask to be virgins, understands it's just that some things hurt so much they cripple. All a man like Henry really wants to do is to fly.

He puts the package down and walks with the KLUK sticker out to his chariot, the Subaru, and whistles a song he heard on Jamie Lee's show while he peels the tape from the back. He starts to think about flying down in his chariot to see her as he affixes the adhesive to the bumper. There's strength flowing from the sticker into the car's engine, into the radio and into the front seat where he will sit when he does take that trip. Other people vacation in Idaho, why not him? The sticker has a mother hen and baby chicks in cowboy boots and hats. Chas comes out to the curb to stand beside him.

Pretty funky.

Yeah. I like it.

What is KLUK?

A radio station.

Kind of funny you work with chickens and you listen to a station called KLUK.

Yup.

Say . . . we're going to be late with the rent again.

Ah.

Sorry. Jim and I have to get it together. It's just that work has been uneven at the grain elevators ever since, you know, his latest detox. And my chair at the new place isn't working out that well. Being the new guy, I'm stuck in the corner, never get any of the walk-ins.

Normally, news of late rent would upset Henry but he's determined not to let anything disturb his mood. He says bye to Chas and floats back inside the house to pick up the glossy of Jamie Lee again. He traces his finger around the edge of her breast, circles in on where the nipple would be. He lies on his bed and takes down his jeans. Briefly, baby chicks and mother hens are in his mind, but they're quickly supplanted by breasts poking out of a blouse, nipples hard against a silky shirt, tousled blonde hair. Then a *thump thump crash* from downstairs, and a shriek from Chas that is so loud he can hear it through the floorboards. At first the commotion excites him, images of Chas at Kits Beach intermingle with imaginings of Chas having sex with Elaine, Chas having sex with Jamie Lee, then all of them having sex together, and somehow he is getting harder, so firm he feels the semen move up, it's going to be terrific, it's mounting, he's ready to fly, until he hears Chas screaming out on the front lawn. Ejaculate spills, but it is hardly what he could call a satisfying event. A stream of warm semen flows down the shaft, the force behind it so minimal none of it makes it past the base where a disappointing puddle forms in his pubic hair. He messes with the pool and he thinks about using it as a lubricant to start over, but he can still hear Chas outside and he knows it's going to be a wasted effort.

No flying for Little Ducky today, he says as he stands and walks to the window. He pulls the drape back enough to see Chas in his wine-coloured dressing gown, bent over broken pieces of a hair dryer scattered on the front lawn.

I was only trying to make my hair look good for you, Chas yells back toward the suite.

Henry looks down at his dangling apparatus. How could such a small flap of skin be so temperamental? He's seen hens and roosters have an easier time of it in the barnyard. And his useless equipment has gone numb again, the tip is freezing cold, as if merely taking it out of his pants with any thought of it going inside someone else, anyone else — and what the hell was that thinking about Chas in the middle of it all anyway? — has killed it. As he stands there he realizes more than just his dong has gone numb, his fingers have too. He's beginning to terrify himself with this confusion. Oh my God, he thinks, this can't be normal. Partly to make himself stop thinking about sex, he pulls on his underwear and walks into the living room.

He finds his mother's Rand McNally Road Atlas on the bottom shelf of the bookcase, flips to the State of Idaho and traces the green line of Interstate-90 with a shaking forefinger to the edge of the Bitterroot Mountains and the black dot that is Silverton. It would only take him twelve hours to get there, maybe fourteen if the twisty bit around Coeur d'Alene causes any trouble. Might be sort of a different thing to do, to travel down there, find out what the Gold Digging Days are all about, check out the local scene, practise taking a few photographs, landscape shots, and maybe even a portrait or two of interesting people like, say, Jamie Lee.

He puts the Atlas back and turns to see the photo of his mother, still presiding over the house, preserved in the silver picture frame on the fireplace mantel — right where she left it. She wears a red sweater in the picture, and she and Henry, aged ten, stand in front of a Christmas tree festooned with decorations. Henry took the picture himself, setting up the new Kodak Instamatic Santa had given him with the self timer. His mother is trying to kiss him, but he's averted his head enough to make the kiss swipe at his cheek instead of his lips. This causes a visible stiffness in his mother's arm that he had not noticed until now. Every time before when he looked at the photo, he couldn't get past how bad the mole on his left cheek looked. His mother used to call it his *beauty mark* and to this day he can't stand how much the mole makes him feel like a girl. He puts the picture back on the mantel.

He wakes at six the next morning, motionless on top of the covers, his mouth dry and his head full of the take-me, hurt-me sound bites of Jamie Lee Savitch. His mind starts working like a slide projector as he runs through a collection of his fantasy girlfriends. First up in the carousel is Debi of "Sister Golden Hair" fame with her swaying ponytail and luscious buttocks, then there's Shannon-or-whatever-her-name-is in her taut T-shirt swatting at a fiery bubble and looking appealing despite his nearly setting them both on fire, then black-eyeliner girl in English twelve, the thought of her white lipstick still gets him, next is Kitty with her smoky sexy Winston smell, still one of the best, followed by Janine with her fermented haybreath and rabbit teeth, and finally Elaine with her orange hair and her mouth full of whipped cream. He's about to go onto Jamie Lee when out of a foggy part of his mind there is a slight nudge from the Chas corner, enough to make his hand jerk and reach over to the night table to pluck up the glossy photo of Jamie Lee. He is holding the photo tight as if his life depends on it when he calculates there is enough time for his Subaru chariot to whisk him to Silverton for the start of Jamie's Friday evening show. Things are slow at work anyway, he thinks, they won't miss me. Besides who there really cares? Certainly not Elaine. He grabs his penis, yanks it hard and with thoughts of Jamie Lee achieves what just the evening before seemed impossible. He is tempted to fall back asleep with the relaxation of it all but knows that if he really is going to make the evening radio show he must leave immediately.

He quickly packs a small bag of toiletries and underwear, his camera, and the *Rand McNally Road Atlas*. He leaves a hurried message on the machine at work, saying he's ill, and puts on an extra sweatshirt before he heads out the door.

Even though it's just past Halloween, there's frost on the windows of the Subaru at 6:30 in the morning. He uses the bear-paw scraper the dealer gave him, moving around the car's windows, making as straight a swath as he can under the circumstances. When he's almost done, on window number seven, he begins to wonder if he needs his birth certificate to cross the border. He rushes back inside to rummage in the drawer of the desk in the living room. On the way out of the room, he turns the picture of his mother face down on the mantel.

South of Bellingham, he has to make a decision. He's been speeding to this point, so he takes a moment at the Sedro Woolley exit to thumb through the Atlas. He can either take the red, single-lane highway from where he is, or he can drive a hundred miles farther south in the wrong direction but be on the green, triple-lane I-90.

He rolls down the window. The sun is up, the air still cool. The car shakes when a transport rumbles by. There could be snow in the higher elevations, and though he trusts his four-wheel drive anything can happen in a mountain pass. He's seen it himself on the news — the tanker on the mountain road tipped into a snow bank crushing a small Japanese car, a tiny import skidding off the edge of a cliff. Why has he bought a foreign car and not a heavy-duty Ford truck? The thought gives him a nervous stomach. He decides to drive to the Nuff 'n Such he can see at the gas station just down the shoulder to try one of their fifty-seven varieties of homestyle donuts. He needs to think this through.

Three crullers and a donut hole later, he still hasn't made up his mind, but he knows he has to get going. Two truckers are ahead of him at the till and he spins a rack of sunglasses while he waits. The fat trucker is capping his coffee when a pair of reflecting aviators whirls past. Henry pulls them from the stand, faces the mirror at the top, and puts the wires around his ears.

Not bad, the checkout girl says.

You think so? Henry answers.

Yeah, like Jack Nicholson.

He buys the sunglasses and wears them out of the shop. When he gets back to the car, he checks his reflection in the window. He does look okay. He checks again in the rear-view mirror. Then, when he starts driving, he begins to wonder how Jack might decide which route to take. Jack would take the most direct route, no fooling around — so Henry points his wagon toward the red, single-lane highway into the mountains.

Soon after Baker Dam, he needs to pee and pulls over at the rest stop. He walks into the cement building, past the urinals, and into one of the stalls. He puts paper down on the seat as his mother taught him to do in public washrooms. *Filthy places. Horrid things can grow on your bum. Ulcers, tapeworms!* He's almost finished when he hears someone come into the bathroom. He shakes himself dry, uses a bit of paper to dab at the end, flushes the toilet with his foot and walks out of the stall.

Can't even make it as far as Diablo, the dark-haired man standing at the urinal says.

Henry takes his sunglasses off, as if he might hear differently without them.

What do you mean?

I mean that dump last night closed the road past Diablo.

It did? How long will it be closed?

I dunno. Could be for a coupla days. Road ain't hardly open this timea year anyway.

What? The atlas shows it as a highway.

Well, could be she's a highway, but that don't mean she's open alla the time.

The man sort of winks and walks out. For a second, Henry wonders if he might have been kidding. But when he walks to the Subaru he can see the big rig heading back toward I-90. He pulls the atlas out again and sure enough when he traces Hwy 20 past Diablo, the thin red line breaks into dashes marked 'Closed in Winter'. They ought to make these things clearer, he thinks. Stupid map showing campsites better than highways — green teepees all over the place obscuring important information.

This time he doesn't fool around. He heads straight for the I-90, pushing the Subaru up over 100 km/hour. The entire state of Washington is yet to be crossed, and precious time has been wasted on the ill-fated Diablo turnoff. When he catches himself tense at the wheel, he thinks about how Jack would be. Of course, Jack wouldn't be driving a yellow Subaru, and Jamie Lee probably wouldn't like that either — she'd want something substantial with tinted windows — so to fill the time he starts imagining how it would feel to ride in the cab of a Chevy, high up on a padded bench seat with matching panels and flip-down visors.

Hunger and a full bladder bring him down at a diner in North Bend. It smells good inside, like roast beef and peas. He leaves his sunglasses on long enough to be sure the young waitress sees him. He's happy when she gives him a big smile as she walks toward the table.

What can I get you?

What comes with your deluxe cheeseburger?

You can have fries or slaw . . . Oh, what the heck, want both? I'll getcha both.

Yeah. Both. I'm hungry.

Uh-huh . . . And to drink? Sweetheart shake? They're on special.

What's a Sweetheart shake?

Strawberries and marshmallow. It's yummy.

Yeah. That'd be good too.

Uh-huh.

Henry can't remember the last time he looked forward to a meal so much as this one. If he stays happy like this, he'll have to watch his waistline. Doubtful Jamie Lee would like a paunch either.

After the meal, he sails down the highway and the wagon scales the Snoqualmie Pass, no problem. The sign at the top says the elevation is 3,022 feet. Just for the heck of it, he tries KLUK. It comes in loud and clear!

That about wraps it up for the Radio Ranch Lunch Hour. I gotta move over and make room for that crazy new guy, High Tech Red-Neck, Billy Wray. He's gonna bring you folks some of the best in the West. And remember if you like country-rock, western swing, or rock-a-billy, this is the station for YOU . . . and oh yeah, if you want to win those tickets for the Opryland Express, take a ride on our fabulous party bus down to Nashville with two of KLUK's favourite DJs, then all you have to do is pick up the phone — NOW — call us here at 666-KLUK . . . maybe we can even talk that little troubleshooter Jamie Lee into coming along . . . WOW . . . look at those phone lines light up, whole lotta people out there want to check out the Ernest Tubbs Texas Troubadour Western Store with Jamie Lee on board. And don't forget the Music Valley Wax

Museum while you're at it . . . Okay let's listen to what should have been a No. 1 hit a few years back take us on down the road OUTTA HERE . . . this is Gary Goodnight singing "My Baby's Gone" . . .

Gary is into his second wail of *baby's gone* when the phantom air waves leave the car and bring Henry nothing but a whole lot of fabulous static. He doesn't care. His mind is turning on the idea of the Opryland Express with Jamie Lee. It frosts him that the lunch guy used her to get callers to phone in. But it sure would be great to travel down to Nashville with her. The gang would probably meet in the early morning, a whole busload of them, and they'd leave right from the station parking lot, Jamie Lee looking her purest pretty in the early light. And she would have stopped to buy everybody donuts and coffee for the ride, or maybe she'd have the driver pull over as soon as they got out of the lot —

But where exactly would the bus be parked? How does one find a radio station parking lot anyway? Radio stations have to be security-conscious these days, lot of important people to protect. And they always do have you phone in to win those free tickets. They never say, Come on down to see us at the corner of Main and Church, never tell you to drive until you see the big old party bus parked out front of the station. Why hasn't he thought of this before? How is he going to find KLUK once he gets to Silverton?

Henry wrenches at the wheel. He is so distracted he moves across a lane of traffic without looking. A speeding pick-up swerves behind him and the driver gives him the finger as he flies past. When he turns to take a look, his sunglasses glint in the side window. The glasses make him feel better, but still he has to turn down the static on the radio, so he can concentrate.

At the outskirts of Ritzville, the soft static changes to the KLUK signature jingle sung in three-part western harmony: *K L - K L - K L - U K   AM   680 . . . Turn on Country.* The sound perks him up.

Hey, partners, you're on board with the High Tech Red-Neck Billy Wray. That's Wray with a W, in case you're wonderin'. My pretty little bride-to-be says when we get hitched she's going to be Ray without the Dubya. What do you think about that? Something about complementing each other without duplicating. She's the one with the intellect. But I'm the one with the high tech.

Billy Wray's voice goes kind of wobbly when he says *high tech.* Henry's pretty sure it's reverb that does that to his voice. When Billy Wray comes back on he's using his normal voice.

It's 4:53 and we're having just a beeeeeautiful sunset here in our new high-tech studios overlooking the lake. I tell you, this afternoon it's so calm and peaceful out there, I just want to pull out some loud and crazy ZZ Top and ZZ right across the water at you. But I don't think the boss man would like that too much, might make him say, "Stop puttin' the freak in frequency, Billy Wray," so this cowboy's going to be good and play a little Kenny Loggins singing "Footloose" instead. Then we're going to fade into newshour with something real pretty, a tune from Willie Nelson just out last year: "What a Wonderful World".

You're listenin' to KLUK radio 680 — all the power of a light bulb just not as bright.

This cracks Henry up. He likes Billy Wray. He's funny and informative, tells you something about himself. Kind of interesting. And he plays good tunes.

He pulls over to have a look at the atlas. It's almost dark, so he takes off the sunglasses. He can see a town named Wallace just past Silverton, and another one just before it named Osbum — what a name — but he can't see any lakes. Which could be good. Might mean the lake near the station is small enough to drive around, and Billy Wray said he was looking at the sunset, so that means he's facing west. The station might not be that hard to find after all.

He does a quick calculation. Assuming he's counted all the markers properly, he still has more than 140 miles to go and part of that is through Spokane and then Coeur d'Alene. He might not make it before Jamie Lee's show starts. His shoulders hunch up. What if he has wasted all this time driving, skipped out on work for no good purpose? The sunglasses on the dashboard calm him. No big deal, he'll meet her after the show. Better timing anyway.

Back on the highway, big fat drops, lazy but steady, begin to fall. Normally this would cause him to hunch his shoulders even more, but again, no big deal. He's got more time now and the highway is good flat blacktop with a new centre line and his wipers are working well.

Neon cocktail signs begin to blink at him. Some are martini glasses with olives sloshing, others are tippling by themselves in the sky, a few are just the names of beer.

Henry has never had a cocktail, doesn't think he really wants one. And though he's only had beer a couple of times, he begins to think about sitting at a bar with one in his hand. He wonders if it would be too much to wear the sunglasses into the bar.

Somewhere past Coeur d'Alene, just at the edge of Kellogg, he spots a giant neon can frothing and pouring golden beer into the parking lot in front of the Shop-Mart. He pulls over to watch the beer for a time before reaching for his sunglasses on the dash. He puts the wire frames over his ears and walks into the mart. It's noisy and bright inside. A pretty but slightly plump woman about his age in a too-tight, red-gingham, southern belle dress walks toward him. Her breasts poke out of the bodice which has been cinched in tight with a drawstring.

Howdy. Welcome to Shop-Mart. What's your name?

Henry.

Hi there, Henry. My name's Charity.

Charity uncaps a felt pen and writes something down on the roll of paper she's holding. She peels a tag off and comes up close to pat it onto Henry's chest. When she's standing near, his heart begins to palpitate. Especially when he senses his mother is hovering nearby. To calm himself he tries to concentrate on the spray of freckles that seems to be painted across her nose. But as soon as he looks at the freckles he wants to reach out and touch her face, or is it the freckles themselves he wants to touch? They're friendly rusty polka dots, practically dancing on the bridge of her nose. *Oh for goodness' sake, Henry, touching a stranger's freckles is inappropriate. I taught you better than that.* He shifts his gaze to the tag she's pressing onto his shirt. His name is neatly printed with a happy-face beside it.

Are you single? Charity asks.

Yes . . .

Thought so . . . But that's good. You can join the party. Singles' Nite at Shop-Mart. All party snacks, chips, dips, soda are half-price for singles. Enjoy!

Another young woman — this one not so plump but wearing too much green eye makeup and a tag that says Mary Lou with two happy-faces — walks up to Henry.

Wanna be my partner in the three-legged singles swipe?

He doesn't know how to respond. He feels torn, like somehow he should be on the road. And what is a singles swipe? Is a person just supposed to let themselves get involved without knowing what is going on, and with *a cheap piece*? Then it comes to him. Jack would play. He wouldn't care what a singles swipe is, he'd just play. Besides, he's already made up his mind not to rush at Jamie Lee, he should have some fun while he waits for her show to end.

Sure. Singles swipe sounds good, he says.

Okay, partner. Let me hog-tie your right leg to my left . . . Jimmy . . . Jimmy . . . come on over here. You and Angie, you swipe with us. Okay?

Jimmy and Angie are tied from hip to calf. They shamble toward Mary Lou, who is bent over just about finished hog-tying herself to Henry. Then Charity at the front door spins a giant egg timer and yells, Aisle three.

Mary Lou drags him to the stack of shopping carts and shouts, Take a cart. Take a cart.

He pulls a cart out of the conga line and they charge, the best they can, their carts banging into each other, down aisle three where Mary Lou begins pulling bottles of vitamins, aspirins, and cough syrup from the shelf. Underneath the cough syrup he sees a bunch of happy-face stickers like the one on his nametag. While he stares at the stickers, Jimmy and Angie swipe by and clean off the hand lotion, then Jimmy bumps him out of the way to take what is left of the vitamins. There's a bit of a scrum around the canned meats and tuna, but Henry manages to snag a dozen cans of smoked oysters and mussels, which brings a smile to Mary Lou's face. Next he reaches down to put a big bag of Huggies into the cart and Mary Lou shrieks.

Put it back. Put it back. Too bulky. Take something else.

He is putting the Huggies back while Mary Lou knocks jars of Cheez Whiz into her cart when Charity with the egg timer calls out, Time — come on over here and let's tote up those buggies.

He and Mary Lou lose by $11.47, and Jimmy and Angie win the maple-cured ham, leaving them to put back the merchandise from all four of the carts. When they're at the vitamin shelf, Mary Lou says, That's okay, Henry. It was your first time. Jimmy and them play singles swipe every Friday so they know what they're doing, get all the expensive small stuff first. You can make it up by buying me a six-pack of Michelob, if you want.

He isn't sure, but he thinks Michelob is a beer. He saw a sign for it on the highway. He goes to the rear of the store and looks into the cooler. Sure enough, there's a bunch of Michelob lined up in bottles and cans. The cans look tastier to him, the silver-gold colour just the way he expects the beer to taste. And even though he wonders if he is being conned, he thinks what the heck, it's only beer. He reaches in and pulls out two six-packs. One for her and one for himself. As he lifts the second pack he notices something hanging above the cheese just to the left of the beer. A pair of fuzzy knit mice is looped over the grill swinging in the current of cold air coming from the cooler. He looks at the mice, then remembers seeing a knitted fish skeleton hanging from the shelf near the cans of tuna.

Mary Lou is waiting for him at the checkout. Want to play swinging taste testers with me? she asks. She points to a large blue swing in the corner where a blindfolded woman is being fed some kind of red chips by her partner.

No thanks.

I'll be easy on you this time. If we lose, I'll only make you buy me a bag of Doritos. She laughs. Half price for Singles' Nite!

No, it's not that . . . it's just that I got a date and I have to get going.

Well aren't you the lucky one . . . Say, before you go, can I have a look at you under those sunglasses. So's I knows it's you when I see you walkin' down the street.

Sure, he says, feeling confident. But as soon as he lifts the glasses, he feels exposed and his face flushes. His palms begin to sweat.

Mary Lou surveys him. Okay, Henry, looking good.

He drops the glasses and feels protected enough to get the money out of his pocket and pay for the beer. That is until he's up close to Charity again and sees her freckles. His fingers flutter and he drops several Canadian quarters on the floor. After he picks them up and plops them on the counter, Charity jokes, Gonna have to charge you twenty percent for those wooden nickels.

What?

Canadian money doesn't work so good here in the U S of A.

Oh, that's okay. Charge me what you need to.

Charity punches some numbers into her cash register. There's a tiny knitted skull hanging beside the cigarettes. The place is beginning to remind him of his mother's Day of the Dead phase. And Charity seems to be taking her time, bent over the moving grocery counter, reaching for something underneath, her bodice drawstring dangling precariously close to the mechanism, threatening to pull her ample bosom into the works. His hands are practically crawling up his sides, itching to reach out, to do what, to stop a catastrophe, to stroke her breasts? Touch one of her freckles? Which is exactly what happens when his hand reaches out involuntarily and hits the big freckle on the right side of Charity's nose.

Ow, she says.

Sorry, I didn't mean to hurt you. I thought your string was going to get caught.

It's okay, it didn't really hurt. Just sort of freaked me out.

She puts the change in his hand and her hand touching his helps to calm him. Then she reaches out to touch him on the chest right around where his heart is and she says, Really, it's okay. Nice to meet you. Come on back sometime. She removes his name tag for him.

He regains his confidence enough to give Mary Lou her beer and walk out. He's able even to put a bit of a swagger to his stride. But as soon as he exits, he can hear his mother's voice, *Stop, Henry — nobody wants to see you posturing that way.*

He grips the beer bag tight. Once he's safe behind the wheel, he takes a can from the plastic yoke. That's when he notices a little knit piece in the bottom of the bag. It has a tag attached to it with a handwritten message: *Beer cozy courtesy of Charity.* There is a ♥ over the i in Charity. He slips the cozy over the can, pulls the tab and takes a sip. Not bad, tastier than he'd imagined. He decides to go back inside and thank Charity for the cozy.

Hey there. You again?

Yeah. Me. Just wanted to thank you.

You like it? Cool. Why don't you sign my invitation list? I'm hoping to have a show of knit things at the art gallery next year, sort of a knit-reactor theme. I'll keep you posted.

Okay.

She pushes a list of names and addresses toward him. He writes his name and address even though he has no idea what a *knit reactor* is. After he's finished, he walks out of the store, without intrusion from his mother, but this time Charity follows him. He's at his car about to get back in when she calls to him.

Hey there, just wanted to say we don't get many folks from Canada. It'd be a real pleasure if you'd come back down for the art show.

While she speaks she holds up a cozied beer of her own and Henry reaches inside his car to get his can so the two of them are able to toast. As their cans touch, there's a flash from behind a nearby parked car.

What's that? he asks.

That's Peter, my boyfriend. He's a photographer and likes to take random shots of people using my knit things.

For what?

For what, Peter? Show yourself, boy.

A dark-haired young man holding a camera pops up from behind a Chevy truck, then disappears behind it again.

He's shy, Charity says. I hope he didn't freak you out. Look I gotta get going back into work. We'll send you the shot. It's nothing weird.

Okay. If you say.

Promise you'll come on down for the show.

Promise.

Thanks for visiting.

Henry finishes his beer sitting in the parking lot. He's not sure what to make of the photo shoot although he has to admit he's a little disappointed Charity has a boyfriend. He felt for a second like they were making friends, and maybe they still are. On balance, weird as Peter is, the evening has been fun so far and taking this vacation has been an excellent idea.

He cracks a second beer as he drives past the Chamber of Commerce. He's starting to feel like he belongs, this is where the gold-digger gal Denise♥ works. There are ♥s everywhere. Couldn't be a better omen for his mission. He clicks on the radio to listen to the seven o'clock KLUK news before Jamie Lee's show starts. For all he knows, Jamie Lee puts a ♥ over the i in her name too. All good things run in threes.

The second beer goes down really fast. He likes it and wonders why he never tried drinking before. Then he isn't sure if it's the beer or what, but the news ends too abruptly and cuts immediately to Jamie Lee.

It's the girl inside the radio bringing you a country devotional for the weekend. Whew . . . it's Friday night and I'm going to play a radio request right off the top. Darryl from out there in Osburn called in and asked me to play "Behind Closed Doors" . . . good choice, Darryl. You and your girlfriend, you chase each other around the room tonight, okay? And you know, Darryl, that's just what I'm wanting to do myself. Get me behind some closed doors later on tonight. But right now, I'm alone in here and I'm feeling kind of soft.

Henry's chest spreads like a massive bald-headed eagle. He wants to swoop down on the radio and caress it with all the lust and passion he's built up inside — that Jamie Lee, she is in a mood all right. He cracks open a third beer and gulps it down greedily as he drives through the town of Osburn, which he realizes he'd misread earlier on the map as Osbum. Another omen: Jamie Lee is talking about the very town he is driving through.

The window wipers slap at raindrops big as mud pies as he passes the Silverton town sign. Then just before Crystal Gayle's "I've Cried (The Blue Right Out of My Eyes)" ends, Jamie Lee's voice seems to jump out from nowhere again.

Hey everybody, the girl inside the radio is in some kind of existential condition. I got a whole mess of tunes guaranteed to put you on edge. First up is Johnny Dear singing "Road to Nowhere", then Garth Yearwood is gonna put his heart on the line with "Can't Get There From Here", and finally the sweetheart of all time, Miss Patsy Cline is going to sing about that bewitching hour when all good things come to an end, you know it . . . "Walkin' After Midnight" . . . Say, all this highbrow talk is driving me to a confession. I'm not really here tonight. I'm out chasing down midnight. Can't wait for it. How about you? Are any of you really out there?

The eagle in Henry's chest starts to thrash, beat its wings hard against his rib cage. Somehow Jamie Lee's mood has switched. He doesn't like it anymore. By the time he comes around the bend in the shore of the lake — which is really just a pond — and sees the red light of a radio tower up on the ridge, he's completely confused. He cracks a fourth beer and has it drunk as Patsy finishes singing. He's starting up the road toward the red light when Jamie Lee comes back on.

I'm surrounded with straps, cords, tapes, reels, headphones, microphones, too much radio stuff. More

STUFF than you can shake a fist at. The whole thing makes me feel looped.

Me too, he shouts. I'm looped too. Friggin' right I'm looped. More looped than you can shake *your* fist at, Jamie Lee.

He hoists his fifth beer into the air. He finishes it and crumples the can as he pulls into the radio station parking lot. The lot is empty except for one other car. He puts on his sunglasses and gets out of the Subaru. His hand trembles when he shuts the door and he has to steady himself for a moment before he can walk to the front of the building. The station looks to be in darkness. He sees the KLUK sign and the hen and chicks in cowboy boots painted on the window, so he knows it's the right building. But it's like no one's here. He decides to return to the car and drink the last beer. When it's gone, he gets out of the car and walks along the side of the building.

At the back, a door is propped open with a chair wedged under it and a single line of light shines out onto the waste disposal unit. A heavy-set man is pushing a large rubber garbage can toward the unit. Henry stands in the dark and watches the man hoist the can over his shoulder. Styrofoam cups, paper plates, balloons, streamers, and a half-eaten birthday cake avalanche into the disposal.

The man scrapes icing off the side of the can, walks back into the building, and returns with a second load. When he's busy hurling champagne bottles into the unit, Henry sneaks inside. He is wandering down the corridor toward the red light over a door, when the janitor yells.

Hey, you can't go in there.

Henry turns around. I'm looking for Jamie Lee.

She's not in there. Are you one of her guests?

What do you mean she's not in there? SHE'S ON THE RADIO!

Hey buddy, settle down. She's on the radio, but she's looped tonight — on tape — not here. Are you one of her guests, or what?

For her birthday?

No, not for her birthday, her wedding. She's down in Wallace getting married to Billy Wray right now.

All the feeling drains out of his body. He's afraid he might pass out if he doesn't move quickly. He runs outside, gets in his car, and turns on the engine. Jamie Lee's voice purrs into the night. He sits as still as he can behind the steering wheel, the voice eddying around him. He tries to force all his thoughts down, deep into his gut, but he can't do it. He feels numb melancholy moving up through awareness, into anxiety and then into a colour — blue electric wire.

Pure panic has a smell — pepper up the nostril.

A taste — red lipstick.

And a sound — thirteen thousand radios all blaring Jamie Lee Savitch.

He grips the steering wheel and shouts, How could you? How could you? . . . What makes Little Ducky fly? I'll show you what makes him fly!

He hits the bridge of his sunglasses with the palm of his hand, floors the Subaru, the car roars across the wet parking lot, skids over a ditch, leaps across a patch of yellowed grass, then smashes into the transmission tower.

A spark flies from the grill and the engine goes dead. Everything is quiet except for the ear-piercing radio.

Henry is aware of someone turning the radio off. He hears a female voice.

Get out of the car, sir.

He unfolds from around the steering wheel and steps out of the car; a crumpled beer can in a cozy falls to the ground. The woman looking at him is wearing a police officer's uniform. She reminds him a bit of Kitty from Arbutus Mall.

Aren't you a sight, she says.

A lens has fallen out of his sunglasses and he has beer all down the front of his sweatshirt.

You okay? she asks. She blinks her flashlight on and off in his eyes. Hit your head or anything?

Henry stares at her. I don't think so.

How much you had to drink tonight, sir?

While Henry tries to remember how many beers he's drunk, it just sort of comes to him, there under the glow of the transmission tower. You have choices in life, and it takes courage to make them, but if you make a choice, that's how you learn to fly. His face breaks into a silly smile.

I'll tell you how many I had, if you give me a hug, he says.

The officer looks over at her male partner sitting in the cruiser. She shrugs.

Let me book you first.

NINE

Show of Feathers

THERE IS A DULL PRESSURE in the front of Henry's head. He sits up and the room tilts. Then he hears himself retch and a voice say, That's what the garbage can is beside you for.

He remembers being told the night before, *If you don't cooperate sir, we'll throw you in the shower.* He can't remember much else, but he must have cooperated because he doesn't feel like he's had a shower in weeks.

From the bed, he asks, Where am I?

The Shoshone County Jail, the voice says.

Oh. He starts to puke again. When the last of all that is in his gut has been brought up, he looks through the bars to see a young deputy sheriff with his feet up on the desk. Inside the cell, there's the bed he's on, a stainless steel toilet, a can full of puke, and that's it. He looks down at his shoes beside the bed. There are no laces.

If I can take ten bucks from your wallet, I'll get you a greasy breakfast, the sheriff says. It'll help with the hangover.

It will?

Should do, sop up the alcohol. Quite the bender you were on.

Yeah, I've never been drunk before.

Really? Be sure to tell the judge that.

Judge? What judge?

You gotta go see a judge before you can get out of here.

I do. Why?

Drunk in a public place. Damage to property. Driving under the influence. You name it. No judges this weekend, but first thing Monday morning we'll get you out of here.

Not 'til Monday?

Like I said.

Do you know where my car is?

Out back. Safe and sound, such as it is.

What does that mean?

Well you hit a transmission tower that was a whole lot bigger than your car, so yeah, the front end is a bit mashed.

Oh jeez. And my other stuff?

Your beer cozies, broken sunglasses, camera, and wallet are right here in my desk.

Any chance I can get the camera back? It'd give me something to do while I'm in here.

Well it's against protocol, but don't see why not, nothing to take any pictures of in here anyway.

I'd be grateful.

The sheriff pulls open his desk drawer and walks to the cell to pass the camera through the bars.

Don't tell anyone I gave this to you, and if you gotta do any serious business in there — he jerks his finger at the toilet — just tell me and I'll turn my head. I'm used to it.

Henry spends the afternoon and part of the next day, until he runs out of film, working on low light exposures. He photographs his shoes without laces, his jail bed, the toilet in the corner and the deputy with his feet up on the desk taking a snooze. Might be an interesting collection, he thinks.

On the Monday morning, a different sheriff rounds up Henry and a couple of inmates from another division and they follow a paddy wagon, sirens going, around the corner to the courthouse. Two guys in shackles shuffle down the hall to a courtroom while Henry and the inmates he came with are ushered into the registry office to wait for the judge to finish up with the more serious felons.

Henry is the last to be dealt with and he expects to be taken to a courtroom, but an officer tells him, The judge is in a hurry. He's missed lunch and he's already backed up for the afternoon, so he'll take you in the anteroom off the registry.

The judge appears with a female clerk.

Okay, Mr. Parkins, what happened?

I got drunk for the first time in my life and they tell me I crashed into a transmission tower.

Why?

It was an accident. I didn't know what alcohol could do to me.

First time offender?

Yes, sir. I've never had any trouble before.

From Canada, right?

Yes, sir.

Okay, I'm going to release you, but you have to sign a Recognizance which means you guarantee you'll pay the radio station back for the damage you caused or you'll appear back here in court. Agreed?

Yes, sir.

I want to make it very clear to you that if you don't pay, the law will come over the border and we *will* have you arrested. Understood?

Yes, sir.

The judge signs a couple of papers and hands them to the clerk, and they both disappear from the room.

Henry waits for almost three hours before the clerk returns. She sets down a number of documents and a pen and says, Sorry it took so long. The radio station couldn't tell me an amount so I've put here *for an amount to be assessed*. Sign, please, and we'll be sure to send you the amount soon as we can.

By the time Henry is back behind the wheel of the Subaru it's nearly five o'clock and before he can drive any distance he has to find someone to check out the car. He's a little shocked by the amount of damage. He doesn't remember hitting anything at all. He drives as far as Kellogg before he finds a gas station that has a light on in the mechanic's bay. The mechanic, a big fellow covered in grease, takes a look underneath and starts to talk while he's still down on the ground.

You'll have to bring it back tomorrow, he says.

Oh no, I really have to be back in British Columbia tomorrow morning.

Sorry, it's closing time.

Isn't there anything I can do?

The mechanic hauls himself out from under the car and just stands there. Henry doesn't know if maybe it's the grease on the mechanic's face, a swath of it along his hairline, but something about the fellow makes him feel like he is a comrade. Even though it's against his grain, Henry makes him an offer.

I'll pay you an extra hundred bucks to stay open long enough to look over the car. I only need to know whether it's safe enough to drive back.

The fellow gestures toward the blue light of Jeffrey's Fry Shack across the street. Fifty bucks and a bucket of chicken with slaw, and you got a deal.

When Henry opens the door to the Shack, a wave of greasy chicken hits him. He thinks he might retch again like he did that first morning in the jail, but he keeps it together long enough to order. He's sitting on a red plastic chair waiting, when Charity walks through the door.

Hey stranger, you still here? Thought you'd be back in Vancouver by now.

No. Decided to stay the weekend. Huh, how do you know where I live?

You signed my invite list.

Oh yeah.

Don't forget to come down for my show, or I'll have to come get you.

Sure. Sure. When is it again?

Early in the new year. Haven't got the exact date yet, but it'll be on a weekend.

Okay.

He wants to say more, but nausea and a dull headache are taking the edge off everything. Charity's order is ready before his and she walks back holding something out toward him.

I was gonna mail this to you, but might as well give it to you now. Turned out pretty good, huh?

She hands him a photo of the two of them toasting with cozied beer cans. Her boyfriend got a good angle on her ample bosom, and the two of them look okay together.

Nice, Henry says. Something good to remember the weekend by.

He's feeling better when he crosses the street back to the garage and his stomach would have stayed settled if the mechanic hadn't been chomping on a chicken leg — bits of still-red muscle and tendon hanging from the cartilage — when he hands Henry the bill for the hoist check, plus fifty bucks.

Should get you back to Canada, he says. But take it in for service soon as you can, the electrical is fragile.

Henry takes a swig of the Coke he bought at the Shack. He is curious to know what the fellow means by *fragile*, but he can't watch him eat chicken any longer, so he settles up and rushes out into the cool night air. Good thing he applied for a visa after the debacle with Elaine at Denny's, or he wouldn't have been able to pay for everything. He breathes deeply once back in his wagon. He turns the radio on just long enough to deprogram KLUK. He knows he shouldn't be using anything electrical, but he can't stand to think his car is in any way connected to KLUK. Then he puts his broken sunglasses into the glovebox and slams it shut because clearly Jack Nicholson is an idiot.

The roads are mostly deserted and he's glad for the peace, though he can still smell fried chicken. He'd had to wait too long in the Shack for the order, and the stench is on his clothes and in his hair. It makes him think about his first assignment at Swift Farms overseeing the spring beak trimming. The farm manager had told him the heated blades were self-cauterizing, *state of the art*. But afterward a lot of birds had neural discharge because the beaks were trimmed too close. Henry filed a remedial order, but Swift objected and got him overruled. He'd done what he could to protest the industry, hadn't eaten turkey or chicken since, but there was only so much one man could do, and buying the mechanic his bucket and slaw had been an emergency.

He starts to tire after midnight, but around two in the morning, just south of Seattle, he is jolted back awake. He thinks he feels the Subaru veer to the right, although as soon as it happens he's not sure. The veer might have been more a tug of his brain after all the trauma on the weekend.

It doesn't happen again and he's thankful when he pulls up in front of the house just before dawn. His neck and shoulders are so tight he has to sit in the car for a few minutes to unwind. And his stomach feels queasy again.

He needs to go inside and drink some milk, settle himself down before he cleans up for work.

When he opens the fridge and swigs straight from the carton, he figures out too late the milk is off. He stands with the carton in hand and throws up into the sink. He hoses the vomit and spoiled milk down the drain with the hand-wand his mother had installed just the week before she died. As he watches the last bits of food swirl around, he yells, GODDAMNIT, YOU'RE DEAD. WHY AM I STILL MEASURING THINGS BY HOW LONG BEFORE OR AFTER YOU DIED?

He shuts off the water and steadies himself at the edge of the sink. She is not still around every corner, waiting to come at him, telling him he's a comfort, while at the same time berating him, saying he isn't strong enough, smart enough, handsome enough. He just won't let this happen anymore.

He stalks into the dining room, sweeps off the clutch of bereavement cards that have been on the sideboard for too long, then picks them up, brings them into the kitchen, and hurls them into the garbage. They land on top of the sour milk container. The last card opens to Chas' scrawled sentiment *we're here to help* reminding him this month's rent hasn't been paid yet.

He starts to clean himself up in the bathroom, but when he checks his reflection — his blue eyes are paler than usual, and his whiskers have grown in a multitude of colours ranging from red to almost white blonde — he can't stand to look long enough to shave. Besides, it might be good to see if the beard gets better with time, it's already half covered up the mole on his left cheek. He changes his clothes, then checks to be sure there is no cheque from Chas and Jim poking out the mail slot. When he finds none, he flies around to the basement suite. He's annoyed to see a stack of sodden newspapers and magazines sitting out on the walk, and is doubly annoyed they are mostly porn, the image on the top one a hairy, bare-chested man on the cover of *Bear Growls*.

He knocks. A few seconds pass before Chas answers.

What brings you here so bright and early?

You know, Henry says. He glimpses inside and can see the walls and ceiling of the living room have been painted black.

Jim appears behind Chas. He is bleary-eyed, as if he's just dragged himself out of bed.

What the fuck?

What the fuh to you, Henry responds. He is super angry now. You're two months behind on the rent and you've painted the suite without permission.

He couldn't quite get the *fuck* out, even in front of a jerk like Jim, but the intention was there and it felt good.

Neither Jim nor Chas say anything.

Have the cheque to me by this evening or you're out, he says. No more hooey about late paycheques.

He walks down the sidewalk alley and points to the heap of wet papers, And get this garbage out of here.

Hooey? Jim shouts down the alley after him. You're such a loser!

He doesn't look back, keeps walking toward his Subaru. He tucks his shirt in, feels his stomach all the way down to the end of the tails. He's pretty sure he's lost weight over the weekend, but still, he's a bit thick in the middle, and he wonders if he might look a little like the man on *Bear Growls*, especially with his beard grown in. He hopes not. He straightens up as his hand glances off his penis and wonders why he's tucking in his shirt anyway. It's only going to come untucked while he drives to work.

He arrives a half-hour earlier than usual to find Chief in his customary morning pose, hunched over a coffee in the lunchroom, rubbing a hand on his bald head while he does the crossword.

What happened to you the last couple of days?

Took sick, Chief. Sorry I didn't call yesterday.

Yeah. Kind of unusual for you not to phone. Bit disappointing really. The inspection in Langley is eleven-thirty. You'll drive out with Elaine.

He doesn't know what inspection Chief is talking about and doesn't care, except he doesn't like the tone of Chief's voice or that he has to assist Elaine. She'll go all snooty on him with her university education. And whatever he thinks, she'll override.

When Elaine waltzes into the lunchroom, she's wearing spiked heels and her dress, slinky red and low-cut, is a little odd for going on inspection. He lets himself fantasize for a moment that she chose the outfit for him. He imagines her standing in front of her wardrobe mirror practising how the dress looks when she bends over.

Hey, Henry, can you take your own car today? she says. I'm going straight from the site to meet Bob afterward.

She keeps chirping on about something, but he isn't listening. He's stuck on the fact that it's Bob she's chosen the dress for. She puts her face right in front of his.

Hello, are you in there? Here's a map to Lightstone's poultry farm. Don't forget your test kit.

How stupid do you think I am? he mutters under his breath.

Rough few days, Henry? she asks.

He looks at her. She's trying to be nice but he isn't in the mood, knows they're not going to get along; she'll finger the avian flu again, won't wait for test results, will sentence an entire flock to death based solely on a couple of soft-shelled eggs and a few ruffled feathers. For months now she's been predicting it's only a matter of time before the virus jumps to humans, and she wants to be the one-woman army to stop it and save the world.

As Henry drives toward Lightstone's farm in Langley, he barely thinks about the fragile electrical. Instead he obsesses about the smell of fried chicken in his hair — why didn't he take a shower? — and how he might mask the smell and whether Elaine has ever had a hangover. He hopes so. But then he has to will himself to stop thinking hangovers for fear he'll throw up again, so he switches to money, tries to calculate whether he has enough in the bank to pay for the transmission tower if Jim and Chas never pay their rent again. Then he thinks about those stuffed manila envelopes from the lawyer, how he really does need to open them because he's having trouble keeping the mortgage payments going without his mother's disability pension, and he knows he still has some death taxes to pay, and perhaps she had other assets he doesn't know about. But he doesn't want to think about her either, not even her money. So he begins to worry about the weight he's put on in the last year and wonders how much a new scale might cost. Once during the drive he even reaches out to turn on the radio, but stops before hitting the knob, then smacks himself in the forehead to try to stop all thoughts of Jamie Lee, except he does manage to wonder if she's ever been to Jeffrey's Fry Shack and whether she had a champagne hangover after her wedding reception.

When he arrives at the Lightstone farm, Elaine has changed out of her spiked heels and is wearing a lab coat over her raincoat. They walk toward the diminutive woman who waits for them outside the barn.

The chickens are in here, the woman says. My husband drew up a schedule before he passed away and this is my first season on my own. I don't think anything is wrong, but the guy from Swift Farms must have thought otherwise. I guess he called you in, eh?

We'll let you know ma'am, Elaine says.

Henry is upset by the response. Elaine's all business when the situation calls for a delicate touch. He isn't always intuitive about things, but perhaps he's more attuned than usual having just swept the bereavement cards from his own home. This woman is grieving. This is a widow they're dealing with. She isn't much older than he is, maybe only ten years, young to be a widow. He likes her manner, the soft yellow angora scarf she wears around her neck, the almond-shaped eyes that open and close with quiet determination. Still, he suspects by the way she hangs back from the barn door that things have gotten out of hand in there.

Let's look, shall we? Elaine says.

He braces himself for the strong get-you-in-the-throat smell of chicken manure that will pour from the barn if he's right. In part to distract himself from the moment, he asks the widow another question before she pulls open the door.

What's your name?

Wendy, she says.

The smell is worse than baby diaper. He knows Elaine is ticking the *unsanitary condition* box on her mental checklist. He asks, How long since your husband passed?

Some months now. I'm trying my best.

I'm sorry for your loss.

Elaine shoots him a look that says *what the hell?* When was the last top to bottom clean in here? she asks.

A while back, before Dennis passed, but he was weak, so we probably didn't do as good a job as we should have.

Wendy's eyelids slide down, bringing a calmness to her answer. Henry wants to reach out and touch the small angora hairs quivering at the edge of her scarf. They're so delicate in the late fall air. But as soon as he thinks this, his hands start to shake. The three of them walk into the barn.

Once his eyes adjust to the dark, he can see the barn is well-built, even has a mesh wall for good ventilation, if anyone bothered to open it, but the floor and the roosting beds are littered with feathers. Many of the chickens are motley, especially around the head and neck. Some have been pecking at each other and look like battered hens, but he doesn't think they are. He decides the widow's husband, Dennis, must have been a decent man. He built a good barn, he tried until the end. A good hosing together with a vigorous pitchfork would make a big difference.

What kind of chickens are these, ma'am? Elaine asks.

He can't believe it — whole lot of good her university education did — clearly most of the motley lot are hybrids with some bantam standard in them. Elaine should know hybrids moult more than purebreds, that these chickens are simply reacting to the boredom of not being fed properly or stimulated enough after their breeder died.

Dennis said they're mostly bantams, the widow answers.

Purebreds then, are they? Elaine is being her best professional stupid.

Suppose so, the widow says.

Excuse me, but a lot of your birds are hybrids, Henry says. It doesn't mean they aren't good chickens. They just moult more and for longer into the season. You've had a lot on your plate. I'm thinking maybe these chickens haven't been getting the exercise they normally do.

Wendy seems to lean into him, almost as if she is a small chick taking shelter.

Henry's chest plumps in an effort to provide her some comfort and for an instant he feels an urge to kiss the sad blinking eyes nested in yellow angora; but then the nervousness and usual flush to the face occur because a woman has come near. He keeps talking to occupy himself.

I'm wondering what kind of food you've been feeding these chickens?

Wendy points to a sack of pellets in the corner.

People at the Co-op told me this stuff was okay. Cheaper than what we used to feed them, but I have to start saving a little now that . . . things have changed.

He reads the contents on the side of the sack.

You know, there isn't enough protein in this meal to maintain laying, he says, or to help the chickens through the moulting season.

They said I could buy low protein so long as I let the chickens out to feed on insects, she says.

And have you been doing that?

Wendy averts her eyes, chagrined.

Elaine scoops up one of the hens, holding it inexpertly, its back leg awkwardly splayed across her belly. She inspects its eyes, picks at some crust at the side of the head. From where Henry stands he can see no evidence of edema. He watches while she begins to tick off the avian flu indicators on her clipboard: edema, ruffled feathers, drop in egg production, depression, loss of appetite. He knows where this is headed.

There's nothing wrong with these chickens that better food and exercise won't fix, he blurts.

Oh come on, Henry, Elaine says. This flock has avian flu and you know it.

No, it does not. These chickens are hybrids. They're moulters. And their diet's not been good.

He knows he is offending Policy Number 4: workers do not contradict one another in the field. He also knows there is a big kill order on in the Department, but the order is largely at Elaine's instigation and he can't stand by while she sentences another flock without proper testing. Especially not this one. He does not wait to hear Elaine's response. He grabs a transport case sitting by the feed sack and shoves six hens into it. They could do testing on-site if they really wanted to, but he's desperate, although not sure why. Is it desperation to save the flock or to prove to himself that he's right about something?

I'm going to take these back for proper testing, he says.

You do that and you're fired, Henry, Elaine says.

You can't fire me, Henry answers.

Oh, yes, I can. Maybe if you'd come to work more often, you'd know I was promoted on Friday to deputy chief inspector. You report directly to me now.

Henry thinks briefly about phoning in to confirm, but knows it's true. When he looks at the six blinking hens in the case, they seem to be saying *Do it. Take us.* He picks up the crate, walks to the Subaru, opens up the back, puts the chickens in and slams the trunk down. The words *you report directly to me* ring in his ears, but the quiet calm of Wendy's face, eyelids opening and closing, keeps him steadfast. Out the open car window he calls to her.

I'll be back with your chickens. You'll see, they'll be healthy and recovered.

He drives as fast as he can down the concession road, dust billowing behind him. He blows by a Swift Farms truck parked at the corner. He wonders why the truck is there, but forgets about it as he merges onto Highway 1 and a strange grating noise starts up behind the right front wheel. The noise worsens as he drives and when he's in the middle lane trapped between a transport truck and a Greyhound bus, the car definitely veers to the right and he feels stuck in the cocoon of the car, believing everything broken down is his fault. The loop of self-loathing makes him think he doesn't deserve help and somewhere in the loop he abandons the idea of taking the chickens in for testing in favour of taking them home with him. Back in Kitsilano, at the corner of Fourth and Vine, he has to pull over for fear the car will hop right up onto the curb by itself. He takes the crate with the chickens out of the back and begins to walk the remaining blocks home.

He's sweating profusely. The chickens are heavy despite their scrawny bodies. As he nears the end of his street, he has to set the crate down. He needs to think how he might sneak the chickens into the house before old Mrs. Krumpskey sees them and reports to City Hall that he's brought livestock into the neighbourhood. When he turns the corner onto 7th Avenue, he's distracted from thoughts of Mrs. Krumpskey by what he sees stacked on the curb. Chas and Jim must have begun their clean-up. He sets the crate down to look at the mound of garbage. None of it is the old newspapers and magazines, instead there's chipped dishes, a scratched bedside table, and a broken lamp — as if random items have been pulled from the suite in haste. Maybe, he decides, they're planning to redecorate and have begun by cleaning out old housewares.

He looks at the chickens. He can tell by the way they cower in one corner that the walk home was stressful. He should get started building a coop, it's nearing 3:00 in the afternoon and in two hours it will be dark. He picks up the chickens and heads down the side alley past the sodden mass of newspapers and magazines. When he gets to the suite, he's startled to see the door is wide open.

He sticks his head into the dark room and calls out, Hello.

No one answers.

He flips the light switch. It doesn't work, but he can see there are more magazines in the middle of the living room and an old coffee table in the corner, and that's about it. He sets the crate down in the room and walks to the kitchen. The sink is full of dirty dishes and the fridge has nothing in it but two dried-out lemons, a head of lettuce in the crisper that has turned to soup, and a carton of milk that he refuses to smell after the morning's episode. They'd worked quickly to get out.

The idea of them taking off without warning, not even a note, hurts. Especially Chas. He thought Chas was his friend. He wonders if Jim bullied him into leaving. But no time to get sunk into that now, he has live responsibilities needing his attention.

TEN

Cry Fowl

H E STANDS IN THE BASEMENT suite living room for a moment to strategize. With the black paint and the curtains pulled, he has to blink like he would if he were inside a roosting coop. He hauls the crate into the middle of the room, closes the front door, and lets the hens out. They run for the corner near the baseboard heater. He turns up the thermostat but when he doesn't hear the usual click, he remembers — there's no hydro in the suite. He decides he needs to get the portable fan heater from upstairs and run an extension cord out his window.

Once the fan's set up, purring out heat, he cleans one of the dishes in the sink and fills it with water for the chickens, then goes to the backyard to search for insects. After ten minutes, he's found only a couple of dead millipedes and one half-dead spider. He knows he has to organize something better, and since he can't get to the nearest Co-op without his car, he walks up to the Chinese grocery store on Broadway where the grocer fancies himself a bit of a medicinal herbalist.

Henry looks over the bins of food out front of the store. Most of it is conventional, apples, peppers, and melons, but there are some dried fish in a sack that he can wash the salt off and mash together with soybeans, bran, and sunflower oil. He scoops several hundred tiny dead fish into a brown paper bag then walks to the back of the store to survey the few jars of herbal medicines the grocer keeps behind the counter. He's looking for some sort of insect, but he can only see dried mushrooms, dried sea horses, and something that looks like tiny elk horns with tufts of monkey fur on them. He asks the grocer if he has any crickets or grasshoppers.

Maybe grasshopper next week. Only ant, the grocer says.

Henry orders a half-pound of ants and is shocked to see the scale price go over thirty dollars.

How much for a half-pound of sea horses? he asks.

Twenty-nine, the grocer says.

It makes no sense that ants are more expensive than sea horses, but he's in no position to dicker. He needs insects, not sea horses. He is almost out of the store when the grocer asks, You have bad blood? Maybe I have better product.

Henry shakes his head no. I need these ants for my chickens, he says.

You chicken? the grocer asks.

No, I'm not chicken, I have chickens.

The grocer looks confused, but Henry doesn't feel like explaining that his car is abandoned at the side of the road, so he can't drive to the Co-op to buy feed for the illegal chickens in his basement, nor does he feel like explaining that he's lost his job because of the chickens, and that there's a warrant out for his arrest in Idaho for a toppled transmission tower, so because of all of that, he can't afford to pay for a cab to the feed store, and he has to buy expensive black ants.

Thanks for the ants, he says as he walks out the door. He blinks in the milky winter light.

It's dark when Henry carries the bowl of mash down his front steps and follows the flashlight beam along the sidewalk toward the suite. He pushes open the door. The living room is already starting to get smelly and a trail of feathers leads from the door to the abandoned coffee table where the chickens have made their roost. They've pulled apart some of the magazines and mixed the paper with the dried grass he had brought in from the lawn. He turns off the flashlight. A few small moulted feathers have stuck to the black walls and ceiling. He's dizzy a moment, like he's space walking in a night sky.

He turns the flashlight back on and weaves toward the row of chickens. The small brown hen has her head tucked into her neck. She opens a bleary eye as he nears and pops her head up. He laughs at her featherless neck. You look so ugly, he says. The hen closes her eyes. He can't help laughing again. This time all the hens pop their heads up. Twelve blinking eyes atop featherless necks stare.

All of you look ugly, he laughs, but the hens look sorrowful. To make amends he begins to give them names. The small brown hen he names Chocolate Kiss. Down the line, Sunshine, Beauty, Lacy, and the mostly white one, Angel. Before he can name the final hen, she hops off the table and walks up to his shoe. She has a large red wattle and comb, and the same wrinkly red skin around her shining eyes. Her feathers are black and white, and a few new pinfeathers are beginning to poke out of her neck. He gives this one the name Pepper. He picks Pepper up and feels her sturdy rib cage. There is absolutely nothing wrong with this chicken. He sets her down and she gives her head a toss. She's winking at him. She's happy. He leaves the mash on the floor and the chickens rush toward it. They like his recipe.

After his own dinner, he checks on the chickens again. When he opens the door a puff of warmish air hits his face, but it isn't quite warm enough, so he turns the fan heater up. He sits in the corner of the dark room by the line of sleeping hens. In time his eyes adjust, and he begins to see more feathers stuck to the walls and ceiling. He can see constellations. It's sort of creepy, but nice at the same time.

Later, while he sits in front of the TV watching a replay of an old Anne Murray special, the freshness of her face reminding him of the widow and the gentle hairs on her yellow scarf, he is aware that his mind is in a new place, it's in what he would call an unfocused attention mode. He decides to let it drift. It's liberating to do this. He wonders if it's because for the first time in his life he's alone in the house, just him and the chickens, no scary sad mother, no brooding Jim, no confusing Chas.

His mental wandering keeps hitting on angora, and eventually he wants to feel some for himself so he decides to see if there is any among Alice's knitting supplies. Despite his new freedom he does try to confine his thoughts to the widow and angora. He doesn't want his mind to wander to the subject of his mother. But as soon as he pulls open the cupboard door, out spill her Day of the Dead figures. Mariachis in sombreros. A dead dog. A dead man holding a dead woman's hand, both of them wearing scarves. Before his thoughts go too deep into why she would knit dead things, he reminds himself that she isn't the only one to knit skeletons. There's a fish skeleton and a skull at the Shop-Mart in Idaho. Charity knits those things, and Charity seems pretty cool. Maybe Alice wasn't as crazy as he thought. Besides, the dead don't look so menacing anymore. He sets the mariachis on top of the cupboard, arranging them so the one with the trumpet is the leader. Then he looks for the bags of wool, but finds no angora, only mohair. He uses it to cast a few stitches onto a pair of No. 9 needles. At first, he's not sure what he's making, he's just knitting, but then it comes to him — why not tiny scarves for the chickens? While Anne and Glen Campbell sing "Bring Back the Love", he knits a black and white striped scarf for Pepper. Then while Anne sings "Snowbird", he finishes a white mohair scarf for Angel.

When all the scarves are finished it's late. He switches off the TV and slips out the front door down into the constellation room to give the hens their scarves. He steps in the pan of water trying to make his way in the dark.

He spots Angel first, her white feathers glowing ever so slightly. He ties the white mohair scarf loosely around her featherless neck, and she sinks her head into it. He saves Pepper for last as he isn't sure she needs a scarf. But she makes such a happy chirp when he brings her scarf near, he ties it around her neck anyway.

Four days later, he has used up all the ants and is nearly out of soybeans and fish, but he believes the hens have grown enough stubble to suggest feathers and that allows him to take their scarves off — all, that is, except for Chocolate Kiss. Her neck is still naked, and the others have been pecking at the bare skin on her rump. He needs to separate her, to give her a chance to heal. He puts her into the transport crate and pulls the crate close to the fan heater.

As he stands looking at her, he realizes that for four days now, up until that very moment, he's not allowed himself to worry. He hasn't picked up the phone when it rings, hasn't answered the doorbell when it chimes, nor opened the mail stuffed through the mail slot; he has not even bothered to call Chief to confirm he's been fired, or to tell him he's quit. Barely even thought about his mother, except a little on the night when he knit the scarves, and most of all, he's not thought about his limp and numb penis, or his tendency to obsess about it. Instead, he's cradled the hens whenever he felt like it, and he's thought about the widow, and a little now and again about Charity, her invitation to come back to Idaho.

He knows he will have to return the chickens soon and goes upstairs to make up their mash. When he brings it down, he tells the hens, Do not brood my lovelies — here's your lunch.

The five free hens in the room move toward the food. Pepper takes the lead, her head and neck outstretching the others by half a hen's length. But when he opens the crate for Chocolate Kiss, he finds her in a strange huddle. One yellow chicken foot is splayed unnaturally behind her. He looks farther into the crate and sees that her head and scarf are entangled in the fan of the heater. He screams. Pepper hops away from the mash and into the crate. She starts to peck at the yellow foot. Henry has to move quickly to prevent Pepper from pecking at any of the open sores on Chocolate Kiss' body.

You're an idiot, Henry, he yells as he takes the limp brown body out of the crate. The scarf burns and unravels as he pulls it away from the heater.

Despite it being a cool November day, sweat pours down Henry's back as he walks up the Fourth Avenue hill carrying the crate and five hens. He opens the Subaru's yellow hatch and sets the crate inside. Not until he's behind the steering wheel does he realize there are several tickets on the windshield. He pulls away from the curb anyway, the car veers and makes the grating noise, and he doesn't care. By the time he's on the highway all but one of the tickets has flown from the windshield and he is talking to himself. He's trying to work out how, without a job and with a suite that smells like chicken manure, he's going to pay the debt he owes for the KLUK transmission tower.

You are a very stupid man, Henry, not to have seen where this behaviour was leading. You *must* make amends.

He's talking to himself like his mother did; and he can't seem to stop her words from flooding his mind. His hand instinctively goes to the radio to find something light to drown out the talk, but when he turns it on there is nothing but static. Then he remembers the fragile electrical, snaps the radio off and slaps himself in the forehead.

He starts to sing, trying to calm himself. The chickens appear to be listening and begin to make happy hen sounds. He sings "Snowbird" and is doing pretty well with it until he comes to the part about the broken heart. Then it's all he can do to stop from veering the car off the road and flying it across the field and up into the sky.

He is very soon weeping so hard he's afraid he'll crash the car and kill the chickens. They've gone quiet again and he hears himself apologizing to them.

Sorry, my little hens — don't brood. Brooding only brings grief and anger.

The last of the parking tickets flies from the window as he's driving down the concession toward Lightstone's farm. Tears stream down his face, he doesn't have any friends and he killed Chocolate Kiss whose poor body is still lying in the basement on top of a pile of discarded *Bear Growls*.

He pulls into the widow's yard and sits behind the steering wheel, completely exhausted. He doesn't trust that he won't cry again, so to distract himself he goes to the back of the car, takes Pepper out of the crate, brings her into the front seat and settles her on his lap. He waits for a line of peace, and although that doesn't come, the heat of her body and her steady breathing does begin to calm him. He's nearly ready to open his eyes when a tapping at his car window rouses him.

The widow Wendy is smiling at him.

Henry winds the window down and holds the hen out.

How do you like Pepper's new look? he asks.

The widow continues to smile.

He wonders if she's still clouded with grief, perhaps on automatic-pilot-smile.

I gave your hens names, he says. This is Pepper.

Pepper looks really healthy. Thank you.

Check out the others, he says.

He's choked knowing she'll see one hen is missing, but decides to address it straight up.

Your little brown hen had a mishap. She didn't make it, but all the rest have new hairdos.

He waits while the widow walks down the side of the car and peers through the back window.

They look lovely, she says. What have you been feeding them?

Secret ingredients from a Chinese herbalist.

Really?

He steps from the car with Pepper in his arms, but his legs feel wobbly. He's not sure whether it's because of the frightening drive, or because he's nervous being around the widow. He can feel his ears turning red and his face is hot, but his palms are not sweaty, and he is in no way close to making his chortling embarrassed hyena laugh.

Come and see the other chickens in the barn, Wendy says. They look better too, and the barn is cleaned up.

He and the widow step inside the barn. He's surprised to see the entire flock still there. He'd been so certain Elaine would issue a kill order.

What happened? he asks.

That lady last week. She seemed to pay attention to what you said. She ran tests and you were right, they were only malnourished. I bought better meal. She points to a sack propped up beside the feeder.

Well I'm glad for that, he says. Glad I didn't lose my job for nothing.

Really? You lost your job? They need more guys like you.

Not sure they'd ever admit that.

Well I could use a good breeder. Any interest? Can't pay much, but . . .

Oh thank you, ma'am, for the offer. It's not the money, it's just . . . I don't consider myself a breeder.

The widow is still smiling away, and the angora hairs on her scarf quiver in the wave of heat coming from the barn.

Henry sets Pepper down on the floor of the barn. She runs toward her old roost making quite a show of tail feathers.

Somebody's happy to be home, he says.

ELEVEN

Bear Growls

THERE'S A SPRING IN HENRY'S step as he walks toward his front porch. The Subaru was shaky but at least it made it back to Vancouver from Langley. And it was nice to visit Wendy. She seemed genuinely pleased to see him again.

He can see a note tacked to the front door. Instinctively, he looks over his shoulder across to Mrs. Krumpskey's house. When the curtains in her living room quiver in that Mrs. Krumpskey way, he knows it's not going to be good. He takes the note down. It's a triplicate copy of an Animal Control notice from the City of Vancouver issued by the Coordinated Bylaw Enforcement Inspector. It's signed by *illegible scrawl* and beside the scrawl there is a number he can call. He spins on his heel fast enough to catch Mrs. Krumpskey's moon face at her window and, in a gesture of self-preservation, he waves. Her curtain flutters closed. Life is a series of reversals, he thinks.

He pushes through his front door and steps on the small avalanche of mail that has accumulated over the last week. A Visa envelope sits on top. He scoops everything up and adds it to the pile of manila envelopes in the kitchen, where he spends an inordinate amount of time examining a white rock from his mother's cactus plant, rolling the rock back and forth on the table and holding it up to the window. It glows almost clear around the edges — like Alice used to when she was sitting at her vanity — and like her, the middle is dark and dense. He sets the rock down, gives it a final roll and opens the Visa bill. It's the first one he's received, so he thinks perhaps he's reading it incorrectly. But after checking several times there's no doubt the total amount he owes is $693.00. He hears Charity at the Shop-Mart telling him Canadian quarters are wooden nickels, but this seems a severe exchange rate for the money even if it's only good for firewood. Then he sees it. The mechanic has put through the extra charge for staying late at $500, not $50, and once the conversion on the dollar is factored in the total is nearly $700. There's a phone number he can call if he has questions or concerns, both of which he has, but he's not sure how Visa can help.

His throat is parched and he needs to get himself a drink of water before he can tackle another envelope. At the sink, cold water running over his hand, he thinks there must have been some sort of mistake. The mechanic was like a friend, he wouldn't intentionally overcharge him. When he sits back down, he looks at the bill again. There's no way from the information on it to find the mechanic, no phone number, no address, not even a real name for the business. The bill just says *Autobody 510013493, Idaho.*

He decides to move on and picks up the next letter. This one can't be good either; it's from the North Idaho Court Registry. He twirls his glass of water a few times before opening. Inside is another triplicate document titled Court Appearance and Bail Bond. He's getting good at reading these things now. This time he zeros right in on the amount. One transmission tower: $8,500 USD — with exchange this means he owes KLUK radio station over $10,000 for the property damage. How can it cost so much to fix a transmission tower? Surely there's been a mistake here too. He keeps reading and sees that unless payment is received by December 31, 1990, he's to appear in court on January 4, 1991, at which time he's to be prepared to surrender himself into custody. Again, there's a phone number he can call if he has questions.

He has questions all right, but instead he picks up the phone and dials Wendy.

About that offer. Like I said, I'm no breeder, but I do know chickens some.

That's okay, I can't pay much so you can learn on the job.

I can start Monday morning.

Good. See you then.

He puts the phone back in its cradle and is about to stand up — the pile of mail too distressing — when he sees a postcard poking from the stack. He pulls it out. On the front is a knitted object that reminds him of the codpiece he learned about when studying Shakespeare in English class. He flips the card over. It's an invitation to come to a Holiday Knit Show at Charity's Mobile Gallery *where hundreds of knit objects, including the ever-popular knit muffwarmer, will be on sale: this year in new leopard and zebra designs.* Under the printed portion of the invitation Charity has handwritten: *Henry — Come on down and see us before Christmas, or if not come on . . .* the rest is a smudge of ink. This time there is no phone number. He turns the card over and he can see now that the object on the front is knit in a leopard motif that looks more like a bikini bottom than a codpiece. He doesn't want to sit and think right then about Charity in her tight southern belle bodice wearing a leopard muffwarmer. He's in a no-touching-self phase. Besides, he has a dead chicken in the basement.

He finds a snow shovel and a small trowel in the garden shed, uses the trowel to make a hole in the nearly frozen ground under the back porch, then scrapes out a bigger space using the shovel. When he lays Chocolate Kiss in the shallow cavity she is nearly the same colour as the earth. He covers her body with the loose dirt and puts one of the patio stones Chas left behind over the grave. He doesn't want neighbourhood dogs to dig her up. He hangs his head for a few moments. It hardly feels adequate but it's better than putting her out with the trash.

Over the weekend he has a good look at the *Rand McNally Atlas.* He figures a route to the Lightstone farm that won't take him onto Highway 1, even though it will be an hour out of his way, through Port Coquitlam and over the Fraser River on the Albion ferry. But until he can afford to have the Subaru fixed, he just can't see himself on any road that will force him to go over forty kilometres an hour.

The first morning, Henry arrives twenty-five minutes late even though he thought he'd left in plenty of time to make a stop for coffee at the deli in Langley that boasts the intriguing combination of Hawaiian Health Food & Ice Cream. The Subaru practically collapses in Wendy's drive and blue smoke billows out the tailpipe when he turns off the ignition. Wendy comes out in the wind and rain to meet him. She doesn't seem to mind he's late. She smiles the widest smile he's seen yet and ushers him toward the farmhouse, an old but substantial storey-and-a-half white stucco building with dark wood trim. The door they're headed for is partially obscured by spindly cedar shrubs that look like they've been rubbed down by deer. Wendy appears to be sympathizing when he explains he had a four-sailing wait at the ferry.

Oh that ferry, so unpredictable. Where were you coming from?

Kitsilano.

Kitsilano, in Vancouver?

Yes.

He's not surprised she's confused by his answer; his route by ferry is very odd. But he doesn't want to get into the saga of the veering, shaking, belching car, so he lets it hang.

Come on in, she says, pushing open the kitchen door.

He feels like he's walked onto the set for *Happy Days*, as if Richie and the Cunninghams are going to arrive any minute to tape a show. The table is a linen-grey Formica with four raspberry-coloured, vinyl-and-aluminum chairs. The floor is black-and-white-checkered tile and, even while he is thinking of the Fonz, a good-looking black-haired teenage boy slides into the room.

Who's he? The boy points at Henry.

That's not polite, Wendy says. Introduce yourself.

The boy ignores her and walks out of the kitchen.

That was Joey, she says. He's kinda moody sometimes.

Your son?

Yeah. And he's late for school as usual.

What grade?

Twelve.

The boy's voice calls from somewhere above Henry's head.

Mom, where are my gym shorts?

Henry cranes his neck to see a loft above with the boy hanging his head over the railing.

Joey's eyes flicker between focusing on Henry with some interest and a thousand-yard-teenage-gaze that could signal disrespect. It's difficult to tell.

They're down here in my bedroom, Wendy says.

What are they doing there? Joey asks.

I was mending them. I'll bring them up to you.

While Wendy is upstairs, Henry does the math — assuming Joey is seventeen and the widow just twenty when he was born, that means she's only thirty-seven, seven years older than he is, less than a decade. Not too much of a stretch. Or is it? What if it's just that she's a young fifty-year-old? Is that too old? More importantly, is he getting ahead of himself?

When Wendy comes back with papers and pen in hand, he tries to act nonchalant, like nothing is on his mind; his hands in his lap are ready to start the day's work.

How old are you? she asks.

Why?

I need to know for these workers' comp forms.

Okay, I'm thirty, almost thirty-one.

Really?

He wonders whether she thinks he looks older or younger, or might it mean she considers him old enough to be in her league? He wants to ask her how old she is and his mouth opens as he begins to form the question, the word *How* half-way out, when he changes his mind.

Hooowwoo's . . . that coffee on the stove?

Fresh. Want some?

Sure.

She puts a cup filled with lukewarm brown liquid down in front of him. While he sips, she talks about the farm. Tells him Dennis inherited it from his father, and even though he loved the land, he'd had to sell a part of it to a development company.

We're one of the smallest commercial outlets in the valley, less than 500 birds, she says. But we've started to specialize in free-range eggs and roasters. So it can be chaotic because the chickens are cage free.

Organic is all the rage, Henry says.

Yeah. It's kind of silly. It's all just the same crazy bird. But your ladies are happier than most.

Guess so. Should we go out to the barn?

When they open the barn door, Wendy shoos the chickens into the yard with a wild swinging of her arms and a funny *foo foo* sound. Chickens rush for the door, but few go outside.

They hate the rain, Wendy says. Push them with your foot, they need to get out and scratch.

Henry looks over the crowd at his feet. After a couple of nudges, the lead chickens get the idea that outside is better than being booted and a blur begins to move through.

Shut the door on them so we can hose out the barn, Wendy says. There's a pair of rubbers over by the post.

Foo foo, Henry says to the last of the chickens.

When they're finished, he helps her coil the thick length of black rubber hose back up — Wendy twists while he walks — and he notices she bumps into him every time he moves past her. If he weren't so unsure about these things he would say she was flirting. To test whatever weak currents there may be, he takes a step away, and within two coils she's back rhythmically bumping her backside into his upper thigh. He's so distracted, he misses the last turn and the end of the hose pushes up the inside of her leg.

Watch where you put that, she says, staring straight ahead as if it were an accident.

I'm watching, Henry says.

She's smiling again and he wonders whether this might be some kind of tic or else encouragement.

An echo drifts down from the rafters, *Don't flatter yourself,* and he lowers his head. Mother again, he thinks. But she's probably right, he is getting ahead of himself. Best to forget it. Focus on the mob of chickens stampeding back through the open barn door.

Well it's lunchtime, Wendy says. Did you bring anything?

A sandwich, he says, but I was thinking I might go into town to try the Hawaiian Health Food deli. Then, in a moment of insolence toward his mother, he adds, Want to come?

Sure.

On the way into town Wendy grips at the armrest of the Subaru.

Why are you driving a car in such a state? she asks.

Long story, he says. Can't afford to fix it right now.

Inside the deli they look over the selection. The refrigerated case holds a small display of grain and rice products all with the same no-appeal porridge look — no doubt the health food component — and beside that there's a larger more colourful display of sweets. Wendy orders a macadamia nut muffin and Kona coffee, which she takes to the back booth. Henry, thinking about his thickening waistline, settles on a coffee and a bowl of the yellowish porridge called poi.

Do you want that with salmon or pineapple? the deli man asks.

Which is better?

Depends on whether you're eating it for lunch or dessert.

Lunch.

Okay, salmon. But it's an acquired taste.

Henry carries his tray to the back booth wondering what kind of taste he needs to acquire for his lunch. He starts to spoon poi into his mouth — it's fermented and musty like it's been stored in a cave. He screws his face up and the deli man catches him.

Told you, he laughs. Want to try something else?

Henry walks back toward the counter. He looks over the desserts and this time settles on a chocolate macadamia cake.

You'll like this better, the man says.

Thanks. Uh . . . what's your name? Henry asks.

Norman from the Big Island, the man says, extending a large brown hand over the counter.

Nice to meet you, Henry says. Never been to Hawaii.

Well you've got a little taste of Kona right there in that coffee and cake, Norman says. He holds his thumb and baby finger up and rotates his hand. Shaka, he says.

When Henry sits back down and takes a sip of the coffee, he feels strong. Revived. Like he's in a coffee commercial. Then, timed as flawlessly as the best commercial in the world, the bell on the handle tinkles, the deli door pushes open, and in walks Elaine. Wendy's back is to the door so only he can see. Elaine is either oblivious as to whom she is walking toward, or she's looking for trouble.

Hello Henry, she says.

Likewise. He puts his head down hoping she'll walk away.

Out here returning Wendy's chickens? she asks.

The chickens came back last week, Wendy says. Henry works for me now.

Really? Well he knows chickens, I guess.

Elaine walks away and sits at the booth by the deli counter. The door jangles again and a bulky, angry-looking man ambles through. He picks up two mugs of coffee from Norman and carries them to the booth where Elaine sits.

Hey Bob, Wendy calls over to him. Who'll be coming by to pick up the eggs tomorrow?

Bob looks up, focuses on Wendy, on Henry, shifts his bulk, puts his head down as if he's not going to answer, then mumbles, Someone'll be out before noon.

Things slowly settle in Henry's mind. This is Bob, Elaine's boyfriend, and he seems to work for some kind of chicken operation that does business with Wendy. But it isn't until he and Wendy are back in the Subaru shaking and veering their way toward the farm that he asks, How do you know Bob?

He's the son of the owner of Swift Farms, she answers. They're my biggest customer. Can't pull off the organic thing themselves cause their hens are in battery cages, so they market my product as their high-end.

This answer doesn't feel good. Maybe he should have challenged Elaine's assertion that the Swift Farms' file had been transferred to her, but it's too late now, not his problem. He doesn't work for Agriculture anymore.

Back at the farm the weather has taken a turn for the worse. Sheets of rain move across the yard, and the wind is lifting up the corner of the tin roof on a small shed beside the barn.

What's in that shed? he asks?

Roosters, Wendy says. Five of them. Four more than I need, but they're rescue roosters from Swift Farms. They don't want the hassle of keeping them cause they fight.

Poor cocks all cooped up, he says.

Really? I don't know about that. Wendy huffs. One day you could build them a run, but in the meantime you better get their roof nailed down before they're drowning cocks.

The wind is fierce and pushes the too-tall ladder over a couple of times before he figures out the clawed feet need to be shimmed to sit straight. He uses a couple of pieces of kindling from beside the house, and when he finally has the ladder secure and is six steps up, balanced at the edge of the tin roof, he takes a swing and drops the hammer. Six steps down and six steps back up, he takes a dozen or so more swings until two nails are secure in the corner of the roof. He's trying to crane his neck to survey the handiwork when the wind repositions the ladder and tosses him onto his right leg; his ankle twists and he's on his ass in the mud. The limp back to Wendy's door is not too painful, but he knows the ankle is going to get worse.

The roof's nailed down, he says, but I fell off a forty-foot ladder. Got any ice?

Wendy laughs. This is good. She seems to understand his humour. And in that instant it starts to pour rain harder than he has ever seen before.

It had not been his plan to use his mishap as an excuse to stay the night but it's just as well. By dark the weather has worked into a gale force storm.

Next morning the worker from Swift Farms comes earlier than expected. He's pissed off the order isn't ready, and he has no trouble expressing his dissatisfaction. Seemingly he has learned everything he knows about demeanor from boss man's son, Bob. He sits in his truck while Henry and Wendy scramble to collect the eggs.

Henry asks, Why do you let Swift Farms push you around?

I need the money, plain and simple, she answers.

He runs his hand along the back of the roosting bar. When he's almost finished the last row, his hand hits a warm body. Once his eyes adjust to the gloom of the laying trough, he can see it's a hen that looks like Pepper.

What are you doing down there, Pepper?

Is there a hen brooding? Wendy asks.

Looks like there might be.

Gotta snap her out of it or she won't lay for weeks. Need to get my egg count up to keep Swift happy. Bring that hen here.

Henry holds Pepper out and asks, Why?

She's going into the panic room.

Wendy pushes open the door off the side of the barn. The room has been mudded adobe style, but the walls,

ceiling, and floor are painted a cerebral blue. Warm air
wafts out. Inside there's an oak table with a wooden box
on it. She puts Pepper into the box.

Henry sits on a mud slab the size of a bed that juts out
from the wall.

A man could sleep in here, he says. It's beautiful.

Dennis did sleep in here sometimes, she murmurs.

Oh.

Then wanting to change the subject, he asks, Why is
Pepper in a box?

New accommodation, away from the eggs and her
brooding. She'll stay here 'til she's over her nonsense.

That night Henry sleeps in the mud room with Pepper.
It smells of chicken, but not too bad, or maybe he's just
gotten used to it, and he tries not to think why Dennis
might have slept here. But his ankle still hurts, and
anything would be better than that first night sleeping
on the living room floor, with Joey making such a big
deal of stepping over him whenever he needed to go to
the bathroom — uttering the same *Jessuschris* sound each
time no matter where on the floor Henry moved to — and
come to think of it, going to the bathroom way more times
than any normal teenager needs to in one night.

The second night in the mud room, he takes Pepper out
of the box and sits with her on his lap. A calm comes over
him. After a time he realizes having a chicken in his lap
keeps his apparatus warm. He might even start to think
about taking it out, and touching it, without freaking that
it will go numb or dissolve, though bits of doubt make

him wonder whether it's creepy to be thinking this with Pepper so close; it's not like he wants to do anything with the chicken, it's just that she's warm and it's better than thinking about, say, his shrivelled five-year-old self in the bathtub, his mother kissing his soapy face. After a time he exhausts himself thinking and just settles into the warmth. He is half-asleep when he feels himself lapse below the busybody monitoring of himself for weirdness and into a zone of comfort without admonishments about inadequacies.

By the third night he's made the room his own sort of nest, bringing in different chickens for a visit, comforted by their warmth and chatter, their feathers beginning to form constellations on the heavenly blue walls. But after the fourth night, Friday night, he thinks he needs to get back to his own place. Who knows what new mess might greet him there, and besides he can't ask Wendy to wash his only set of clothes again.

On the Saturday morning, the Subaru starts easily and no smoke comes out the rear, so he decides he can risk stopping for some pie and a morning visit with Norman before heading to the ferry. He's disappointed to see Elaine and Bob sitting in the same booth as before, just down from the deli case.

What brings you to Langley on the weekend? she asks.

Morning, Elaine.

He doesn't owe her any kind of explanation, and four nights in the mudded constellation room have emboldened him.

I'll take a slice of banana pie and coffee to go, he says to Norman.

Shaka, Norman says.

Henry extends his own babyfinger and thumb and rotates his hand like Norman before picking up his pie. He can hear Elaine snicker and Bob mutter, What a moron. He ignores them.

Less than a mile down the road the Subaru jerks so badly the pie slides off the dash and the takeout cup tips over. Rivulets of coffee mix with pie and run down the plastic floormat, disappearing under the seat. The car barely makes it back to Kitsilano.

Henry is around back checking that nothing has dug up Chocolate Kiss, when he hears something behind him. A momentary flashback to sneaking kids with snakes in hand, prepares him for almost anything.

Henry, I finally found you, Chas says.

Hey! What brings you here? His new boldness makes him ask, Why'd you take off?

It was Jim's idea. He was so mad at you that morning.

Do you always do what Jim says?

We broke up actually.

Um-huh.

I like the new beard, Henry. Looks good.

Henry reaches up to touch his face. He hasn't had a good chance to look at himself lately, with the boy Joey always at the bathroom door nagging to get in. But he knows that a few days without a razor has let the beard come in thicker.

We left the place in sort of a mess, Chas says. I've been wanting to help clean up, but you're never here, never answer the phone.

I've been busy.

Henry puts the key into the keyhole and the suite door swings open.

Wow, we didn't leave the place in this big a mess, Chas says.

No, Henry answers, coughing.

The pile of magazines and chicken scratch sits right where he left it. The smell is worse than in the barn. Together they put the suite back into some semblance of order, with Chas flinching more than actually working the stainless lifter through the chicken poop. And even though they're dealing with yucky stuff, there is something else in the air that Henry can't put his finger on. Then it happens.

He is carrying a pile of the magazines toward the door when an issue of *Bear Growls* falls between the two of them.

You look like him, Chas says.

Henry stares at the cover and says nothing.

Come on, Chas says.

Then somehow Chas is on his knees, head hanging, arms at his side. Henry can only think his penis will surely dissolve if it goes anywhere near Chas' face. And yet this man, this other person who is not crazy, this other person who has nothing to gain from befriending him, seems to have a thing for him. This much at least he has to respect.

I don't know what to say, Chas. I don't think this is something I am interested in.

I know, Chas says. But you should know that's why we took off so fast. Jim thought something was up.

It wasn't, Henry says.

He sits on the coffee table and Chas stays on his knees in the middle of the floor. The two of them wait until the mood in the room feels safe enough for someone to speak again. Finally, Chas gets up. Let's get these magazines out of here.

As they carry bundles to the curb, Chas says, I've been crashing on a buddy's couch since we broke up. But I have a new chair. I can make rent going forward. And I'll do what I can to make up what I owe you.

The smell of ammonia is going to be in the suite for a time, Henry says. You could camp out in my mother's room until it lifts.

The words are out of his mouth before he thinks through the implications. He can't grab them back.

TWELVE

Tisket a Tasket

ON THE MONDAY MORNING WHEN it's time to go back to Wendy's, Henry has trouble starting the Subaru. Chas, who has come out to see if there is anything he can do to help, jumps away from the car when throat-closing blue smoke fires out the tailpipe.

Oh God, what kind of fuel you got this baby on?

It's not the gas. It's a long story.

Lucky for you, I'm not working today. I'll drive you. I wanna catch a look at this chick you're into anyway.

Because the Mustang is so fast and because they can take Highway 1, Henry and Chas arrive back in chickenland, downtown Langley, a good half-hour before Henry needs to start work.

Pull over here, he says. Good food, except don't order the poi.

Norman greets them with a friendly wave and announces, Specials today are mango sticky rice and coconut-banana pie.

What part of that is health food? Chas asks.

All of it! Norman grins. My specialty is smiling faces. Chas rewards him with a smile, and Norman laughs again. See, I told ya, all of me is good for the smile.

Henry's relieved to see Elaine is not in the deli, though he's pretty sure it's Bob sitting in a Swift Farm truck parked outside the door.

It's health food, Chas says as he drops two slices of coconut-banana pie on the table.

They eat the pie in silence, then Henry starts to talk about his idea to market free-range eggs and chickens for Wendy in Kitsilano. Cut the middleman out, he says. He's a real jerk named Bob. His dad is the owner of Swift Farms. Brutal what they do to their chickens. It's a battery-cage operation.

If you say so, Chas says.

As they exit the deli, Henry jabs his thumb in the direction of the Swift Farm truck. That's Bob, the bigwig's son.

Creep, Chas says. You see the colour of his eyes? Never trust a guy whose eyes are gunpowder grey.

They drive out to the farm and, even though Henry is early, Wendy is in a panic again about getting eggs collected. She comes running out of the house before Chas has time to turn the car off.

Thank God you're here. The Swift pickup is moved back an hour, they say they never adjusted for daylight savings. I don't know, does this make sense? The chickens don't adjust. Oh hello, she says to Chas.

This is Chas, my roommate, Henry says.

Follow me, both of you, she says. We can use an extra hand scooping.

As they walk toward the barn Chas whispers, I don't think you should have said we're roommates.

What do you mean?

Chas pirouettes. My friend, you are naïve. She knows a good gay couple when she sees one.

Do you think?

I know.

Hurry up you guys, Wendy says. Chas, you work this row and Henry the other side. I'll get the lamps going. She hands them each a big wicker basket and runs to the ultraviolet table.

Chas sings, Tisket a tasket, a green and yellow basket.

Stop it, Chas. Henry is suddenly nervous. As if he's responsible for the social networking of this clutch of unlikely people working to scoop eggs. He wants to make light of everything, like Chas does, have fun with it, but it seems so serious and beyond him.

He is thinking about the rest of the words to the basket rhyme *I sent a letter to my love* when his hand hits a chicken that refuses to move off her egg. Scram, he says. The hen pecks at him. He tries to pick her up but she steps sideways and pecks again. He's surprised when she moves that there's no egg under her, and he notices she's holding her body in an awkward shuddering position. He checks her eyes. She looks healthy. But she shudders again, this time as if she's trying to give birth to the egg, but can't.

Wendy, come check this hen out, he calls. I think she's egg-bound.

She sticks her head in under the roosting bar. Yeah, she's got an egg stuck.

Now what? he asks.

You're the doctor, she chides. She hands him a container of Preparation H cream.

Doctor Love, Chas chimes from behind. This is getting interesting! His eyes light up.

Lubricate up to your knuckles, gently reach in and pull the egg out, Wendy says. She talks as if this is all very matter of fact.

It's not until Henry is in up close enough to the chicken's rump to sniff her eggy odour that he realizes he is about to put his fingers into a vagina. The Preparation H burns a little and for a second he loses all sensation in his index and middle finger. But what else can he do but pull his fingers together and plunge them in? He's ready to feel sick, but instead it's soothing and moist inside the chicken. Like going into a warm cave. He can feel the egg and his fingers just naturally form around it. His body knows what to do even if his mind is misfiring. The rhythmic contractions of the chicken as she helps to expel the egg tap into some primordial part of his brain. It's okay.

Careful not to break it, Wendy says. You'll have to pick out all the pieces if you do.

No problem, Chas says, he's got it.

The chicken lets out a loud cluck and a triumphant Henry holds up the egg.

He looks carefully at the hen. She's pretty, a docile buff Orpington, with profuse and soft feathers the colour of orange marmalade. She ruffles right down to her leg feathers in appreciation that the ordeal is over then stands on the walkway looking for all the world like a yellow zinnia in full bloom.

Little Flower, Henry says.

A tisket a tasket, Chas sings.

They walk out of the barn toward Joey who's down on his haunches looking under the Mustang. He straightens up.

Nice pony car, he says. Yours, man? He looks at Henry for the first time as if he might be a real person.

No, it's his. This is Chas.

Joey runs his hand along the fender. Real beauty. How much does a car like this cost?

Depends, Chas says. This one's in good shape so almost the same price as new. Maybe ten grand.

Wow. Ever think of selling it?

All the time, Chas says. Just can't bring myself to do it.

Never mind that, Wendy says. What are you doing home, Joey?

The teachers are threatening job action so the grade twelves walked out in sympathy, he says.

Very altruistic of you, Wendy says.

Whatever. Gotta get going over to Lucy's. See ya'all later.

Joey hops on the bicycle he's propped by the back door and takes off.

When Chas departs, Henry and Wendy stand alone in the yard.

Who's Lucy? Henry asks.

One of several girlfriends, Wendy answers, though Lucy seems to be the main squeeze right now — that boy learned a few too many tricks from his father.

Hope you don't mind, I brought a few things. Henry picks up his overnight bag. My car's in no shape. Chas will be back to get me on Friday.

Are you a couple? she asks.

No. No way.

Just wondered.

Later that night in the mud room, the words *just wondered* resonate in Henry's head. He's trying to put himself into the meditative trance that helps with that neural mistake — his brain. Flower is with him this time. She is comfortable, and loose thoughts of rhythmic pulses of warm water float in his mind, all vaguely sexual and he's not pushing any of it out of his head. Thinking of Wendy, he is half-aroused in what he assumes is a normal-male-ascending-into-full-erection state, when he hears an odd scratching on the other side of the wall. He thinks at first it's mice at the feed station, but the sound is too loud. Then he hears a couple of the chickens cluck.

He walks out of the room and into the main barn. Something bigger than a mouse slinks in the corner. He follows the slither and catches sight of the back end of a mink disappearing into the gloom. On the floor behind it lies a chicken's head.

Henry stamps his foot and hopes the yell scares the mink enough to send it flying out whatever hole it slid in through. Then he notices one of the doors to the barn has been left open a crack. He watches the mink slip out before walking to the door to look across the yard. The light is still on in Wendy's bedroom.

He can't help but notice the curtains are not drawn. He's semi-erect and the notion of Wendy on her bed brings him to further attention. He slows his pace, not wanting to appear menacing, and stops when he is close enough to notice the veins in the dried leaves on the tangle of clematis outside her window. Through the veil of leaves he sees she is naked on her bed. He's now fully erect outside the window of a nude woman, perhaps not the best time to ask about a mink. A pickup truck blasts along the road, rips the night open. Then there is only the moonlit field, the veins in the clematis and space enough for Alice's voice to creep in.

You're disgusting, Henry. A Peeping Tom.

Back off, Henry says to the night as he walks across the yard toward the barn. He means it, his mother is in no way right about what's going on.

When he opens the mud-room door he finds an upset Flower. She has dropped a few feathers while he's been gone. He scoops them up and showers them over himself. It feels like progress that he's able to sustain his erection and maintain a strong thought of Wendy, her nipples erect — or were they? What does it matter? He can imagine they were if he wants. He takes off his clothes and lies down on his mud-slab bed, drawing himself up into a handful of feathers.

Thank you, he says when it's all over, his hand languid at his side, a bright-orange feather stuck with semen to the side of his leg.

Early next morning, Henry collects eggs for the Swift pickup, and then, because he has time, he picks out a number of luminous feathers from the nesting box. He runs his hand over the plume on the top of the head of one of the fancy breed chickens. Her head flicks from side to side like a makeup brush. That's when he gets the idea. He takes one of the plume feathers and sticks it to the mud wall using a dab of albumen from a broken egg. At first the individual barbs mat around the edge of the shaft and the feather doesn't look good, but later when he brings in another handful, the egg white is dried and the quill sticks to the wall. The barbs splay yet the down floats free. It's an interesting effect.

By the final night of the workweek, the mink has not returned and he has created his first installation. He dims the light in the mud room and allows his eyes to adjust. Yes, he says as he looks at Orion's Belt in formation. The longer he lies on his bed, the more the room swirls with beauty.

So, did you get laid? Chas asks.

Henry sits uncomfortable in the passenger seat. They're driving back to Kitsilano and Chas is full of chatter. Henry doesn't want trouble, doesn't even want to think about answering. He's tempted instead to tell Chas about the beautiful room he's been building, but decides to wait and show it when it's finished. He simply says, It was a good week.

When they come to Macdonald, Chas keeps driving along Broadway and stops at the Greek grocery and deli down near Alma Street.

Are we having souvlaki for dinner? Henry asks.

Could be, Chas says. Let's go.

In the shop, a large Greek man about thirty-five years old with a bushy black beard nods in greeting from behind the deli counter.

Chas holds his hand out in Henry's direction and says as confidently as he might if he were presenting a prize rooster, Aristedes, meet Henry from Lightstone Poultry. Henry has confirmed he'll be able to supply you organic roasters and free-range eggs beginning this January.

Chas keeps on talking about all kinds of crazy things — how much the price of grape leaves has gone up, whether Aristedes has any fresh souvlaki, whether he's going to buy a ski pass up Grouse Mountain, whether he thinks the Canucks are going to win the Stanley Cup. And after Chas and Aristedes exhaust everything they know about hockey, they drift into stories about wild nights of drinking retsina and eating raw chicken livers with their hands. Henry knows it's intentional, meant to keep him from opening his mouth, exclaiming he can't promise any free range orders, and he is set to interject, when Aristedes addresses him with a highly charged appreciation of life.

I love chicken so much I could fuck it, he says. You bring me good kill, Henry, and I make you the best spanakopita in town.

Aristedes presses on them a dozen dolmathes, a slab of saganaki, and two bottles of retsina from the back, before he walks Chas and Henry to the door.

Good eating and sexing on the weekend, he shouts as they walk down the sidewalk.

What was that about? Henry asks.

I told you you wouldn't be sorry I came back, Chas says. I've already lined up five other outlets in Kitsilano, all of them ready to start receiving free-range products in January. And there's lots more in Vancouver still to tap.

Back home Chas sets about frying up the saganaki, and setting out the dolmathes.

Henry pushes open the door to his mother's room and is upset to see how much it looks as if Alice is still here. The makeup table is set up again with her bottles, jars and brushes — Chas must have kept that box of cosmetics — and other than Chas' silk robe hanging on the back of the door, and his rosewood trouser press in the corner, the room looks like it always has.

He returns to the kitchen where Chas has poured two glasses of retsina, and set the bottle on the counter. Henry sits at his regular spot and Chas takes Alice's seat and holds out his glass in a toast.

Despite his better inclination, Henry toasts Chas and takes a sip of the wine. He screws his face up and coughs it back out. Why do you drink this?

It's cheap and sorts of goes with a debauched evening, Chas says.

We're not going down that road.

Ahhh! Why not?

Henry's mind starts to spin. He had nothing in mind when he said *going down that road*, nothing except the social awkwardness of sitting across the table from a man who is now his tenant, a man who used to be Jim's lover, and is *not* going to be his lover. But still that man is smiling like he thinks he's going to get lucky.

Henry picks up a piece of saganaki from the fry pan. It's a warm gooey cheese that hangs limp and flaccid from the end of his fingers. He moves it quickly toward his mouth, too late for Chas' warning that it will be hot. He burns his lip, but is glad of the distraction.

Ouch, Chas says. Want an ice cube?

No, it's okay.

Henry stuffs a dolmathes into his mouth to keep it occupied.

You're a real stoic aren't you, Henry? Chas says.

I am?

Sure, you had that whack-nut for a mom and you never complained.

She wasn't a whack-nut.

You know she was off.

So what?

Well you were kind of slow to defend yourself against her, and then she went and died, and well you needed somebody to . . . You know, we would have moved out years before . . . Jim wanted to . . .

To what?

Well, it's tough being raised by a crazy. I had one semi-sane parent at least. Don't get me wrong, Alice tried her best. Just the same, I know how easy it is to get hung up on your own thoughts when you've had a weird start.

Yeah, it was weird sometimes.

It occurs to him this is the first time anyone has ever really hinted at what he sometimes suspected, that he needed protecting, needed to have a mirror held up by someone on the outside, someone who was sane. So far the only mirror held up was as foggy and distorted as a funhouse mirror.

Chas stands up to get himself another glass of retsina. He slugs back the white liquid. Rat's piss, he says.

That's when things stir, or perhaps not so much stir as move involuntarily in Henry's underwear, just the smallest bit, certainly not so much a commotion or an arousal, in fact so slight that even while it's happening, he has to wonder, Is it really or is that just a fold in my underpants? And is my subconscious mind on Wendy, or Jamie Lee? Yes, even Jamie Lee, or maybe, no, maybe it is rat's piss that sets me off, even rat's piss would be okay.

All in all no matter how trivial, how insignificant the little jump in his anatomy, he is not listening to Chas anymore.

Don't you agree? Chas says.

No. I mean yes. I mean maybe.

Are you listening?

Trying to, what were you saying?

I was saying don't let your obsessions get the better of you. Obsessions can become a habit.

I'll remember that.

Keep fleet-footed. One step ahead of your thoughts, Chas adds.

Henry wishes he had been listening. This sounds like good advice, but he doesn't want a rewind on any part of what has just happened.

Later that night, after Chas has finished the bottle of retsina, Henry's glass included, and they are in the TV room watching reruns of the *A-Team*, Henry pulls out a bag of wool from his mother's craft cabinet, looking for something to do with his hands, occupy his mind, keep one step ahead of his thoughts.

I just love this, Chas says. He points to the shelf where the dead mariachis are displayed. Can you teach me to knit a dead Mr. T?

Okay. Sit across from me so you can mimic what I do with the needles.

This is the way his mother taught him. He uses the memory of her lessons to keep one step ahead, to remind himself not to think too much about the position the two of them are in, legs splayed, facing each other like lovers, dicks practically touching — *make sure you work through the loop not the bumpy part when you form a stitch.* Only problem is that dicks practically touching is exactly where his thoughts devolve no matter what lesson snippets he conjures to block them. Added to that is his mother's high-pitched scream, now in the room with them — *teach him how to knit and that's all, don't let him touch your anus.*

Chas picks up casting-on quickly and except for a · couple of dropped stitches does well with garter stitch, but he has difficulty with purling.

Pay attention, Chas. You insert the needle over top for the purl.

Henry regrets his word choice. Inserting over top sounds lewd. He does a quick mental pant check and is relieved he is unmoved by the suggestion of insertion, but right away he wonders why he's even thinking that. Internally he repeats the advice *keep one step ahead of your thoughts*, but is struck by its duplicity. The advice itself is a thought. Everything is starting to feel as painful as a knitting needle under his fingernail, and he lets out an audible sigh.

Sshhh, Chas says wagging his finger at the TV. This is the part where T crushes the crystal skull.

Henry uses this interruption as an excuse to shift his position, so his knees are no longer glancing off Chas' like shy lovers. He is almost giddy to find his dong feels as flaccid, and not nearly as hot, as the saganaki he dropped earlier into the fry pan.

He wills himself asleep quickly that night so he doesn't have time to start obsessing about whether he might be gay as well as crazy.

THIRTEEN

Mink Patrol

HENRY SITS IN THE CONSTELLATION Room — that's what he officially calls it now — and thinks about the pile of headless chickens he found stacked behind the nesting box that morning. He thought he'd solved the problem after he plugged the holes in the foundation and began bolting the barn doors at night, but in fact he'd locked the mink in the night before. Beside the stack there was a smaller messier heap of heads that looked like they belonged in a voodoo priest's tool box. What would a head look like here in the Constellation Room? Not good, he decides.

He loves the room. Yet when he looks around it, he can't help but wonder what others might think. It's certainly weird. Maybe obsessively crazy. Wendy has respected his privacy and not asked to see it, not even after he told her he might do a bit of decorating. Nothing permanent, he'd said. But just the same the room is central to him. It's where he lets his thoughts splay like plumes from the quill, where he consoles himself by making radiant feather constellations. In the evening, he sorts through piles of feathers, picking out the pearly ones, the sparkly ones, those that radiate warmth and contrast with the grey and black pin feathers he's arranged into the black holes beside the white dwarfs and the luminous planets of love. All of it transports him away from his puny life. And away from a new misery that has struck him very hard.

It hit so deep and with such precision, he had to sit up in bed the first time it happened to let it drain from his mind.

Had his mother done more than just admonish him to keep his *filthy private parts clean?* Had she molested him?

A moment of rubbing and jerking in a soapy bathtub came so clear to him he could even hear the rhythmic lapping of water on the side of the tub. It all fit with the courting, the sexual dancing in his bedroom, the jealous rages whenever he mentioned a girl. He feels sick every time he recalls it, but also, in some unfathomable twist, he begins to doubt it at the same time. Could it be true or is this just another creepy and weird obsession he's adding to his list? When he thinks about it, like he is now, he wishes desperately he had a father, an uncle, a trusted neighbour, anyone — even Tom from the old days — he could ask. How had she really been when she was around him? Is this why he can't get a proper erection? He tries to push the thought away, but can't. He just sits there feeling sick and sorry for himself. Aware that he is in desperate need of some healing magic, he takes off his clothes, grabs a handful of the feathers heaped beside his bed, lies down and builds a nest around his poor broken apparatus. It helps. He can feel a dry warmth radiate from his balls.

He lies on his back and mentally fills in the points of the star cluster above him to form a shapely maiden in a Southern Belle dress. Charity at the Shop-Mart, he thinks, her big breasts. His equipment stirs, pushes a few of the feathers aside. There's lots of work to do to sort this out, he thinks. Too much to let this continue right now. So he wills himself to switch to more practical problems — like mink in the barn.

Wendy, after he'd showed her the stack of heads, told him there was no easy way to deter a mink short of trapping it. To prove she was serious, she'd handed him a set of legholds.

Really, Wendy? Those things look barbaric.

And ripping the heads off our precious chickens and sucking out their blood is not?

Please, Wendy. I promise I'll check the barn three times a night and set the trap if so much as one more chicken goes missing.

To honour his promise, he gets off the bed and puts on his jacket.

It's cold and clear outside. Ice has formed on the water dispensers and a skiff of snow covers the yard. He walks around the barn and is just about to head back in when he hears the sound of someone crying by the farmhouse. It's Lucy, Joey's girlfriend.

Hi there, he calls out. Are you okay?

Hi, the girl says, wiping a tear from the corner of her mouth.

Henry has met her a couple of times passing through the yard, but this is the first time she hasn't been with

Joey. She is shivering and he doesn't know what to say next. It's none of his business why she's crying, and not being very practised at consoling teenage girls, he asks, Want to help me with my mink patrol? It's warmer inside the barn.

Okay, she says. I could do that while I wait for Joey.

Come on in here, then. You stand by the front door and I'm going to slam the back door really loud to see if it scares anything out of the barn. Let me know if you see something dark and slinky.

Ew, sounds gross.

It's not, it's only a small animal.

Slamming the door is not part of his usual mink routine, so when he does it, several hundred chickens flap awake and fly off their roosting bars with one giant squawk. Only the docile Orpingtons have some semblance of calm. But then Lucy screams and even they hop from their bars and flutter into the middle of the barn.

If he had slowed down enough to think about what he was doing he'd have remembered the sleeping chickens, all of them with highly susceptible ears and easily put off balance by anything vibrating their tiny cochlea. He might calm one chicken by petting it and covering its eyes, or in a pinch by holding it upside down, but what is he to do with hundreds of flapping chickens? All he can think is to make a cooing noise, and he sits in the middle of the barn making a sound as close to a mother hen as he can muster. The racket begins to lessen, but it's taking a while, and he starts to feel like he's going to sprout feathers himself. When he finally opens his eyes he's happy to see most of the hens back on their bars and things pretty much back to normal. But where is Lucy? The barn door is still closed, so she hasn't run outside. He pushes gently on the door to the Constellation Room and finds her sitting on the table, transfixed.

What is this place? she asks.

My meditation room, Henry answers.

It's wonderful. Heavenly, she says. It's the first time since I left home I've felt really happy.

Home? Where do you live?

Here in Langley, but home was Yugoslavia. I miss my baba.

What's a baba?

My grandmother.

Lucy holds out the hot water bottle with the chicken cover on it that he knit over the weekend.

What is this? she asks.

It's a meditation comforter, he says.

The comforter is something he modelled after his new favourite hen, Flower. He'd interwoven it with a set of golden feathers just like hers.

Really? How does it work?

Sit on the side of the bed . . . er, well yes, it is my bed. Sorry, is this weird?

No. Like I said, it's heavenly in here.

Okay, then it's better to rest with your back against the mud wall and put the chicken bottle on your lap. Stare at the constellations until your thoughts drift to somewhere peaceful. I'll go and finish up in the barn while you try it.

A couple of nights later, just as Henry is finishing up his early evening mink patrol, Joey comes to stand at the barn door. He's wearing his Grateful Dead Wonderland Jam-Band T-shirt. Ever since Henry recognized the logo, Joey has decided he is okay. Joey's eager to hear as much about the 60s as Henry can remember. Henry plays it up, never really telling him he was only a kid and not a real hippie in the 60s.

Hey man, I heard your room is pretty cool. Mind if I check it out?

Okay.

Henry pushes the door to the room open. A small golden feather flutters down from the new Ursa Major constellation he's installed. As the feather approaches a candle burning beside the bed, it swirls back up toward the ceiling and catches on the edge of the Virgo constellation where it hangs like a golden nipple, almost at the spot where he imagines the virgin's breast is.

Wow, this place is cosmic, Joey says.

He stands for a few moments looking, then flashes Henry a peace sign. Carry the beauty with you, man, he says as he departs.

Next morning Henry is in the yard remembering what Joey said. He's about to batten down the hatch on the rooster's shed, and he's feeling beautiful thoughts about the day. That is until a hawk circling the barn distracts him. Hawks and minks go after the same prey, he thinks, so he walks toward the barn to check. After he satisfies himself there are no mink in the area, he decides to let the hens out for a dust bath.

What's left of his good cheer turns to dismay as he watches the roosters, quick to detect the scent of fresh chicken, stampede from the shed he's forgotten to finish battening. Some of the roosters hit on three or four different hens within seconds, and the poor hens, most of them virgins and none of them strong enough to fight off the sexual advances, just stoop to take the weight. Those not mounted sprint in circles, overturning feed pans, defecating everywhere, and flapping their useless clipped wings. Henry runs at a cluster, shrieking and corralling roosters away from chickens but, no matter how hard he runs or how loud he yells, the biggest rooster, the buckeye, will not be deterred. Eventually, he has to remove the cock's talons from the feathers on a chicken's neck and kick him toward the shed. The marauding frenzy is over in a matter of minutes, but it leaves him exhausted. He's bent over sucking on a bleeding forefinger when Wendy, who's been watching from the kitchen, comes out to make sure the shed is latched properly this time.

I'm sorry, he says.

Well, she says, we're going to have a bunch of fertilized eggs and useless brooding chickens to go along with the ones the mink killed. How are we going to make the orders you and Chas have lined up for January?

Let the fertilized eggs hatch? He can feel his nervous, stupid laugh coming. Something he hasn't felt in quite a while.

Hmphf hmphf hmphf, he snorts.

The laughing stops only because the freshly scuffed dust has filled his nostrils and made it hard for him to breathe. He's anxious, though. How else is he going to earn a salary if the farm can't afford to keep running? He hates that he's pissed Wendy off. He looks down at his feet hoping the barnyard muck will give him inspiration, but nothing comes clear except that he needs to buy a new pair of shoes, these are permanently stained with chicken shit.

He looks up to see that Wendy's mouth is pulled tight.

What? What are you thinking about?

You manning the incubator, she answers. Chicks in winter are not going to be easy. You'll have to rotate the eggs at least three times a day.

Show me the switch. I'll turn it on.

If this doesn't work, you're gonna have to make us eggnog with fertilized eggs. Pick the embryos off the side of each yolk, one by one.

She demonstrates the minute movement with her fingers.

Sorry I can't help you with the mess, she says. I've got to drop a load of eggs off. See you after lunch.

She walks toward her car then turns. Oh yeah, I gave notice on the Swift Farm's contract yesterday effective January 1. So you guys better make this work.

Inside the barn, Henry tries to compose himself. There's too much to clean up after the maraud for him to be focusing on the new business. To begin with, he has to change the water in the dispensers. They're full of feces dropped by the panicked chickens trying to escape the randy roosters. As he fills the watering can, his spirits begin to lift. Physical labour is good. By the time he's filling the twelfth can, he's even thinking cheery thoughts about eggnog — sugar, cinnamon, nutmeg, his favourite flavours. As he dumps the dirty water from a dispenser behind the barn, he lights on an idea to host an eggnog party in the Constellation Room. It will be Christmas in a couple of weeks and Joey's girlfriend, Lucy, called the room heavenly. He could invite Aristedes who could drive out with Chas; it would be fun to have him so long as he doesn't talk about violating chickens. And if Aristedes comes that settles the rum question, there'd have to be rum for the eggnog.

He picks up a watering can and is on his way out into the front yard to clean the feces from that dispenser, when he sees something — a dead chicken behind the stack of transport cases. At first he thinks one of the chickens has been killed by a rooster and dragged behind the case, but as rambunctious as they are, roosters don't usually murder hens. With each step he sees another dead chicken, bodies piled up one on top of the other like a cord of firewood, the mink's biggest stash yet. The closer he gets to the transport cases the sicker he feels. He yanks them away from the wall and is doing a dead count when a car pulls into the yard. Unbelievable timing. It's Elaine.

Hey, Henry, she calls.

Hello, Elaine. Why are you here?

Just a routine follow-up.

What do you mean? There's no such thing as a routine follow-up.

Where's Mrs. Lightstone?

She's gone to town. You should come back when she's here. Call to make an appointment.

Come on, you know better than that. I've got authority to come anytime onto a premise that sells commercially.

Elaine walks toward the water dispenser, which is covered in poop, islands of feces floating in the liquid. She kicks at a mound of feathers in her path.

What happened here?

Bit of a barnyard scrap. I left the roosters' shed open, that's all.

That's all. I would have thought you knew better than that.

I do.

And the feces in water, is that something you know better about too?

Of course . . . but you see some of the hens got excited. That's not unusual.

It's not usual. It's downright unsanitary. You know feces in water is one of the best ways to transmit avian flu.

If there *was* any flu to transmit.

Elaine walks toward the barn and he runs in front of her feeling a lot more like a chicken being chased by a rooster than he would like. He beats her to the door and stands in her way.

What are you hiding?

Nothing. You don't have the owner's permission to come in.

Looks like reasonable cause for me to come in.

He lets her push him aside. He knows she can cite him for obstruction, which is only going to make things worse. An Orpington pullet stands in the middle of the barn looking especially bedraggled; a great many of her tail feathers are missing and she's suffered a small injury from her tryst with the rooster, a scarlet drop of blood hanging from her rump. Elaine bends down to inspect the chicken, makes a clucking noise with her mouth and a note on her chart, then, as if she is some sort of dead-hen-tracking dog, she marches straight for the corner where the headless chickens are stacked.

What's this, some of kind of ancient Langley ritual? Monument to the dearly departed?

We had an issue with a mink.

What are you doing about that?

We have to set a trap, I guess.

You guess? Dead corpses in the roosting box, feces in the water, extreme feather loss, untreated injuries due to gang rape — not sure how I'm going to write this one up.

The Orpington comes to stand beside Henry. She looks up at him, and then as if commanded by him trots over to Elaine and plops chicken shit on her foot.

Better add unruly chickens to your write-up, Henry says.

Elaine does not reply. She takes a few photos then walks to her car. The Orpington trots beside her, drops into a hole in the dirt, and spins. A dervish of dust blows over Elaine like Saskatchewan farmland during a drought.

Don't think I don't know your visit is no coincidence, Henry shouts after her. We terminated Swift's contract, and your boyfriend is no doubt unhappy about that.

I don't know what you're talking about, she says, closing her car door.

FOURTEEN

Constellation Room

I T'S THE LAST FRIDAY BEFORE Christmas, the day of his party, and bales of hay are set around the table in the centre of the Constellation Room. A large bowl of eggnog sits beside a bottle of Captain Morgan and beside that a plate of shortbread and butter tarts. Henry has lined up his gifts on the bed: a hot water bottle with a knit chicken cover for each guest — two orange, two white, two pepper — and one chocolate kiss for a special romance wish. He knitted one a night during the past week. The knitting itself didn't take long, it was interlacing the feathers and affixing the knit heads that took time. Each bottle is freshly filled with hot water that should still be warm when he's ready to give the presents; they're under the blanket so the surprise will not be ruined.

He paces the room waiting for the guests to arrive, anxious about throwing his first party. But, more than that, he's incredibly ticked off with what's stuffed into his pocket. Four sheets of paper burn a psychic hole into the side of his hip, to say nothing of the very real blood on his thumb and forefinger that he acquired tearing out the staples Elaine had used to tack up the Notices of Disposal — kill orders — on the front and back doors of the barn and the roosters' shed.

She appeared in the barnyard just before five o'clock, pulled out her red staple gun, stapled up her greetings, and slipped away. The notices, issued under the federal Health of Animals Act, say: *All the animals in the infected place, to wit the Lightstone Farm, are to be killed and disposed of within twenty-four hours from the date herein.*

Henry knows the definition of animal extends to even the fertilized eggs incubating this very moment behind the Constellation Room. He also knows it's an offence to take down a notice issued under the Act. But he's already seen a defect: Elaine in her rush forgot to date them; still, this is going to be a sticky one.

He is tapping at his pocket when his first guests arrive. Lucy and her mother, awkward as new colts, stand in the doorway.

I told you it was beautiful, Mom, Lucy says.

Oh, Mr. Henry, Lucy's mother says.

Hello, my name is Henry, he says. He's embarrassing himself. The mother already called him by name.

My name is Vedrana, she says. So good to meet you, Star Man. You have made monument to the beginning of the universe.

Thank you, he says.

He hears Chas and Aristedes in the barn and motions to Lucy and Vedrana to help themselves to eggnog and goodies. In here, he calls.

Chas is wearing his best houndstooth coat and Aristedes' grizzly beard has been trimmed back to Pavarotti-sized whiskers encircling his mouth. Aristedes' eyes look especially fierce and happy, and Chas seems even smaller and more delicate than usual. He's tucked in nicely beside Aristedes, but they unlink arms as they approach. Henry is pleased Chas appears to have found a relationship with a real bear, although he hadn't guessed Aristedes was the type.

You both look festive, he says.

Incredible, Chas says, looking about.

Aristedes is tongue-tied. When he is ready to talk he says, This place brings the joy of tears to me.

By the time Wendy and Joey arrive, the rum has been cracked and Aristedes is singing a Greek carol blessing the room and all that are in it. He leads everyone in a round of carols and, when he's finished, he motions toward the special cake he's brought, promising a coin in every piece.

Shall I sing another? he asks.

Without waiting for an answer, he breaks into "Jingle Bells" with Lucy and Vedrana joining in while Wendy and Joey snack on the goodies.

Chas sidles up.

You seem sort of stressed out. Is the party making you tense?

No.

He points to the papers sticking out of Henry's pocket.

What's that?

Nothing.

Look, I don't want to break the mood, but I might have an idea what's going on. We stopped at Norman's Hawaiian on our way here and that skinny broad you used to work with was there with her boyfriend.

Right.

That boyfriend's not too bright. This farm's condemned, isn't it?

You heard that?

And he's going to use it to drive the price down.

What?

Would I make this shit up?

Come talk outside. Wendy doesn't know anything yet. I don't want to wreck her Christmas.

Carry on with the singing everybody, Chas calls to the room. Henry and I are going outside to look for Santa.

Chas looks like an angel under the outside light. Henry inclines his heads toward him while they talk.

You're sure it was her?

Yeah, I'm sure, skinny broad with a bad dye job.

Maybe I should speak to Chief. Would you be willing to back me up if I go to him with this information?

Of course, our new business depends on it. And look, I don't mean to make things worse, but you're coming back into town with us tonight. Right?

Why?

Well, you have a mound of mail you didn't open last weekend and this banker dude keeps calling, saying it's urgent you get in touch.

About what?

Don't know, but I'm guessing you owe his bank some money.

Oh, maybe there isn't enough in my account for the mortgage.

And there's one other thing. The city wants into the suite to have a look.

Oh God. Let's go inside, this is too much.

When Chas and Henry return to the room, steam is rising off their bodies from standing in the cold. Aristedes has cracked one of his bottles of retsina and he's got everyone in a conga line. A slightly inebriated Joey breaks in to announce it's time for presents. He wobbles out of the room and across the yard toward the house. Henry shoots Wendy a look — he doesn't think she should let Joey drink. He told her so, but she said, It's not your business.

After a minute, Joey weaves his way back into the room. He holds out a box toward his mother, pulls the lid off and says, I'm going to skin it for you, Mom.

Wendy seems genuinely relieved when she sees the dead frozen mink, but Henry's practically numb with the spate of bad news. He just wants the party to be over. All the others start pulling out gifts. Chas has a card for Joey with a Mustang car on it and twenty dollars inside.

Start saving, he says.

Thanks, man, Joey answers.

Wendy gives everyone something from Norman's — pots of Hawaiian pineapple marmalade, boxes of macadamia nuts.

In a bid to get it all over with, Henry uncovers his chicken bottles with a Ta-Da and Merry Christmas to all and to all a good night. But everyone is too festive to catch on. They all coo and hug their gifts, and start another conga line, each carrying a new feathered friend while they dance. It takes him another hour and a half before he's able to shut the party down and ride back home to Kitsilano, sullen in the back seat of the Mustang.

On the Monday morning, Christmas Eve, Henry does not go out to the farm. Wendy told him to take the holiday week off, she and Joey could handle things, so long as he was back by January 2nd to help with the hatching chicks. He sits at the kitchen window and plays with the phone cord. A stack of opened mail is at his elbow. It's taken him the entire weekend to work up the energy to tackle it. On the top of the heap are the four kill orders, under those a foreclosure notice from the bank's lawyer, a bylaw infraction from the city's lawyer, a notice from the Court in Idaho reminding him of his January 4th appearance date, a Visa bill with an additional $54 in interest, and a Christmas card with poinsettias from Mrs. Krumpskey. Her handwriting is so bad he thinks at first she has written *Baby Jeans pays for Henry*. When he finally reads it properly, he feels no joy that *Baby Jesus prays for Henry*.

He picks up the phone and dials Chief's number at Agriculture. The phone rings and rings. He tries again, same thing. He's waited all weekend to make the call. Then he remembers that it being December 24th probably means the stingy government has given everybody time off again in lieu of a real Christmas bonus. He drums his fingers on the pile of kill orders. He picks the phone up again and this time calls City Hall. A pleasant-sounding receptionist answers, Season's Greetings.

Greetings, Henry says. Bylaw inspector's office please.

I'm sorry, sir, that department is closed for the holiday. Is this an emergency?

Not really, he says.

He puts the phone in its cradle and rips up the first copy of the kill order. Somehow there is a balance between the unavailability of any of his potential saviours and annihilation. Although he *is* the Star Man.

He dials again, this time to the bank manager. The call is answered by a series of bizarre clicks and rewind sounds while an answering machine attempts to receive, then kicks in with the tail end of a message . . . Holiday.

Happy Holiday to you too, he says, tossing bits of the kill order over his head.

Next he grabs the foreclosure notice and dials the number of the lawyer at the bottom of it.

Patrick Madeira, a voice says.

Henry is not prepared for anyone to answer but, now that he thinks about it, it figures the foreclosure lawyer would be working Christmas Eve. He begins to form a question, but he can't do it. He hangs up on the lawyer's voice asking, Anyone there? He folds the remaining three kill orders into tiny squares and puts them back on top of the pile. The shredding game really isn't any fun.

What's going on in here? Chas asks.

You're not working today either? Henry says.

You should talk, sitting in your pyjamas with a mess of confetti around you. Any coffee made yet?

Listen, do you feel like driving down to Idaho at the end of next week? Take a couple of days off, do a three-day weekend thing.

What are you talking about?

I've got something I need to take care of down there and I could use a ride. Besides, you sorta still owe me for rent from last fall.

I guess I could do that, a drive in lieu. Can Aristedes come?

Sure, the more the merrier.

Christmas Day, Henry wakes up alone in the house. He feels like a block of stone, entombed, completely unable to move any part of his mind or body. He lies very still for a long time. He has felt sad, nervous, anxious, tense, sick to his stomach, and weepy, but he's never felt this sort of hit-by-a-Mack-truck-stuck-in-depression before. Except maybe for a time when he was a highschool dropout with no job. But this is different, this feels more adult, more grim. For the first time in his life he is seriously worried his mother's bipolar has hit him. Dr. Davis once told him that Christmas week is the busiest time in psychiatric emerg, and that he should watch his mother carefully that week. He understands why now. He even starts to think about offing himself. How might he do it? Are there books on it in the library? He heard that gassing yourself is painless, but the Subaru is probably pretty useless for that as all her gases seem to fly out the backend right now. He knows the expression *sucking on a tailpipe* but he doesn't believe that is actually how it is done. The only thought that gives him any relief is a silly one: he has access to a lot of chicken methane gas. He feels certain that wouldn't work as his body is so used to it it would probably just think *another day at the ranch*. Still the silliness of death by chicken gas makes him feel okay enough to get up and cook himself some Christmas oatmeal with a little cinnamon and brown sugar. He sits at the table for three hours.

As the week wears on, his emotional stability comes and goes. Chas and Aristedes spend most of their free time with each other, sometimes tucked away at Aristedes' condo, and sometimes holed up in Chas' room. When they're in, Henry thinks he'd prefer it if they were out, until they actually leave and he is alone in the house, which then seems cavernous and drafty. Mostly, all he does is worry. He calls Wendy a couple of times, ostensibly to check on the chicks. They still just look like eggs, she tells him. But will they come on time? he asks. Like clockwork, twenty-one days from conception, she says. The truth is he's worried about the chicks, he's worried about himself and worried they'll be born late, on the day he has to leave for Idaho, he's worried his promise to Wendy to be there as soon as they start to hatch will be broken. Such a slim margin of error. What will it matter if he offs himself? Many times in the week his cycle of thought ends on this one.

Between worried calls to Wendy, he tallies up columns of numbers, trying to make projections about the new business and his debts. But the numbers never come close to balancing, even when he projects profits at double what they already have contracts for. There's no doubt he's going to have to sell the house or let it go on foreclosure, but where will he live? It would be presumptuous to think Wendy will let him stay forever in the Constellation Room, and then there is the worry that Bob will actually convince her to sell the farm.

On the Friday at the end of Christmas week, Henry checks the mail to see what new disasters have arrived. He rips open the envelope from Agriculture Canada expecting another worry. Instead he reads that vacation pay is owed to him, but they can't calculate the amount because there's some confusion over his final date of departure. The boss of the HR department, a woman named Sue, has added in handwriting at the bottom *call any day over the holidays if you want, someone has to be here!* Henry doubts that, but by the Monday morning curiosity as to how much might be owing gets the better of him, and he calls.

Agriculture Canada, a man's voice says.

Chief? Is that you? Henry asks.

Yeah, who is this?

It's Henry. What are you doing there on New Year's Eve?

It's a long story.

I'm sure it is. How be I come out and hear about it in person? I've got a couple of things need discussing.

How 'bout you do that.

Henry rides the bus out to Still Creek Drive with the unsettling kill orders in his top jacket pocket and the vacation pay letter in his jeans pocket. When he gets to the office the chief spends the first five minutes sucking on a soda can and whining about being the only one who has to do a day's work over the holiday season, then launches into a painfully long story about how the union negotiated a two-week Christmas holiday for its members in lieu of the government not fulfilling the usual usurious hourly wage request, and how the chief being management was not included in the bargain, so when the Deputy Minister issued a directive that no government office could be closed for a period of more than four consecutive work days, Chief was the one pressed into service.

What about Elaine? Henry asks.

Ahhh. She already had a holiday approved so I got stuck with it, Chief answers.

Just as well, I'm here partly to discuss something that concerns Elaine.

Boring. Okay, shoot.

Henry lays out the background, emphasizing Elaine's relationship with the creep Bob, and the conversation Chas overheard involving the plot to take over Lightstone's Farm. And then he produces the kill orders.

Chief smooths out the creases with his hands.

Whatcha been doing with these, Japanese paper folding?

It was a moment of frustration, Henry replies.

Chief takes a big suck on his soda before he strolls to the filing cabinet where office copies of the orders are kept. He walks his fingers across the tops of the files, rifles through the in-basket on the top of the cabinet, and comes back to his seat for another swig of soda.

Nothing there, he says.

Maybe Elaine took them with her, Henry says.

That's a technical default then — leave it with me. Chief gestures with his hand and knocks over his soda. Pink liquid fizzes out of the can, spills across the desk, and is sopped up by the orders. Aw hell. Chief wads the orders into a ball of soaking paper and pitches them into the garbage can. Okay? he says. Gone.

Sure thing, Chief. As always good doing business with you.

Then why'd you quit? Chief asks.

Well that's the other thing I came about. Henry produces the vacation pay letter.

Chief rubs his bald head while he reads the letter. He looks amused and says, You don't really think I know about this vacation pay stuff, do you? You'll have to call HR on this.

Umm. Henry smiles back at him.

On the ride home Henry ruminates about what Chief said. He'd been so focused on the kill orders, the implications of the word *quit* hadn't sunk in. But as the bus makes its way down Lougheed Highway, he begins to wonder. Did Elaine ever tell Chief that she'd fired him? Did Chief really think he'd quit? He feels like he's in too deep with the new business plan to contemplate returning to work, but still thoughts about quitting and being fired rumble through his head until he begins to feel woozy swinging on the bus pole. At the corner of Broadway and

Main he gets a seat, but by then his head is pounding and Alice is talking to him. *You're the cause, Henry. You never stand up for yourself.*

His sore head starts to turn annoyance into a starburst migraine. Blue and red stars shoot across his eyes. By the time he's off the bus, it's all he can do to walk home and get into bed, though in a weird way he's relieved it's only physical pain. It's a lot easier to handle than that psychic pain he's been feeling most of the week. And thank goodness Chas and Aristedes are out somewhere celebrating New Year's Eve.

Henry awakes New Year's Day to a panicked call from Wendy.

Either we miscalculated or the chicks are arriving a day early, she says.

What?

I can hear them chirping inside their shells. Get out here.

He sets the phone down and pads bleary-eyed across the hall to Chas' room. He knocks, knocks again, and after a few seconds sticks his head into the room. It's quiet. Either Chas is not there, or he's died under the mound of covers from too much *piss of the rat*, as they all now like to call retsina. Henry suspects he's not there, but he pokes at the covers anyway. They deflate. His head pounds as if he's the one who's had too much retsina. Tiny flecks of light shoot across his vision. There's no way he can take a bus all the way to Langley.

He picks up the phone.

Any chance you can come and pick me up? he asks Wendy.

Someone needs to stay here and watch the eggs. I'll send Joey.

Joey?

Yeah, he got his license just before Christmas. Don't you remember?

No. Is he safe?

Course he's safe. Gotta go.

He scribbles a note for Chas to remind him they need to be on the road to Idaho by 9:00 AM on Thursday. Then he sits at the front window, waiting and worrying. What kind of driver can Joey be with a one-week-old license? He can't remember ever seeing him at the wheel of a car let alone hearing anything about driver's lessons. He knows from his own lessons that, aside from those who are drunk, the number one cause of deaths is new drivers improperly merging onto the highway.

After centuries, Wendy's small grey Toyota approaches too fast down 7th Avenue, Joey hunched behind the wheel. Joey tries a headfirst park in a spot that's too small to take even Wendy's car, and the stars of Henry's migraine shoot again. Joey lines up to try a second time. Henry flies out the front door in his hard-soled shoes, onto the icy porch, where he slides off the edge, and down three steps to land on the end of his tailbone. He hops up in that older-guy-makes-a-fool-of-self-in-front-of-cocky-teenage-boy way and hobbles toward the car. Good thing Joey can't see the feathers he put in his underpants this morning.

Man, that was spectacular, Joey says.

Thanks and Happy New Year to you too, Henry says.

No, seriously, are you okay?

Sure. Sure. Not a problem. I do that every morning as a wake-up call.

The truth is, his rear end is throbbing, his head is pounding and his knob has gone numb — something the feathers are supposed to prevent. As if that is not enough, once they start driving he has to grip the armrest every time Joey takes a corner because of the speed at which they travel. Joey actually lays rubber at one corner.

You're driving kind of fast. Lots of cops out this time of year looking for drunks, Henry says.

Good point, man. I only had a couple of beers before I left. Hair of the dog, you know. But you can't be too careful.

Now that Joey mentions it, Henry can smell alcohol. He looks around to see if there's an open bottle in the car, and tries to relax when he sees none. But as they approach the highway on-ramp at Willingdon, heavy rain pelts the car and Joey begins to drive so slowly Henry worries about the merge. Almost at the highway, they traverse a huge puddle of water, and a tsunami hits the windshield.

Henry is certain now that he broke his back in the fall, possibly severed all the nerves to his penis. He grips the armrest and closes his eyes.

Why are you screaming? Joey asks.

Henry opens his eyes. They are on Highway 1 proceeding at a proper speed, light rain hitting the windshield, and Joey has both hands in the proper 10-2 position on the wheel.

That wall of water sort of jolted me, Henry says.

You freaked, man. Sometimes I dunno what my mom sees in you. Get it together.

Yeah, okay.

And no more screaming. Okay, man?

Henry adds to his list of concerns the affections of the widow. Or is that what Joey meant? Maybe he just meant it in the sense of him being her business partner, her worker, her farmhand — a friend even. He's not sure now where he wants it to go. He's tempted to ask Joey more, but lets it drop. It's not fair to drag him into it.

Wendy has set the eggs in the incubator so he can see the pencil marks where he's indicated which mother hen he guesses goes with which egg. There are forty-six eggs in total, almost as many as chickens the mink killed. He's touched she's put the eggs this way, because she thinks it's nonsense. She's told him hens brood each other's eggs and it's impossible to know which belong together. He puts his ear down to Flower's egg and hears nothing.

They don't all hatch at the same time and not all of them are going to hatch, she says. Listen to Pepper's egg, but don't turn any of them, they need to be left still now.

He holds his head over the egg marked with a *P* and sure enough there's a soft peep. When he pulls his head up he can see the egg and a few of its cousins rocking, as if the chick inside is starting to flex. Wendy hands him a plastic spray bottle.

Mist them, she says. It keeps their shells soft. I'm going inside to make us lunch.

What do I do if one starts to hatch?

Just watch. Don't panic — it takes time.

While she's gone he looks around at the small maternity ward she's set up. There are bowls of water, Q-tips and an extra heating lamp on a cookie sheet. Beside the lamp is a bottle of disinfectant and a bottle of champagne. While Henry contemplates this, one of the eggs gives a hard rock and a hole appears at the large end of it. By the time Wendy returns with a plate of corned beef sandwiches, there is an audible chirping coming from the table.

Did one of them hatch? she asks.

No, but there's a big hole in one egg.

Keep watching, in case any are born with yolk stuck to the rump.

What?

The yolk is all they have to eat at first and if there's any stuck, the rest of the chicks will peck it to death.

Really?

Would I lie?

Maybe.

By mid-afternoon one chick has pecked a hole big enough for Henry to see its eye. The more the chick struggles, the more it looks like a dinosaur emerging. The chick's yellow down is slick with albumen, its eyes and feet huge in proportion to its scrawny body. Once the chick is fully exposed it lies on its side, gathering the strength to stand up. After about an hour, when the chick finally stands, Henry crows.

Now you understand why I have the champagne, Wendy says.

She pops the cork and pours two glasses. She hands one to Henry and they clink glasses. He takes a sip. The bubbles go up his nose and he shudders.

You don't like it? she asks.

It's okay. It's just I'm not much of a drinker. But hey — Happy New Year.

Can't be any worse than last year.

No, I suppose not.

Wendy finishes her glass and they both look down to watch another chick struggle up onto its feet. Now there are two babies to look at, but Henry is feeling stuck. He knows he should say something wise about life and passages, but his backside is sore and his headache is returning. He's been standing for a few hours now and is feeling as discombobulated as a chick tottering on new legs.

Why don't we do this in shifts, Wendy says. You can rest, if you want, and take over later.

Okay. You sure?

I'm sure.

He starts to head for the Constellation Room.

Wendy calls, You know, neither one of us really has to be here all the time, so long as we check now and again.

He can see she is tired too. The best thing he can think to offer is a spot in the Constellation Room.

Do you want to lie down in here? he gestures to the room.

Okay, she says.

Sweet Jesus, Henry thinks, how do I the deliver on this one? I can't, I mean I don't, I don't function properly. But here it is, the test, and I've got feathers in my underpants, a bruised butt, and a paralyzed penis.

He follows her into the Constellation Room. She lies on his mud-slab bed.

What now, he wonders, what if it won't move, what if it doesn't know how, what if my mother did suck my dick? Figure something out, push on it, jam your hand into your pocket, think about breasts, there you go, you can feel it, push, yeah, now get on that bed.

Wendy looks up and says, This is not what you might be thinking. I don't want to *do* anything, I just want a little company. It's been a hard year.

Henry's head is swimming as he walks to the edge of the mud slab. He picks up his hot water bottle and holds it out.

Let me get some hot water, he says. It will make you feel peaceful.

He plugs in the electric kettle at the incubation table. The two chicks that have emerged roam through the unbroken eggs, trailing each other, not too closely, not enough to crowd, but near enough.

By the time he returns with the bottle Wendy has scooted over to make room for him, but she looks half asleep. He hands her the bottle, and she puts it on her stomach, smiles, and closes her eyes. He lies down beside her and watches the bottle move up and down. It's reassuring and he is starting to feel comfortable enough to get up on his elbow and lean over for a kiss. A kiss should be easy enough, only a touch on the lips. He's almost ready to do it when he hears gentle snoring synchronized with her rising and falling belly. He kisses her anyway. She does not respond. She is asleep.

Now that he has a moment on his own, not panicked by performance anxiety, he runs over in his mind what he would do next if she were awake and returned his kiss. He would give a stellar performance, rock hard, as long as it takes, whatever *it* is. His hand goes to the top of his belly, gently rests on the edge, rubs carefully and things firm up, and what would he do if . . . uh, uh, uh . . . his hips thrust toward the ceiling like a teenager's, out of control and with no sense of place. His superhero ejaculates while he struggles to keep silent so he won't wake Wendy. He hasn't had this happen since he was fifteen, and even then not so easily.

Relief floods his body. This is a type of success. This is something he can be proud of. He needs to bank this feeling. He is almost not a virgin anymore. His body is relaxed enough that he falls into a partly awake, mostly asleep state, but it's hot, very hot, like being under an ultraviolet lamp, and it's crowded with bodies, all of them in the same sticky space, swimming in a viscous substance, all elbows, nipples, mouths, testicles, kneecaps. His own rump among them has yellow yolk stuck on it and all the other bodies want to peck at him, and his nose is full with that smell, what is that smell? he knows he's smelled it before, even as he is asking himself he is down the drain of the kitchen sink with his mother's hand-wand, and then in the kitchen cupboard by her pots and pans, the cymbals and tympanis that accompanied her disturbances, then

inside her cold-cream pots and lipstick tubes — all of it
smelling so, well, the only word for it, so eggy.

Henry sits up, his heart racing. A ruckus in the barn
has awoken him. He rushes out to find Flower who has
escaped from behind the barricades. His rear end is stiff
and sore from where he crashed earlier on the steps,
and his underwear feels sticky and itchy, but he has to
ignore all of this because Flower has hopped up onto the
incubation table and is trying to peck a hole in one of the
eggs. Several of the eggs are rocking now, including the
one marked in pencil with a small flower, though that's
not the one she's pecking at. No matter, she has to get out
of there. She's in danger of burning her feathers on the
heat lamp. He picks her up and sets her on the floor. She
fights him, pecking at his hand.

What's going on? Wendy asks as she walks out of the
Constellation Room.

More chicks are hatching, he says. Check that Flower
is okay, she got close to the lamp.

Wendy picks the hen up and holds her still against her
belly. She gives her a once over and sets her down on the
other side of the barricade. Flower squawks.

She's okay, Wendy says.

Henry looks down to see another shell is almost off
except there's something wrong with the chick. It's on its
side and the eye is not open like the others. He watches
for a few more seconds, waiting to see if it pops opens.
The chick is alive, its feet curling and uncurling as if it

wants to grab onto a roosting bar, but still the eye does not open.

Wendy, come here! What's up with this chick?

Which one? she says, putting her head over the table.

This one. I think it's blind.

Naw, that happens. Is there any warm water left in the kettle? Put some on a Q-tip and clean off the eye.

He pours a half-inch of warm water into a bowl and dips the swab into it. He wipes the Q-tip gently across the chick's eye and the chick flutters it open and closed a few times.

Wait 'til it stands up to see if the other one needs doing, Wendy says.

It takes the chick a few minutes to wobble onto its feet but when it does the other eye is closed too. He sets the bowl of water in the chick's track. Down at chick level, eye-to-one-good-eye with it, he sees that not only is the other eye stuck, but the chick also has a cross-beak. He wipes the second eye open.

It's okay, little chickie, I'll make sure you can eat too.

Wendy comes and puts her hand on Henry's back, You're a gentle man, Henry. I like you, but . . .

But, what?

But . . . I mean I'm not ready to go there yet. Maybe it wasn't always the best marriage with Dennis, but it's not been a year and I'm still sort of mixed up.

Henry thinks in many ways he could just as easily be the one saying he's not ready, that he's mixed up. But what's his excuse? How is he supposed to say *my mother was crazy, which makes me crazy, and now I can't have sex?* Is that even an excuse? He knows he's different, but it's not anything anybody else can see and he doesn't even know how to describe it to somebody else. It would be so much easier if he'd been born with a shrivelled leg or a damaged heart. Then people could say *treat him with care, he's not like us.* He looks down at the newest chick.

I think we should give cross-beak a name, he says. How about Henry?

What if it's not a he?

Henrietta then, he says. We have to treat her with care, she's special.

Hours later, after thirty-eight chicks have been born and he is alone, undressing in his room, he discovers feathers stuck to the shaft of his penis.

You're special all right, he says to his feathered appendage. You're chicken.

FIFTEEN

Brooding Machine

THURSDAY JANUARY 3RD, HENRY WAKES alone in the Constellation Room and stares at Ursa Major. The feathers at the end of the nose have fallen off and Henry feels almost as empty-headed as the Great Bear above. Tomorrow he will be in court in Idaho. This could be his last day as a free man. He has no idea how he'll satisfy the transmission tower debt, or how he'll convince the judge his venture in chicken sales is a sure thing. All he can do is try. Eventually he drags himself out of bed. He needs to check on the chicks, make sure they have enough mash and water, before heading over to tell Wendy he has to take a couple of days off.

The chicks have doubled in body weight again overnight, and even Henry Cross-Beak is growing longer and fatter.

As he crosses the yard, Henry decides to use a technique he learned at Agriculture. When staff asked for a short leave, they'd go vague about the reason, saying little other than *I need time for a procedure.* Right away everyone knew not to ask because clearly if it was something simple, like an ingrown toenail, they'd just say so.

Wendy is at the kitchen table with eight cards in front of her, and a book at her elbow titled *Luscher Colour Test*. He watches her place the purple first, the green second, then flip the others and rearrange them.

What are you doing? he asks.

I'm putting the cards in order of my favourite colours. They interpret my personality, she says.

She makes a calculation on a piece of paper and starts to read from the book.

It says I'm fearful I won't achieve all that I want, and I need sex as a stress relief. Ha ha, she laughs. Could have fooled me.

Henry laughs too but isn't sure why. Somehow their not having sex has loosened her up, made her want to talk about it. And all he wants to tell her right now is that he needs a few days off.

Ah, Wendy, I need to use the phone.

Sure.

He dials his number in Kitsilano. While he waits for Chas to pick up, his neck and shoulders begin to cramp. What if Chas is not home? What if Aristedes, who threatened to kidnap him until after the Epiphany, has wooed him away? What if Chas, in his enthusiasm for Aristedes, has forgotten his promise to drive Henry to Idaho? His shoulders begin to feel like they are being pulled toward each other by some powerful magnet. He's about to hang up when a man's voice on the other end says, Huh.

Hey. Who is this? Aristedes?

It is, my friend.

Is Chas there?

No.

Where is he?

Out.

When will he be back?

Dunno.

Henry's neck cramp is getting worse. His head feels like it's being pulled down to his right shoulder. He bends into the phone as if by pushing on it, he can make this all work.

When did he leave?

Dunno.

He's just going to have to say it in front of Wendy. Tell Aristedes he has to find Chas and make sure he gets on his way out to the farm to pick him up so that they can drive to Idaho for court the next morning.

You know, he says, Chas has to drive me somewhere today. Remember?

No. Wait. Maybe. Look, sorry, I'm pretty bad hungover.

Wendy looks up from her coloured cards and starts motioning with her hands that she needs to speak with him. He turns his back on her so he can lean further into the phone, give it all his attention.

Aris, can you get Chas to call me back? I'm at the farm. We have to be on our way soon.

I'll try, my friend.

I'll drive you, Wendy says.

No you can't, Henry says. I'm sorry.

What? Aristedes asks.

I'm not talking to you, Henry says.

Then why did you call? Aristedes asks.

Sorry, please just get Chas to phone me.

He hangs up and sits down at the kitchen table. He flips over the red card and buries his head in his hands. From underneath his hand he asks, Is this the card that says you'll drive me to Idaho?

From up in his loft Joey calls down, Say no, Mom. He's a crazy passenger.

Mind your own business, Joey, Wendy says.

Henry tells her what he can manage to spit out about the court appearance and the transmission tower, while Wendy busies herself with packing for a weekend away, walking back and forth between her bedroom and the kitchen holding up various outfits, asking him whether he likes the pink or the purple sweater, the black or the blue jeans. She's happy and excited, and natters on about how it's time for her to get out of Langley, how the farmer next door can be on call, and they can transfer the chicks into the brooding machine, so it'll be easy for Joey to take care of them.

Joey calls down, I'm not sticking around to take care of a bunch of stupid chickens.

How 'bout if I pay you twenty-five bucks? Henry asks.

Okay, I guess.

I'll pay as soon as the first chick sells.

There's always a catch, man, Joey says.

There always is, Henry agrees.

Wendy's pulling on her boots when the phone rings. She listens for a bit and holds the handset out to Henry.

I'm on my way, Chas says.

Okay, see you soon.

Wendy looks disappointed. He can't tell her he doesn't need her to come.

How would it be riding with Chas? he asks.

Good, she says. Fun to go in a Mustang.

Great to go in the Mustang! Joey corrects from upstairs.

Not you, Wendy says.

I know. But I'm gonna get my hands on a pony car one day soon.

Henry follows Wendy out to the barn to see what the brooding machine looks like. She walks to a shelf by the transportation cages and takes down an oversized carton with a painting of a pineapple field on it. He is expecting something to come out of the box — a special poo-extracting, down-washing, mash-dispensing gizmo. But when she lifts up the sides of the box and drops a piece of cheesecloth into the bottom, he can see it's empty. Nothing in it but cheesecloth.

This is a brooding machine? he asks.

It'll do. Keeps the predators out and Joey can change the cheesecloth easy enough. Just set the heat lamp over top, add some water and mash, and away we go.

Just before ten, Chas pulls into the yard and honks. Henry is surprised, given the earlier conversation, that Aristedes is with him.

How did you manage the time off from the deli? he asks.

My big sister, she runs things better than me anyway.

Makes better béchamel too, Chas adds.

Henry carries the bags to the trunk. Compared to the back seat, it's a treasure chest of space, room for everything, despite the bottles of retsina Aristedes has stashed there. He slams the lid and catches a glimpse of Joey standing outside the kitchen door. He looks a little forlorn. It's been a tough year for him too.

Chas flips the bucket seat forward, and Wendy scrambles into the back.

Cozy in here, she says.

Henry folds himself in beside her.

Wendy rolls down her car window and calls to Joey.

If the chicks huddle together, it means they're cold. Turn the heat up, she says. And no more than half an inch of water in the jars. You don't want any drowned chicks.

Happy Epiphany, Joey, and do everything I would do, Aristedes shouts as they pull away.

Out the back window, Henry watches Joey's uncertainty turn to a grin.

Last thing Henry sees as they retreat is Joey playing air guitar out in the yard.

Once they're through the border — thankfully with no issue over the purpose of the visit — Aristedes, who is navigator, fumbles with the map, turning it upside down and right side up before attempting to explain the route through Diablo, the same one Henry had to turn back on in the fall because of the snow. Henry makes a noise from the back seat that even he thinks sounds like a whimper.

What now? Chas asks.

We can't go that way. Not this time of year, Henry says.

Ah, the seat of the back driver, Aristedes says.

Henry says, I've been this way before. Look at the map, the road is closed in the winter.

Why should we believe you? Wendy asks.

Really. I can't miss this date tomorrow. I could go to jail.

Jail! Aristedes roars. Aren't you fancy, my friend.

Okay, we won't go through Diablo, Chas agrees.

Henry closes his eyes and wishes there was a good road map for his life. The sky is grey and so is his mood. He pretends to sleep for as long as he can, the heat in the car helps, and except for a pee break in Ellensberg, and a dinner stop in Coeur d'Alene, he pretty much fakes the sullen-criminal-in-hiding thing until they're in Wallace cruising for a room. They pass the courthouse, an imposing boxed-wedding-cake structure that takes up the entire block at Bank and 7th Street, and looks more frightening than it did the first time he was there — the snow on the dark mountain behind bothers him. It's late by then, after ten o'clock, and the motel's sign is blinking no vacancy. They drive by a quaint historic hotel, but Aristedes and Chas decide to pass.

Too small to fly under the radar, Chas says.

Gay men in cowboy land. Gyro mess, Aristedes adds.

After circling town a couple more times, they pull up in front of the squat two-storey sandstone hotel at the end of Cedar Street. Old-fashioned brass sconces adorn the doors and give the place a big city, tarted-up look, sophisticated enough to provide anonymity. Chas holds the oak door open for everyone. Aristedes heads straight for the lounge, and Chas steps up to the clerk.

Two rooms with double beds in each. Yeah? he says, turning toward Henry and Wendy.

For the last part of the journey, Henry has been moving between sleep and anxiety, apprehensive about this moment. What kind of room should he and Wendy ask for, and what will happen when they get there? He really needs to sleep to be sharp the next morning. He's about to shrug out a *yes* when the clerk saves him.

Sorry sir, there's only one room left. Might be the last one in town, what with the skiing being so good. Are you here for the skiing?

No, we're here for a court hearing, Wendy says.

Well then, I'll see what I can do to make you comfortable. How many are you?

Four, says Henry. He wants to take control of the conversation, make sure no one says anything more about court.

I can set you up in the queen room with two cots. Would that suit?

In the morning Henry can barely wake up and his tongue feels thick as a sausage.

It's probably the Ativan I gave you last night, Chas says.

When they walk the three blocks to the courthouse, Henry realizes he might still be a little stoned, which surprises him — the pill was so small. His legs are on autopilot as they come up the courthouse steps where a few people are sucking on last minute courthouse-jitter cigarettes; two bored-looking cops loiter near the top. Wendy, who looks sleepy, is first through the glass and metal door. Aristedes and Chas file in after her. Henry is last. The heavy door slams, and the clatter echoes down the long corridor. Inside there seems to be the sound of many feet drumming on the floor, reverberating, even though it's only a woman walking toward them on the marble floor in high heels.

Henry holds out his court document. Excuse me, where can I find this courtroom?

Right there. She points to a mahogany door.

Chas says, It's hard to believe you need so many courtrooms in a town this size.

Oh, there's loads of people get themselves into trouble around here, she says.

Her shoes clack on the floor as she moves away down the corridor under the high ceiling and past several doors.

The four of them sit at the back of the courtroom on a hard bench. They might be in a church, what with the bible on the witness stand and the high wooden desk like a pulpit at the front. There are already a dozen people in the room, all of them silent except for one guy with sideburns the shape of a Texan boot, who seems fussed about the length of the list for the morning. He's trying to convince the clerk to rearrange the appearance order.

The DA has no objection to me going first, he says, pointing to a slight young man sitting at the front of the room running fingers through his greasy hair.

The DA doesn't respond.

The clerk says, I'll ask the judge.

Henry takes comfort from this if it means *he* won't have to go first. Just then the doors behind the wooden desk open. A diminutive man with a round head and in ill-fitting black robes walks through to sit in the pulpit chair.

All rise, the clerk says. Order in the Court on Friday the 4th day of January in this the year nineteen hundred and ninety-one, Judge Stanley Hinds presiding.

The judge picks up a piece of paper and says, I want to start with the detention list.

The clerk says nothing, the DA runs his hands through his hair, and Sideburns lets out an audible whoosh of frustration.

The clerk stands and calls, Henry Parkins.

Henry floats out into the aisle.

The judge gestures him to come forward.

He walks toward the front and the DA begins, If it please the court, the details are in the remand record . . .

The judge holds up his hand.

The DA stops speaking.

The judge picks up another piece of paper and studies it.

Henry's head whirls with random words — *baby jeans, baby jeans pays, baby jesus, baby jesus prays* —

The judge is talking again.

So, Mr. Parkins, am I to understand that you drove down here from Canada looking for one of our local celebrities, got yourself drunk, crashed into a transmission tower, destroyed private property, nursed a hangover in our jail, promised to pay us back? And now you're reneging? Is that right?

Henry nods.

For the record, Mr. Parkins, yes or no?

Not exactly.

Well what then?

Henry doesn't know what to say. Words are swimming — *Mother caused it, Mother made me, you're such a bad boy, cluck, clucking disaster, you're going to jail Henry* — but nothing will come out his mouth.

Well?

I don't know, he finally answers.

Do you have a job?

No. Yes.

What does that mean?

I was working. I am working. I'm starting a new business.

So, you have capital?

No, not really.

Assets?

A house, but it's in foreclosure.

Lord above. Well I hope you brought your overnight bag because you're going to jail, Mr. Parkins.

Henry looks to his left to see Aristedes standing next to him.

If I pleased the court, I am Aristedes Giannakos and I am Mr. Parkins' guarantor. I run the best Greek delicatessen in all British Columbia and Mr. Parkins grows the best chickens. He'll have you the money in six months. I put my word.

We're going to need more than your word, Mr. Giannakos. Are you prepared to post bail?

Yes. I have all the money you need.

The judge turns to Henry. So you're a chicken farmer?

Yes, sir.

Have much trouble with avian flu up there in Canada?

No, sir.

Good. Do you believe in clipping wings?

Henry is on home turf now, like he can talk a little. He tells the judge, You only need to clip one wing. If you do that, it throws the chicken off balance and it can't fly.

Okay then. Mr. Giannakos, speak to the cashier, see what you can work out. And Mr. Parkins, you straighten up and fly right from now on.

Yes. Thank you, sir, Henry says.

The four of them walk toward the back of the courtroom. Aristedes turns to give a polite bow to the judge, the door crashes behind them and they're in the hall.

I don't know how to thank you, Henry says.

I'm proud of you, says Aristedes. Enjoying yourself so much you go to jail!

I'll get the money back to you soon.

I know this, my friend.

Back at the hotel it's late afternoon. Everybody but Henry has had at least two glasses of retsina and is starting to feel happy. Aristedes, who has had several glasses of *piss of the rat,* hits Henry on the back, and says, Stick your chest out to crow. You're free. Show us around. Where do you go to drink here?

Well, I bought the beer at Singles' Nite in Kellogg, Henry says. It's Friday, so it should be happening again tonight.

Well then, it's to Kellogg we go, Chas says, putting on his jacket and fishing in his pocket for car keys.

Wendy insists Henry sit beside Chas to navigate. Henry feels guilty because he's thinking about Charity, wondering if she'll be there, if she'll remember him. She probably will, they had their picture taken together. The thought of her pretty smiling face makes him feel shy, and what about Wendy in the back seat? How will this all go down? It's so complicated. They should turn around, but since everyone else is in such a good mood, it doesn't seem fair. They drive the dozen or so miles to Kellogg, stopping to treat themselves to double-bacon cheeseburgers, passing the corner where the mechanic's shop was, a For Lease sign out front — no wonder the guy cheated on the bill; even so it still makes Henry mad thinking about the Visa. But when he sees the neon can spilling golden beer into the parking lot and the overly bright fluorescent lights inside the place, his palms begin to sweat.

Pull over here, he says.

Really? We're going to Singles' Nite in a strip mall? Chas asks.

You'll see, Henry says. Tell the woman with the rusty yellow freckles you're single.

Charity is spinning the singles wheel. This time she's wearing a green gingham multi-layered southern belle dress and old-fashioned lace-up boots. Her hair has been dyed ginger and piled on top of her head in what Henry believes might be a bouffant. She looks even prettier than he remembers, and slimmer.

Hey there, welcome to Shop-Mart! she says. I'm Charity. Give me a second to finish up here and I'll be right over, folks.

She hasn't really looked up. That's maybe best.

Chas and Aristedes disappear to the magazine rack and Henry ushers Wendy to the back to hunt for the knitted mice that hang by the processed cheese slices. When they get to the cooler, the mice aren't there anymore, but in their place is a giant knitted Swiss cheese wedge with a small mouse peeping out one of the holes.

Isn't it cute, Wendy says.

A set of couples is in the midst of a singles swipe. Two beefy men with outsized women hog-tied to their right legs push shopping carts around, a small crowd of onlookers cheering them on. The big man with the red face wrenches a bottle of hand lotion from the hand of the large blonde woman on the other team. The lid comes off and a waterfall of pink spills to the floor. The crowd cheers. The blonde shouts, We have a default here!

Above the cacophony, Chas' voice explodes, Unreal, two of you in the same room!

Henry turns and sees Chas wildly gesticulating at him, Come on over here, Henry. We gotta do this. It's tomorrow night.

Chas holds a card out. Henry approaches. On the front is a picture of a knitted Airstream Trailer with the words KNIT REACTOR printed below it.

What's tomorrow night? Henry asks.

Hey, I know you, Charity says.

Yes, I was here in the fall. From Vancouver.

Yeah. I sent you an invitation. You came. That's so cool. Nice to see you again.

Henry flips the card over and reads: *Charity makes her knit art to bring attention to all things that fail the honor test, whether it be the home of a murder victim, or the lowly war declarations of George Bush (may he never succeed).*

Henry's a knit artist too, Chas gushes.

You never told me that. What's your focus? Charity asks.

I don't know. I don't think I have one, Henry says.

Sure you do, Wendy says. He works with feathers and wool. He makes beautiful meditative environments.

He made a Constellation Room, Chas adds.

Aristedes stands with them now. Henry can tell by the way his bearded mouth makes a big O, he's going to say something wildly inappropriate, and hugs himself in fear of it.

He makes best knitted chicken bottle, Aristedes says. Wait. I go. I come back.

Henry lets go of himself, nothing bad came out, and everybody laughs when Aristedes swings back into the Shop-Mart with the bottle on his head and the knitted chicken neck swaying rhythmically in front of his face.

It's not supposed to be a head adornment, Henry says.

He takes the knit chicken from Aristedes and nestles the neck into the body to make the chicken look like it's sleeping.

Everyone take turns stroking the black-and-white feathers, admiring the handiwork.

Can I include it in the show? Charity asks.

Sure, says Aristedes. We fill her with more hot water and she plumps up even better.

SIXTEEN

Dirty Annie's

OH MY GOD, HENRY SAYS.

It looks great, doesn't it? Charity says. She sidles over to the Pepper knit chicken bottle, which has been placed on a plinth in the centre of the Shoshone County Gallery. But it is the guest in the corner, the one wearing the silky western cowgirl outfit, that's astounding him. Her hair is a bit darker than in her pictures, but there's no mistaking the perky breasts. And what's more, Jamie Lee is prettier in real life than she is in her promo photos.

His foot gives an involuntary jerk in some sort of fright or flight response when Charity introduces them.

Henry, this is my good friend Jamie Lee. She's master of ceremonies tonight.

Charmed, Jamie Lee says. Aahhh-eehhh.

His hand collides with hers in a handshake. Likewise, he says, not trusting himself to say more. Besides he's not sure what she said there at the end. Maybe she knows who he is, and is exclaiming about it. But how could she know?

He tells himself to stop being paranoid. Then when Jamie Lee speaks to the woman behind her, he is pretty sure she gives the same little aahhh-eehhh sound after she's finished. Soon enough he realizes she makes the sound nearly every sentence or two. He wonders how she gets away with not doing it on the radio. To his ear, the sound resonates in the same range as the notes so-la from the song "Doe a Deer" that he used to sing in elementary school.

Everybody circulates with drink in hand, oohing over the art, even though most don't understand what they're looking at — Henry included. But he reads the title cards and all the statements, and he's tingling with excitement, fascinated by the connections Charity has made, the colours in the room, and of course, the people — Charity and Jamie Lee make quite the pair. He has to keep himself busy so he doesn't stare too much. He does the circuit again and this time he understands, he gets it how innocent knit objects can stand for something else. The knit airstream trailer replicates the home of a recent murder victim from Silverton, a young mother killed by an angry husband. He is reading a statement tacked to the wall near a knitted machine gun — *some places where there's been a war, whether physical or spiritual, need to be covered up, others need honoring, either way the knit medium works* — when he hears the familiar radio voice.

Good evening, ladies and gentlemen.

Jamie Lee is standing on a small stage, holding up a glass of white wine, with Charity beside her.

Everybody get yourself a glass so we can toast my good friend Dora, I mean Charity. Gee, Charity, it's hard for me to get used to that. All those years living next door to each other, Charity was Dora to me. A toast to my good friend, Dora-Charity, in her artistic triumph.

A young man appears at Henry's elbow and holds out a tray full with glasses of red and white wine.

To be polite, Henry takes a glass of red and hoists it with everyone else and without thinking takes a swig. It tastes a lot better than retsina.

Jamie Lee rattles on about Dora and art school, Dora and tattooed freckles, Dora and southern belle dresses, Dora and her photographer boyfriend Peter, so notoriously shy he's outside right now shooting the event through the window. Never once does she make the so-la sound. That is, until the end of her tribute.

To Dora and Charity, she says. And to her new found artist friend from British Columbia, Henry Parkins. So-la.

He takes a big gulp of wine. She knows his last name. Someone along the way must have mentioned him to her — this crazy guy Henry Parkins who stalked her all the way from Canada and crashed into the KLUK transmission tower. Now she knows he's that guy. He downs his drink and grabs another from the young man's tray.

Somebody has decided to join the drinking team, Wendy says, smiling away.

No, not really. Here, this glass is for you.

Thanks, I already have one. But if you're sure you don't want it, I'll take it over to that guy playing guitar.

Now that he bothers to notice it, the rock-music-trying-to-sound-jazzy is loud; a big man with long blond hair streaked with grey, hands the size of baseball mitts, is hunched in the corner over a beat-up Les Paul guitar. Henry watches Wendy put a glass of wine on the amplifier and the blond man smile at her as he switches his song from "One is the Loneliest Number" to a jazzy version of "Lay Lady Lay". It's corny enough to make Henry sorry he gave up his wine, so he goes in search of another.

He's beginning to have a good time, except for the stress of being in the same room with Jamie Lee. But the wine helps, especially when he's sidelined by the lady from the Arts Council with the droopy eyelids and a hat that's hard to look at — jewelled cats and penguins dangling from the brim — who chats him up for a donation. It isn't until he gives her ten dollars he doesn't really have that she moves on to other victims. When his eyes lock with Jamie Lee's across the room, only social protocol keeps him from running. He's not sure what he sees in her eyes. Disdain? Possibly fear? Not good, whatever it is. Besides, isn't she married to Billy Wray? He just has to ignore that she's in the same room with him. Come to think of it, where is Billy Wray?

We're going over to Dirty Annie's, Chas says.

Aristedes points toward the door. Dirty Annie's, he repeats.

What about Wendy? Henry asks, ready to follow them anywhere.

Aristedes laughs. I think she enjoys the music. Yes?

Wendy waves and mouths the words, See you later.

Come on. Let's skedaddle, Chas says. Charity is coming, soon as she's finished schmoozing.

The red-tiled floor at Dirty Annie's is sticky with spilled beer. The smell of french fries and a griddle that needs its grease pan changed wafts out of the kitchen. The bar is crowded with men drinking beer, shouting to be heard over one another and a sound system that screeches Creedence Clearwater's "Bad Moon Rising". Two big men at the end of the bar, one of them wearing a trucker's cap, turn to watch Henry, Chas, and Aristedes settle in the only free booth. A tired-looking waitress comes over.

Ginger ale, says Henry.

Millers. Chas signals to himself and Aristedes.

But when Charity and Jamie Lee walk through the door, Aristedes stands and whistles the waitress back.

A dozen ouzo, he says. On fire! he adds.

I dunno if we have that, the waitress says.

You do, my friend, Aristedes says as he hands her twenty dollars. On fire, pretty lady.

Charity wants to sit on the inside of the booth so she squeezes past Henry, and when Jamie Lee perches on a chair at the end, his head pounds. He can't believe he's wedged between Charity and Jamie Lee.

The waitress, flushed and harried, carries a tray of flaming drinks toward their table. All the men at the bar are laughing and yelling, but there's a silence above the heads of the two big fellows watching. Aristedes takes one of the flaming drinks and stands to toast Charity.

Opa! To our new friend, the artist, Charity.

Aristedes downs his drink in one go and takes another. Everybody now. Opa!

Henry picks up a drink, but he hesitates too long and the flame singes his moustache, and the air fills with the acrid smell of burnt hair.

Oh, the stink. You must do it again, my friend, Aristedes shouts. Opa!

Practically the whole bar is watching now, so Henry picks up a second glass and downs it. The ouzo is surprisingly sweet and warms his gut. He feels emboldened, almost confident enough to talk to Jamie Lee, who is cooing something about the smell of burnt moustache and making a little so-la every now and again. Very pretty, very musical, a little so-la right out of the middle of the doe-rae-me scale. Would it be okay to break out in a full *doe a deer, a female deer*? But his lip stings and he's not really quite ready yet, so he sips on one of the cold beers from the tray the waitress brings to follow the ouzo. He holds the chilled glass to his lip between mouthfuls and listens to the cross-chatter between Charity and Jamie Lee. He keeps hearing the name Billy Wray mixed in with so-la. Maybe Billy Wray is coming to join them. Then he hears Charity say, I told you — you shouldn'a married him so quick.

By the end of a second beer, his lip is feeling better and he's quietly singing *doe a deer*, while he listens and learns that Billy Wray has another wife, or maybe two, and he's moved back to a place called Plentiful, where he wants Jamie Lee to join him. Aristedes picks up on the tune and begins to sing aloud. He would probably have carried on with the full score from the *Sound of Music* if the mean-looking guy in the trucker's cap hadn't come over and told him to shut the fuck up.

There is another beer in front of Henry and while he sips he's aware he's beginning to ramble on to Charity about sex, about getting laid, about not getting laid, never getting laid, but in fact desperately *wanting* to get laid. He hears himself tell her, It's so complicated to get everything going in the right direction. She says, You know, baby, it's really not that hard, you just do it. She leans into him, her bosom propped by her southern belle bodice directly below his face, her freckles beckoning. Their two heads are so close for a moment that he thinks, We're kissing. They aren't really, he's just feeling a thrill like they might. Her thigh keeps pressing into his and seems to follow him whenever he moves. She even says, This is sexy, all of us crammed in here, isn't it? He feels his hand creep up over the edge of the table toward the vee in her cleavage where the cinched bodice threatens to pop a nipple. But Charity has a boyfriend and he shouldn't, so to divert himself he looks over at Jamie Lee. My God, he has never been so revved in his life. His body shivers when he takes a sip of beer, any beer, whoever's beer is handy.

You're cute, Henry, Charity says. Then she leans over and really does give him a kiss.

After a third, or perhaps it's a fourth beer, his state of mind is a little less focused on his nether region, on anything, so he is able to ask Jamie Lee to give him one of her radio pitches. He waits to hear if she can do it without making the so-la sound.

Hey there, she sings, *it's country time here at Dirty Annie's where I'm sitting with two premiere artists. And I don't mean country-western singers, folks. No, they ain't that, but one of them's a chicken farmer who makes beautiful stuff with feathers. And he's hurtin' and flirtin' with me, sittin' right across from me grinnin'. And we'll get right back to him soon enough, but first let's hear a little of Canada's Good Brothers singing their number-one hit, "Doin' the Wrong Things Right!"*

Jamie Lee's purring mouth makes Aristedes go again, and he breaks into "If I Were a Rich Man" and everybody at the table joins in. As for Henry, beer and excitement have suddenly overtaken him with the urgent need to pee, and he pushes his way out of the booth and starts to laugh when he realizes how unsteady he is. The room tilts as he pushes on the saloon-style doors into the washroom.

Inside there's only one stall, locked, so he walks up to an empty urinal and tugs at his pants. His fly is stuck, the zipper won't budge. He looks down to see a fringe of orange and white feathers poking out between the teeth. He threw in an extra handful that morning, for what reason he can't remember, but at least he understands now why the men at the bar were laughing. He gives a good hard yank on the zipper and a cascade of orange and white feathers falls to the floor.

After he's finished peeing, he stands for a moment, unsteady on his feet, and picks one last feather off the shaft of his party favour. A hand grabs his shoulder.

I knew you were all fucking fags, a voice says behind him.

A blue-jeaned leg and boot come flying through the air up onto the tap of the urinal. The tap flushes. Once. Twice. Water gushes down the drain. Henry has a sick feeling in the pit of his stomach. The boot comes off the tap and a hand presses on his shoulder and hauls him down onto his knees, then flat onto his back. The guy with the trucker's cap plants the boot on his shoulder and pins him to the floor. Henry tries to lift his head but it gets shoved back down. Hard. Then two sets of hands drag him across the black and white ceramic tiles, through the spilled urine, the muddy melted snow, and shreds of sodden toilet paper. His butt, still black and blue and sore from his fall down the steps, seems to be the fulcrum. His pants and underwear get shoved farther and farther down his legs with every tile.

He likes it in the ass. Did you catch a sight?

Yeah, all the colours of the YMCA.

Fucking fudge packer.

The door to the washroom is kicked open and Henry is dragged across a hallway and smashed against an emergency exit. It's bracing cold outside. He is picked up, hauled a distance across the yard and heaved into a frozen mud puddle. The weight of his body, butt first, cracks the skiff of ice. His butt is too sore to feel cold, but his shoulders and back react to the freezing water seeping under his sweater. There are three of them now staring down at him, all of them faceless, the light from the parking lot making eerie halos around their heads. Dark angels come for a feeding, fingernails like razor blades. Cut the head from the snake. Trucker cap raises his arms above his head, clasps his hands together like a ball peen hammer for the final blow. Henry does not defend himself. At least he won't have to off himself, these pricks will do it for him.

But there is a merciful one in the circle. He stops the doubled hands and forces Henry's mouth open with a pickled egg.

Feel like a cock to you?

The guy with the cap starts to retch. He stumbles a distance over to the wall where he begins to vomit. Henry can see the puke steaming under the light. He's grateful for it because it distracts the men and for a time he can hear them over by the back door of the building, two of them laughing, while the trucker continues to spit.

Eventually the night is silent.

Henry is too confused to get up, stays on his back and stares at the sky. The longer he looks, the more he sees. Stars begin to bloom in the lingering waves of violence. It's fascinating. He tries to process what has just happened, but the harder he thinks the more difficult it is to weave any sense from it. As soon as the stars start to align in a way that might speak to him, a new wave passes through and shuffles everything. Eventually, a cloud drifts across the sky like a curtain in a theatre and he descends into disappointment. It is so much easier to sink than to float. His face is wet. It can't be tears, he thinks, I don't have the energy to cry.

He comes apart the same way he was put together. Fumbling. He tries to spell the word for what it is he wants to feel, but he doesn't know the feeling, so how can he spell it? He knows he's disappointed, but what is that feeling he's itching to have? How can a person want something they've never had and don't understand? He is so disappointed he can't even name the feeling he needs to find. He thinks he'll just give up.

I didn't teach you to give up. The words float above his head.

He is so incensed his mother would come to him now and say such a thing, he spits the pickled egg out of his mouth to yell. Shit! You did! All you ever did was teach me to give up. Sometimes I think you were waiting for me to go mad . . . fucking clucking mad.

Henry waits in the silence for his mother to answer. When nothing further comes, he begins to think silence might be the answer. So he pushes on silence. He'll grow a shell around himself, live in complete silence. Yes. He's ready to go with safety in silence, when a female voice off to the side presents the option of him not giving up.

So you're having trouble getting laid?

Henry looks in the direction of the voice and sees the old-fashioned lace-up boots, the crinoline on a southern belle dress, a halo of good light surrounding a bouffant of ginger hair.

It's really not that complicated, she says. Getting laid is easier, say, than sticking your dick in that mud hole you're lying in.

Huh?

Actually you look even cuter out here, she says. Roll on out of that puddle.

As soon as he moves onto a patch of dry grass, she stands over his face, brings her body down. He can see she has no underwear on. When she is near, he can smell her. She smells different than he was expecting, less like an egg and more like a green apple after you peel it, sweet but tart. She lowers herself and he nuzzles her with his nose, then with his tongue and she makes a little sound like a puppy having a dream. She pivots and uses her mouth to warm him up. Henry does not know whether it is the contrast between the warmth of her mouth and the cold of the night, or just the sheer energy of everything, but he surrenders to her and doesn't allow himself to think. At last, she sits on top of him. She seems expert at what she's doing, and soon he arches and is unashamed for long enough to let her . . . He tries not to be noisy about it, but he can't help but call out at the end, Joy, fucking joy!

After he's quiet, she asks, You okay?

Yeah.

See? It didn't fall off. Lust is easy. I'll leave you to pull yourself together?

That'd be good.

This is just between you and me, she says. Nobody else needs to know.

Especially Peter, right?

No, not especially him. He probably photographed the whole thing, but then that's him.

Henry listens to her boots crunching through the snow toward Dirty Annie's back door. He's not upset that Peter may have photographed them, it's sort of exciting. Makes him want to go again, but he knows this has already been inappropriate enough. The clouds have parted and he watches the stars instead. This time he doesn't want to tear them down, they're peaceful, easy to look at. Stars shooting, planets blinking, the whole galaxy shifting. Light years in front of him. Then, whether it's a hallucination or not, he can't say, but he's certain he sees a constellation of a mother hen with a chick. It's as if new stars have been thrown up in the sky as a reminder to the people of the world to be good to one another. He watches the vision for a time and begins to grid it, mind map it, until it's not just that he has memorized how it looks, he's memorized how to build it. And he knows he will. He will knit a massive chicken cozy, big enough to cover his mother's house. A place where attention needs to be brought and things need to heal. The smell of Shalimar floats through the air.

That's a good idea, Henry. Let go of broken things.

SEVENTEEN

On Fire

ON THE WAY HOME FROM Idaho, in the back seat of the Mustang, Henry develops a kind of certainty that going forward he will be able to use his equipment as intended. How to use it is no longer the question, the question is simply with whom? At this point no one is excluded. He squirms with pleasure when he thinks about virtually every person he knows, even though he is displacing balls of wool each time he changes position. Every inch in the car is crammed with yarn from Charity's extra stash. She and Peter drove it over to the hotel that morning with promises to get started knitting squares and send them to Canada to add to the house cozy. Charity christened Henry Canada's first knit reactor and reminded him it is an honour to be an artist. Henry isn't so sure, but acknowledges he is sort of thrilled to be starting this project in tandem with the new chicken business.

By the time the Mustang pulls into Wendy's yard, everyone is glad to get out of the car. It's been a lot of driving under cramped and hungover conditions. Joey is even happy to see them.

Too much chick tending, he says.

And not the kind of chicks you want. Right? Aristedes jokes.

Right on, Joey answers.

Henry, Chas, and Aristedes leave Wendy and Joey with hoots and hollers, and promises to get the chicken business going in earnest the next day.

Back in Kitsilano, it takes the three of them half an hour to unload the wool from the car. When they're done, most of the floor in the TV room is covered with yarn. Aristedes picks up a large ball of orange wool and a couple of knitting needles. I'll practise with my sister, he says, She can knit the balls off a pompom toque.

What does that mean? Henry asks.

Get out of here, Chas says, kissing Aristedes goodbye.

Henry watches and decides kissing is important, but he could not kiss either one of them. This is useful. He is limiting his candidates.

The three of them work well together in chickens. The urban professionals in Vancouver can't get enough of the free-range products. Projections by the end of February are so good, Wendy feels confident rebuffing the ridiculously low offer made by Swift Farms, made even more ridiculous when Chief calls Henry the day after the offer is presented to ask whether he'll be a witness if Elaine presses forward with her action for wrongful dismissal.

The first thing Henry spends money on is getting the Subaru fixed, so he can move back home and use it as a delivery van. But there's not enough money to make his banker happy, and he has to attend a foreclosure hearing at the beginning of March to find out how long he will be able to stay in the house.

The judge, a woman this time, looks bored with the proceeding, although a little surprised that Henry showed up. She gives him, and the twelve other mortgagors who did not bother to show, until the end of August to redeem their mortgages, otherwise their properties will be sold.

Good to have a deadline, Henry thinks. Time enough to get the cozy finished.

Henry and Chas spend long evenings in front of the TV knitting. Squares come in weekly from Charity and Wendy, some even from Joey and Peter, and after a month of Chas nagging Aristedes to get started, he brings in two cartons of squares made by his sister together with instructions to crochet them together into afghan-sized pieces so that when the chicken is dismantled, blankets can be made and donated to the poor.

I told you she could knit balls around you, Aristedes says.

I still don't know what you mean by that, Henry says.

Some evenings Henry and Chas talk about Alice while they knit. It's as if Henry's orgasm in the mud puddle released a geyser in him and he is able to talk like never before. Eventually he works up to asking Chas whether he thinks it possible his mother could have done something to him.

I have no one else to ask, Henry says. You're the only person I know who knew her.

Well, that would be wicked bad if it happened. But even if it did, you gotta move on. Are you sure it isn't some kind of false memory?

What?

Something you make up to help you cope, Chas answers. Maybe it's easier to believe your mother was messed up sexually than to believe she was mentally ill.

This kind of conversation proves healthy for the knit project; their curiosity in the subject keeps Henry and Chas in their chairs with needles flying. So much so that by the last Saturday in April, they are ready to begin erecting the cozy. They start by laying the chicken breast on the lawn. The squares are arranged to overlap like feathers and the chicken looks a bit like the hen Chocolate Kiss who'd died tangled in the heater, although mottled with white like Angel had been. From the roof, Henry hoists the breast panel over the porch and up the front wall. It goes up easily and he ties it down around the edges of the eavestrough and gutter drains. The plan is to get all four sides up before stitching them together. He is at the side of the house securing the second panel when Mrs. Krumpskey shouts from the curb.

I've called the police!

What for? Chas shouts back.

Public disturbance, she says stepping onto their front lawn.

Henry says, How is this disturbing you?

This is unsightly. You and your mother —

You're talking about my mother, he snaps. My mother who died nearly three years ago. Enough! Go inside your house and don't look out your window.

By the time the police arrive, Henry has secured the head of the chicken to the chimney, so at least that much is clear about what he and Chas are doing. The male police officer is first out of the squad car. What in gawd's name is that? he asks, pointing to the roof.

It's kinda cute, the female officer says. My kids would love it.

Mrs. Krumpskey comes back over to stomp around and make allegations of public disturbance, nuisance, endangerment, and every other quasi-criminal term she can think of. Her grey hair is wild off the side of her head, and her support hose is balled at the ankles. The two police officers let her exhaust herself. The female officer finally says, Sorry, ma'am, there's nothing criminal going on here. But we'll write it up for the bylaw officer to look into.

This seems to be enough for Mrs. Krumpskey who turns to Henry and says, See.

Get off our knitting, Chas says to her.

She jumps off the panel she's standing on, streaks over the lawn faster than a woman her age should be able to, across the street, and up her front steps. She slams the door.

The officers are taking down Henry's address and phone number when Aristedes pulls up in his deli truck.

Henry, fearing what might happen next, is relieved that Chas knows enough to keep Aristedes busy at the truck until the cops pull away. Good thing too, because Aristedes has brought his final box of knit products — a set of pendulous orange balls.

For the bum bag of the chicken, he says, holding them up triumphantly.

Don't let Mrs. Krumpskey see that, Chas says.

Something for the kids to play with when their parents look at the cozy, Aristedes says.

I never saw a hen with nuts before, Henry says. Besides, nobody but Mrs. Krumpskey and us are gonna be looking.

Wait to see, Aristedes says confidently.

What are we going to call this trans chicken? Chas asks.

How about Angel for Chocolate Kiss, Henry says.

Ooh very artistic, Aristedes coos. And don't forget, eighteen roasters and a baker's dozen for next week.

He drives away leaving Henry and Chas to stitch up Angel for Chocolate Kiss. Three of the four sides are finished when they call it quits for the day. The unsecured west panel flaps gently in the breeze and they go into Chas' room to see if they can anchor it from the inside. There, with each flap, light from the setting sun bounces off the vanity mirror.

I have an idea, Chas says.

What? Henry asks.

Chas starts to pull Day of the Dead characters from the knitting cupboard, the drawer in the coffee table, and the dining room hutch.

Before we close this chicken up, let's celebrate your mother. This cozy is for her. She deserves a pageant.

The number surprises them. Nearly two hundred. An impressive collection — women with babies, men with brooms, trombones, and guitars.

But it's the small boy with a plastic chick in his arms that stops Henry. The little fellow dressed the way he used to as a child. A shy smile on the boy's white skull face. He is holding one of the chicks from the farm set. Henry picks it up and rubs the clay face. How delicately his mother painted the faces. He opens up the knit cardigan. There's a little heart stitched onto the boy's shirt and an embroidered *xoxo Mom* underneath it.

Henry puts on the Santana album and the two of them set up the Dead figures while "Black Magic Woman" plays. To the sound of a wailing guitar they make a procession of Dead figures beginning in the television room, following the wainscoting down the hall and into what was Alice's room. They encircle her vanity with female characters.

Let's stitch these figures onto the cozy, says Chas.

Really?

Sure. Let them hang out. Your mom had a great sense of humour, he says.

You think so?

God yes. That whole Cruella de Ville phase? Alice with the green fingernails? That was funny.

It pours rain the next day so Chas and Henry don't get around to attaching any of the Dead. Instead they place a strangely shaped cow on the grass to be sure the clay face doesn't dissolve in the wet. On the Monday, when Henry stops at home for a quick lunch between deliveries, he's happy to see the cow looks pretty much unchanged despite the sopping rain. He's at the counter bolting down a plate of leftover ratatouille and dolmathes, when he looks out through the flap he and Chas created at the kitchen door to see Elaine and Bob in the backyard. They're circling the house, trying to figure out a way in.

What do you want? Henry calls through the flap.

Hi Henry, Elaine says, as if they are friends.

Bob and I wanted to talk to you, she says. What are you doing anyway?

Not your business, Henry answers.

Can we come in?

Nope.

Okay, can we leave an affidavit here for you to sign?

About what?

About me being unfairly fired from Agriculture.

No. In fact, I'm going to testify against you.

Fuck you then, Bob says.

Bob! Elaine exclaims. That's not helping.

Just then the phone rings and Henry says, Gotta go. He lets the flap fall.

The man on the line says his name is John and he is calling from the city. He wants to know when it would be convenient for him to drop over. It's odd. The fellow sounds upbeat. Mrs. Krumpskey's complaint is anything but exciting, but best just to get it over with. He agrees to meet with John the next day after he's finished delivering chickens.

Could I come at 4:30? John asks.

Okay. I guess I can speed my day up a bit.

Good. We want to get a look at your structure in the daylight.

On the Tuesday at two minutes past 4:30, Henry hears laughter in the backyard. Two men and a woman are poking at the giant balls on Angel for Chocolate Kiss.

Hi, he says. You from the city?

He's surprised the city has put three people on the case. He knows it's like any other government, not always that efficient, but really, three bylaw inspectors seems over the top.

I'm Kate and this is Alex. We're here from the Outsider Art Fair.

And I'm John, the other fellow says. From the city.

This is fantastic, Kate says.

Can you tell us what inspired it? Alex asks.

Well, he says, I was lying in a mud puddle outside a bar in Idaho and I saw a blueprint for it in the sky.

Incredible, Alex says.

Wow, Kate says. That's wonderful for the biography.

What biography? What's this about? he asks.

A ringing sounds starts to come from inside Kate's handbag. They all watch while she pulls out a device that looks like a TV remote and pushes a button and begins to talk. It's the first time Henry's been up close to a mobile phone. For some reason he doesn't trust it.

Sorry, she says, stashing the phone. Alex and I are from the International Outsider Art Fair. We're based in

Chicago, but we've chosen Vancouver as the next host city, and —

Alex interrupts. We're just so excited to see your piece. We'd like to feature it on the posters and invitations. Did you build it for the fair?

No, I built it for my mother.

She must be thrilled, Kate says.

She's dead, Henry answers.

Oh. Nice. A memorial! Kate says.

The fair runs for the month of August, Alex says, through Labour Day weekend. This can be a centrepiece.

Well, you have a problem then, Henry says. The house is under foreclosure, due to be put on the market at the end of August.

Can you do something about that? Kate asks John.

I'll look into it, John answers.

Good, so you will sign on? Agree to be part of the fair? She looks at Henry.

Well, I'm an outsider, I agree with that much.

Fabulous. There is possibility in everything, she says. Her purse bleeps again.

When Henry tells Chas about the fair, his only advice is to shave the beard. Bit of a cliché to be a bearded artist, don't you think? Chas says.

Henry agrees and since summer is coming it might be good to have the winter growth off. He snips with scissors at the longer pieces; the mostly blond tendrils fall into the sink and cover the pink porcelain. After he's removed as much as he can with scissors, he picks up the razor. He tackles the left cheek first. Once it's clear of whiskers, a trickle of blood flows from the bottom of his mole. He dabs it with a piece of toilet paper before he starts scraping the right cheek. When he's clean-shaven he stands back to have a look. Thinner in the face than he remembers — but okay. And who is it that he looks like? Someone. Tom's father. He had a mole at just about the same place. Maybe a mole suits a grown-up better than a child. Like a distinguishing feature. He stands back even farther and is struck by how much he looks like Tom's father. Could it really be that simple? Had the answer been living next door for so many years? He stands straight before the mirror, new strength in his spine.

The media team from Chicago seems to know how to rev up an event. Arts reporters from everywhere begin phoning Henry for interviews. He barely has time to get his chicken and egg deliveries done. After he tells one reporter from the *New York Times* he's not an artist, he's just a chicken farmer, the myth of the farmer with the *Artistic Oeufre* — a not-so-clever phrase coined by the wretched reporter — grows. Fair organizers appoint a publicist to help him take calls, and it's a good thing because soon he is the poster boy for several special interest groups. The chicken farmers of British Columbia ask for his endorsement, as do various performance artist groups, the feminist crafters and — after Aristedes points out to one art critic visiting the house that this is a hen with balls — a transgender support group.

Crowds arrive to visit the giant chicken cozy covered in Day of the Dead figures well before the fair officially opens. Charity and Peter come up from Idaho to help with a satellite display to be run out of a tent in the backyard to which other knit reactor artists have contributed, including a display of Charity's muffwarmers with new designs in flamingo pink, mink brown, and a special one with knitted flames called *Dirty Annie*.

It isn't until Henry sees Charity emerging from the tent, her breasts perky in a peach-coloured bustier, he's reminded he's hardly had time to think about sex. That's a good thing, he thinks. Or is it?

By the time the fair is ready to open on the August long weekend, the lawn at Henry's house has been trashed and the foreclosure bank, which has attempted to bring an injunction to prohibit further wasting of the property, has been temporarily shut down by the city throwing money at it.

On the Saturday of opening day, media crews, reporters and crowds of onlookers choke off the street.

Henry can't believe it. He's to be interviewed by TV personality Terry David Mulligan, *the* Boss Jock at CKLG back in the day. It's a good thing Mulligan has a lot to say, mostly an artspeak treatise on *craft as performance*, because Henry is tongue-tied in his presence. He's just about to attempt an answer to Mulligan's question, How much time do you spend knitting? when Mrs. Krumpskey — who's been beside herself with the noise and the confusion and locked inside for most of the month of July — bursts from her house.

I'm calling the cops, she screams.

Henry, awkward and hyperaware that there's a live mike in his face begging for a response, is adrift in a mixture of humiliation, intimidation, and anger. He leans forward and shouts, Craft off, Mrs. Krumpskey.

The crowd roars in appreciation and Mulligan can't help himself but start to dance, mike in hand, singing a breathy rendition of "Super Freak". A reporter from the *Vancouver Sun* uses his mobile phone to call in Henry's response as a headline for an article that is syndicated around North America that afternoon.

Henry's interviewed by the *Vancouver Sun*, the *Seattle Times*, the *Los Angeles Times*, the *Coeur d'Alene Press* and a bunch of art magazines he never even knew existed. Invitations come in asking him to participate in arts festivals across the Pacific Northwest. Kate and Alex counsel him to hold out for the big ones, especially for an invitation from the Venice Biennale — which never comes — but Aristedes, now Henry's self-proclaimed manager, gets in touch with the *Athens News* and tells them Henry's next project will be the construction of a giant knitted womb that spews Greek incantations. The National Gallery in Athens responds with an invitation to create a special exhibit with the womb as its centrepiece . . .

On the last night of the fair, after a month of too much activity, Henry and Chas are quietly watching a news special featuring some of the highlights, including the Mulligan interview, the crowd roaring at Henry's *craft off* comment, and a shot of the devastated Mrs. Krumpskey.

Oh that's not right, Henry says. I have to make it up to her. Maybe I should invite her to take the inaugural snip at the closing gala tomorrow.

Are you sure that's a good idea? Chas asks.

I'm not sure of anything, but I'm going to ask her.

When the special is over, Henry gets up from the television, goes out the back flap and across the street to knock on Mrs. Krumpskey's door.

She opens it a crack. What do you want?

Would you like to come over tomorrow to help dismantle the chicken?

No. She closes the door firmly.

Henry sleeps badly. It's not so much her closing the door, it's the karma that bothers him. Karma is a concept he's been introduced to by some of the people he's met in the art world and he's concerned his unskillful treatment of Mrs. Krumpskey will lead to bad events in the future.

By next afternoon, cars are parked down side streets halfway to Jericho Beach and people have driven from as far away as Seattle and Portland. Wendy and her guitar-playing boyfriend from Idaho arrive, Joey and Lucy drive in from Langley with Norman, who brings macadamia nut pie. Chief from Agriculture is there, giving his usual thumbs up.

The one who takes him aback though is Orville Johnson. He's there with his hat in hand, the same hat he wore to Alice's funeral.

I saw you on the telly, Henry, he says, Thought I'd come around and congratulate you. I'm proud of you.

Thank you, Mr. Johnson, Henry mumbles.

Call me Orville.

Okay. Thank you, Orville.

I don't think you know as many people care about you as what they do, Orville says, as he surprises him with a hug.

Thank you again, Orville. Come by when all this is over.

Orville nods and scoots out of the way of an over-serious young journalist trying hard to look arty in a black turtleneck and leggings, who's with the TV crew arriving to film the snip that will mark the end of the fair.

As the various city officials line up to get their faces on camera, Henry gives up on the idea of Jamie Lee showing up. But he won't let go of the good karma of inviting Mrs. Krumpskey. He takes the official scissors across the street and mounts her porch steps.

You're sure you won't come and do this for me? he shouts through the window.

The curtains part. She shakes her head no.

The mayor is coming, he says. You'll be on TV.

Oh, she mouths.

The curtain falls, and it's several minutes before she pops her overly rouged face out to ask, Do I look all right?

You look lovely, he says.

She follows him across the street and around to the side of his house where the crew is set up with lights under umbrellas. The mayor is there, getting a touch of makeup.

Mrs. Krumpskey blushes and holds out her hand. Pleasure to meet you, Your Worship.

Can we get this rolling, barks one of the crew.

Henry passes her the scissors and points to a spot on the stitching up the west panel and Mrs. Krumpskey cuts.

A small cheer goes up.

Then Henry snips off a Day of the Dead man holding a bouquet of flowers and hands it to Mrs. Krumpskey.

A louder cheer goes up.

May blessings come to you, Mrs. Krumpskey says.

By the time the gala is finally over and the orange city barricades are removed from the ends of the street, the chicken cozy looks ragged. It won't be properly dismantled until the following day when the local cable station's cherry-picker is available. Henry is exhausted. He, Chas and Aristedes have retreated to the backyard where Aristedes has moved his grill in from the street. Rain threatens. It is the last supper before Angel for Chocolate Kiss comes down and the house is properly listed for sale.

Henry's reclining lawn chair is wedged under one of the giant knit tail feathers. His eyes are closed and he's not thinking much. A musical aahhh-eehhh is coming from around the corner and, just like the first time, when he was driving across the Lions Gate Bridge, he is listening to Jamie Lee's voice.

There you all are, Jamie Lee says. Aahhh-eehhh.

Wow, you came. He can't say anything more just yet. He's busy filling his memory with the sight of her coming around the corner of his cozied house.

Dora, I mean Charity, said I had to get up here before the chicken comes down. It's spectacular. Aahhh-eehhh.

It is. It is stupendes! Aristedes splashes the grill with ouzo.

Chicken fat mixed with alcohol flares, and one of the orange balls catches on fire.

Opa! Aristedes shouts.

The yarn flames up the back of the chicken. Chas rushes for the garden hose, and Aristedes throws on a bucket of water, but to no avail. In a matter of minutes, the flames are out of control.

Jamie Lee pulls out a mobile phone and pushes 9-1-1.

The giant chicken house is on fire, she says.

Let it burn, Henry thinks. There is indeed possibility in everything.

HENRY

eventually

I F YOU BACK THINGS UP, a lot of what happens leading up to the trial is good. Take, for example, the acrylic chicken ball fire. Although the fire burns a hole in the roof of the kitchen before it's put out, it's a badly constructed extension of the house, easy to tear down and rebuild. By the time the smell of smoke clears and the reconstruction work is finished, the real estate boom has hit and the house sells for enough to give the bank all its money with some left over. Henry moves to the top floor of a three-storey walk-up in a tidy but modest apartment building near the corner of Fourth and Alma Street. And for a time he works from there in the chicken business, but he and Chas get out once Joey's old enough to come on board.

After the Outsider Fair, Henry's career as an artist blooms so fast and with such force he believes he can make a decent living as an artist. He gets away from knitting and begins to spend more and more time with photography, ultimately a better medium for his collecting nature: the collection of cameras, lenses, and filters, and of course the hundreds and hundreds of images. Few things can compare with the satisfaction of holding a contact sheet full of photos he's taken himself. And, although he eventually comes to like the convenience of digital, there's much about the new technology he laments. Too easy to break the chain of collection, to forget, or to neglect to reproduce the images.

His first professional show is a small one at the Exposure Gallery in Vancouver where he exhibits photos from the fair. He tells Charity about the show and she tells the people at the Shoshone Gallery who invite him down for a remount. While there, he pitches the idea of showing the grainy black-and-white images from his weekend in jail after the KLUK transmission fiasco. The show is critically acclaimed — the reviewer from the Idaho College of Art magazine particularly likes the image of the stainless steel jail toilet juxtaposed with a shot of the deputy sheriff, his feet up on the desk sipping a milkshake — something about *the conscious aesthetic of interior landscape rooted in waste* that Henry didn't really intend. Still, with such artistic success, he believes he is on his way to making a name as a photographer. And in slower times he will make a modest living shooting weddings, bar mitzvahs, christenings, and graduations.

The shows in Idaho allow him to rekindle the romance he'd started with Jamie Lee at the end of the fair. They get together every few months, mostly on American holiday weekends, and then more and more during the week after Jamie Lee loses her job at KLUK. Once she turns forty, she becomes increasingly anxious about her appearance and her public persona, and as the anxiety increases so do the number of times she lets aahhh-eehhh slip on-air. She and Henry are on and off for a couple more years — when they are *off* occasionally he meets other women, usually at wedding shoots — but mostly he holds out for Jamie Lee. Ultimately though she sinks into a funk about everything, including Henry, until finally she writes him a letter declaring their romance off for good.

He adds it to the collection of letters he's squirrelled away — most a lot nicer than the kiss-off. He holds it all together with a red ribbon, her old promo photo on top and underneath an envelope with a telephone message tape that contains her sleepy voice.

I'll be driving up tomorrow to see you. I'm feeling a bit lonely.

At first, when their romance ends, his old doubts and insecurities threaten to swarm back in. Chas and Aristedes are on a break, so why not Chas? But their liaison is a disappointment, brief and furtive. Chas puts on his silk robe afterward and broods in a chair.

Oh well, he says, you did warn me, you never thought you could go there.

Henry partly agrees, saying he thinks he is probably bisexual, to which Chas says he doesn't think he is that either.

Henry is fifty-two at the time the YouTube shot at Jericho Beach goes viral, and the accounts of his trial hit the newspapers. He's had sex, and mostly enjoyed sex, mostly with women and mostly with Jamie Lee, but at this point in his life what's mainly on his mind about sex is that he's *had* it. It's neither here nor there for him. Difficult for him to believe, considering what he has gone through to get to this point, but the truth is he's settled into some weirdly bored state with the matter of sex. For whatever reason, it feels normal to him to be alone. And, as far as he can see, given the amount of porn there is on the web, a lot of people have caught up with him on the advantages of solitude.

Then there's the surfeit of fathers Henry thought he had leading up to the trial. After he hears that Tom's father is back from Ecuador and living in the old neighbourhood, he keeps half an eye out for him. But when he finally runs into him in the produce section of Safeway, the resemblance is not as strong as he remembers and there's no special connection. Old Mr. Lawson pushes his cart on down through the bananas and seems just so sad.

He does begin to meet up with Orville though, another old man now. They see each other at least once a week. When they get around to talking about it, Orville confirms he and Alice had a *thing* for a couple of years, and he'd also had a brief proposal period — not a marriage — with Henry's aunt.

Don't get me wrong, he says, there's no way I was ever seriously inclined to marry either one.

Why not? Henry asks.

Skittish couple of birds. But your mother, she was one hell of a good dancer. Lots of fun.

Orville drops his head and looks at the floor before he adds, Course she stopped talking to me after she went round the bend. Then I had that problem with the booze, when the black dog came to visit.

What's that?

Depression. Does the dog ever visit you?

Mmmm. Once or twice, but mostly not too bad.

Me too. Not too bad, now.

Orville eventually acknowledges it's possible Henry is his son. They know there are things such as DNA tests, but why confuse the truth with the facts? The truth is both settle into believing Orville is Henry's father, and Henry cares for Orville as would a son.

When Henry raises the subject of whether his mother might have touched him inappropriately, Orville looks at him and says, God, I don't think so. She loved you, in her own crazy way.

So here's how it goes, the trouble at Jericho Beach. The day starts like any other. Henry eats a bowl of muesli, drinks a glass of orange juice, and gathers up his Hasselblad and Canon Rebel. It's a beautiful day, early September, perfect to do reconnaissance for the Chong wedding he's scheduled to shoot the next weekend. The couple has chosen Jericho for the formal portraits, and Henry is happy because he can walk there. The old Subaru is still on the road, but she's shaky. Besides, it's good to get out and walk, helps a person to think. But in no way is he hounded by the black dog, nor is he thinking about sex when he leaves his apartment for the beach that morning.

After he's scoped out the willow trees near the duck pond, the wooden bridge at the pond, and the beach itself, he's sitting on the grass arranging his equipment by the bulrush where the red-winged blackbirds nest. Someone has left behind a small group of stones collected from the beach and he picks up a green one that is almost translucent. He is looking through the stone when three naked children run out of the rushes, two boys and a girl — small golden, galloping ponies. He reaches for his Canon so he can document their joy, the glow of light around their heads. He abandons his cases and tripod and soon he's running with the children at a pace toward the beach, shooting as he goes, when the older boy stops to look at him. Hmm, Henry thinks, maybe what I'm doing isn't so cool.

He smiles to reassure the boy, and because the wind is picking up, he doesn't hear the mother's words, only her tone. The kids are dancing around, hooting and laughing, their naked little bodies jumping up and down. Then the mother is right beside him shrieking. And Henry does not understand why she is videotaping him with her cell phone.

The trial wouldn't have even made the newspapers, if it hadn't been for the second-year law student at the university law clinic telling her supervisor, Professor Jon Bakon, about this *interesting situation* in her new intake file involving child pornography. Professor Bakon listens for a couple of minutes, then pronounces he will step in as defence counsel, and do it without charge if Henry will agree the Civil Liberties class can attend the trial and study it as an example of the interface between criminal prosecution and civil rights.

Despite Professor Bakon's belief that he is indeed the star of the proceedings, it is the attractiveness of several of the students in his class, coupled with their tendency to speak loosely outside the courtroom, that initially attracts the press. One young male student eager to catch the television's camera — a pale apricot sweater casually thrown over his shoulders, his hair expensively and evenly cut — tells a reporter that Henry has been in jail in the United States for stalking a woman. This prompts the reporter to ask, Whose side are you on anyway? To which Professor Bakon jumps in to add, That's the deal with this case. It's so difficult to tell.

But the thing that really gives the case its notoriety is the furor that erupts over the YouTube the mother posts of the events at the beach. For several days letters to the editor in the *Vancouver Sun* rage on about whose liberties really have been offended. What was the mother doing posting a video of her nude children laughing and dancing while she shouts at Henry? Isn't she the one who is promoting the pornographic side of things?

In the end, it is Henry himself who is responsible for his defence.

Although Henry has been in court before, it is the first time he's ever properly taken the stand and been cross-examined. When the prosecutor begins by asking about his living circumstances, he admits he lives alone and that yes he does sleep with his dog, a small black poodle named Beau. But when the prosecutor holds up his hand in an attempt to stop him from saying anything more, Henry ignores him and goes on to say that it's just a man with his dog sort of relationship. He even draws a laugh from the courtroom when he says that without the dog he'd never get up in the morning. How every morning it's the dog that pushes him with its knees, telling him it's time to wake up. The prosecutor says he doesn't think dogs have knees, and the judge, a woman who until she speaks looks too old to even be alive, tells the prosecutor he's lost sight of the puck. In response to which the prosecutor switches to his main point.

Why is it, Mr. Parkins, that you didn't seek permission to take the photos?

The work requires me to act quickly, Henry says, and to seek permission later. I would never use photos of any nature without permission.

Except for your own warped purposes, shoots back the prosecutor.

Something makes Henry talk, right over the prosecutor.

Forgive me for not understanding, he says. Forgive me my own childhood that didn't give me the insight to understand mothers. I had no warped purposes in mind.

It's this statement that lights Professor Bakon on fire. He stands and adjusts the glasses on the end of his nose before quoting Henry in his closing argument.

Mr. Parkins had no warped purposes in mind. He told us that today. So let's talk about what this case is really about. It's about the public's fear of a man who takes pictures of beautiful subjects — children whose mother herself has chosen to present them to the world. She is the one who disrobed her children. She is the one who let them run nude in the park. Mr. Parkins caused no harm. It is his civil right to make art, and an infringement of his liberty to prosecute him for doing so. The courts are clumsy vehicles for understanding the complexity of such a situation.

Professor Bakon stabs the counsel desk with his index finger to indicate he's finished, and sits down. The judge closes her eyes for a moment then sets a half hour adjournment. When she returns, she's combed her hair, and applied fresh lipstick.

Mr. Parkins, stand up, she says.

Henry stands. The judge continues.

I want you to grow up, get a real job, and stop sneaking around in the bushes taking photos of kids. You're behaving like a dumb cluck, ignoring your responsibilities. You need to start using your talents for the greater good, and get on with it. I don't know if any of what I'm saying will impact, and it might even be a bit ignoble of me to say so, but at least I got this off my chest.

She turns to the prosecutor. And I don't know what your department is doing wasting court time with flimsy cases like this. The mother's the one who set this thing off. Once things snowballed with that ridiculous video of hers — the judge turns to the mother, Is there something you can do to take that off YouTube? — we all got stuck here taking this thing forward. No conviction for Mr. Parkins. Is there anything you want to say, Mr. Parkins?

Nothing, your honour, Henry says. Just thank you.

Don't thank me. It's my job.

On the way out of the courtroom, Henry asks Orville, What does ignoble mean?

Orville claps his hat on his head and says, Who the hell cares? You got off, son, like I knew you would.

When Henry gets home to his apartment, he looks up *ignoble*. But for days afterward, the thing that sticks in his mind is the judge's line about getting a real job. After a couple of weeks, he makes a small pile of the press clippings he's collected on a plate in the middle of his kitchen table. He takes a photo of it then sets a match to it and opens the window. When the last of the acrid smell is gone, he picks up the phone and dials a number he hasn't dialled in years.

Hello?

Hi Wendy, it's Henry.

He drives to the farm in the Subaru, still yellow but faded and with one blue fender now, worried how it's going to be when he sees her. Whether she knows about the trial, whether she's seen the video and thinks that he's a nasty man. Then he's standing at her back door and she's opening it.

Come on in, Henry, and get some coffee. Good timing. Joey is just on his way over.

If she has read the articles or seen any of the news clips or the video, she doesn't let on. They make small talk for a while. She's been single all these years, things didn't work out with the fellow from Idaho, and then life just got busy.

Henry doesn't say much. Finally he simply blurts out, Any jobs I can help with around here?

I'm sure there are, she says. Joey's so busy. He's going to be a father again. Did I tell you — they're having a second?

Of course this makes sense, but still Henry is taken aback. Wendy is a grandmother. And there's indeed something new in her face. Before he can think further, there's a familiar toot outside and she rises from the table.

They're here, she says.

He follows her out into the yard and over to Chas' old blue-glow Mustang. Its roof is down and the lively Joey is behind the wheel. Sitting beside him is a woman. Once she takes the scarf from her head, he sees it is Lucy.

Still got the Mustang? he says. Looks mint. He bends over to have a peek underneath.

Course it is, man, Joey says. I take care of things. Joey pats the back of the white leather bucket seat behind the very pregnant Lucy, and flashes his trademark lock-your-daughter-up grin.

Nice to see you, Henry, Lucy says. We miss you around here.

A small boy with a round head and a mop-top of black hair pops up from the back.

Hi!

Hi, Henry says.

The boy, suddenly shy, puts his head down before looking back up.

This is Dennis junior, Wendy says. Chive and cheese omelet okay for lunch today, kiddo?

The boy nods.

Inside, on the kitchen counter, there's a basket of eggs. Wendy points to them, You can start with these after lunch, she says to Henry. You know the routine, check for yard dirt, give them a brush.

They all sit at the table. The air is full with sweet onion and fresh egg.

Dennis holds out a small pebble.

Henry peers. It's a pretty pebble, the colour of a goldfish.

He wants you to have it, Lucy says.

Why thank you, Henry says.

Dennis moves his plate toward Henry. Squirt the catsup.

Lucy raises her eyebrows, What do you say?

Squirt the catsup, *please*.

Henry retrieves the squirt bottle from the counter. He is lost a moment looking over the basket of eggs. The satisfaction in the sight of all those round ends, how he'll arrange them into cartons, all pointing forward, he's sure he'll never tire of that. A type of infinity sits between the numbers. Room in there for everyone.

ACKNOWLEDGMENTS

So many have helped me along the way. They include all the early readers, especially Ruth Rowntree (thanks Mom for catching all my typos), Patricia Rowntree (thanks for being a supportive sister and not saying the story was weird), Jeff Turner (thank you for listening *ad nauseam* to my angsty stuff), Kathy Page, Marilyn Potter, Andrew Boden, Shelley Saltzman, Kevin Chong, and Keith Maillard. I'd also like to thank Dr. Carina Perel-Panar who *shrunk* my protagonist and enabled me to write him with real backbone, also my publisher Thistledown Press for letting this novel see the light of day, and especially for the gift of my editor, Michael Kenyon. And finally thank you to Cortes Community Radio, which kept me company during many long rewrites, and where I first heard the wonderful expression *all the power of a light bulb just not as bright.*